SNOW BOUND

ALL THAT GLITTERS

SNOW BOUND

ALL THAT GLITTERS

C.J. BRIGHTLEY

Paperback ISBN 978-1-954768-09-3
Ebook ASIN B0F1HB9M4Q

Published in the United States of America by Spring Song Press, LLC.

www.cjbrightley.com
www.springsongpress.com

Cover design by MoorBooks.

DEDICATION

For everyone who has longed to be fully known
and deeply loved
Psalm 139

Also by C. J. Brightley

A Long-Forgotten Song:
Things Unseen
The Dragon's Tongue
The Beginning of Wisdom
Children of Wrath

Erdemen Honor:
The King's Sword
A Cold Wind
Honor's Heir

Fairy King:
A Fairy King
A Fairy Promise

The Wraith:
The Wraith and the Rose
The Shield and the Thorn
The Frost and the Flame

Other Works:
The Lord of Dreams
Twelve Days of (Faerie) Christmas
Heroes and Other Stories

Eleria:
The Silent Prince

ACKNOWLEDGMENTS

Lovely friends, you truly are the best! I thank God for bringing you into my life. Sarah, Carolyn, Suebee, Chloe, Megan, Anne, and Jen, I love you all so much.

FOREWORD

Snow Bound is set in the world of Eleria. Other books in this world include *The Silent Prince* (part of the Once Upon A Prince series), *A Long and Valiant Hope* (forthcoming), and other future titles.

CHAPTER 1

The snow gleamed pink and gold and silver in the first light of the sun. The wind had left drifts against the north and west side of the lodge nearly to the eaves.

A forlorn tendril of smoke wafted from the hole in the roof and straight up into the clear morning air, for there was no breeze now. The morning promised to be bright and sunny.

The door was on the south side of the lodge, and on this side the snow drifts were smaller. Ivarr forced the door open against the powdery weight.

When he had shoveled some of the snow into a bucket, he put the bucket inside atop the heavy iron stove. He strapped on his snowshoes and went out to check the traps.

The eldest of the eight children, Gytha, was already awake. Most of the younger children slept in the loft above, but the older girls, the youngest, and the parents slept below. There were windows on the lower level and in the loft, but they had no glass, only tightly fitted wooden shutters that opened to the inside of the lodge. The windows were kept closed all winter unless the snow drifts became so high that Ivarr could not get out using the door.

This winter had been especially long and hard. Game had been scarce in the fall, and the frigid temperatures and heavy snow had come early. Nevertheless, Ivarr had stored up plenty of firewood, which was neatly stacked against the outside of the lodge beneath the wide eaves. Every evening he brought in more wood to dry near the stove so that it would be ready for the morning. The lodge itself was a spacious structure, but much of it was devoted to the animals and the storeroom. At one end were the animals: the henhouse to the left and the four-footed animals in a separate section to the right. The center of the house was the living quarters, with a large loft and a wood stove in the center of the main room below. The sleeping quarters were separated from the living area by curtains hung from the bottom of the loft, but these were usually left at least partially open. At the other end of the structure was the storeroom, which held all the family's food stores, soap, rope, cloth and thread, and many other necessities for a smallholding.

The trees crowded close, only a few dozen yards away from the lodge on the north side and farther away to the south. The cleared area grew rich grass for grazing in the summer and an orderly garden, as well as provided space for carpentry, laundry, and other chores more pleasant in the open air during the warm months. In winter, this expanse was covered by snow.

While Ivarr made his daily trek into the forest, Gytha used the hand mill to grind wheat berries into flour and then made little flat cakes for the younger children. At eighteen, she was old enough to be married soon and pretty enough to help her family with a good match.

At the end of the previous summer, Ivarr had received several offers for her. The richest of the suitors was Torvald Hilmarsson, who had offered a new lamb and a sow near farrowing.

"He's not a bad man," Ivarr had said helplessly. "You could do much worse."

"Please don't make me," Gytha had pled. "He's older than you!"

Her father had run his hands through his hair and turned away. "Who do you want, then?" His voice was low. "That fool Hjalmarr? He's in no position to keep you fed through a winter, much less help your mother and the little ones if something happens to me."

Hjalmarr was a perfectly nice young man only a few years older than Gytha. But only his age made him suitable; he had neither money nor looks nor wit to recommend him. Still, she had never heard anyone say ill of him, other than that he was dull, and she said, "I would prefer him over Hilmarsson, if I had to choose, but I'm not ready to marry, Pabbi. Please let me have one more season with you."

"The littles are eating more."

"I'll eat less, then!" Her beautiful eyes were bright with emotion. "Please, Pabbi."

"That's not what I mean, Gytha!" Her father frowned. "I don't want any of you to go hungry! Marrying a man who can provide for you would give you a good life. Hilmarsson is a decent man, and he would treat you well."

But she could see the discomfort in his eyes.

"At least let me wait until spring to decide?" she had pleaded.

Ivarr had said nothing else about it in the days that followed, not a word to pressure her or make her feel guilty.

Through the long winter, though, the foolishness of refusing to marry had become painfully clear. Their cow got milk fever and died, and the following week a lynx got into the hen house on the other end of the lodge and killed all their chickens. The two goats produced less milk during winter, barely enough for two cups a day for the youngest children. The older children and the parents added water to their milk until it was nearly clear. The bag of wheat berries from which Gytha made their flat cakes and porridge dwindled day by day so that she looked at it worriedly. They had gathered acorns in the autumn, roasted them, and ground them into flour, which they had stored away in case of emergency. She added a little of this flour to the wheat flour.

Hlif, Ivarr's wife and the mother of all the children, added more acorn flour than usual to the porridge for breakfast one day. When Gytha caught her eye, she said quietly, "It fills the stomach for a time, and it will make the flour last longer."

One day Ivarr said that milk turned his stomach, and he preferred plain water to drink. Hlif said the same. Ivarr glared at her ferociously. "Drink your milk," he muttered. "You need to keep up your strength."

She raised an eyebrow at him in challenge. "And what of you?" she said, her voice so soft that the younger children, arguing happily with each other about the game of knucklebones that dinner had interrupted, did not hear her at all.

He shrugged carelessly and sat back. He shoved his bowl, still mostly full, toward her. The thin, milky porridge and tiny bit of salt pork on the top was barely enough to sustain a child, much less a man who worked as much as he did. "I'll be all right."

He stood and moved to sit by the tiny fire. He took up the drum he had made the previous winter, just a rough ring of wood with a piece of rawhide stretched over it, and settled down.

"Brinja, come and show me what you've practiced."

The youngest of his children scrambled onto his lap happily. She patted the drum, practicing the rhythm he had taught her. "Good!" He smiled and kissed the top of her head.

Gytha tried to think everything was all right. Everyone had days when they weren't very hungry.

As winter wore on, the food stores dwindled, and the traps were empty far more often than not. Most nights, Ivarr pushed his bowl toward one of the children or his wife.

By midwinter, Ivarr had grown desperate. He chopped holes in the ice on the river and set nets for fish, but very few were active in these coldest months. He went hunting in the woods to the north and brought back ducks several times. Once he returned with a brace of rabbits from the traps, stomping the snow from his boots and sighing with relief when he stood close to the fire, thawing his frozen hands and face.

It wasn't enough.

Ivarr grew gaunt and grim, and even when he smiled at the children, there was not much joy in it. The lines of fatigue in his face grew deeper. Hlif and Gytha ate very little, and they took turns walking the upper town asking for work. Their lodge was in the great forest, looking down upon the upper town through the trees from a slight elevation. There was not a proper road, of course; there were not enough people to need a road. But Gytha's family all knew the path well, for they had walked it a thousand times.

In the summer, it was a pleasant, pine-scented walk of an hour or so, with the mountains far away to the west sometimes visible between the trees. The path to town was roughly parallel with the river, and many smaller paths ran into the whispering forest to the best fishing locations. The shoreline itself was rough and rocky, and in many places not easily traversed, but Gytha and her siblings had explored it for many miles in both directions in warmer months.

Now, with snow thick on the path and the icy wind whispering and snarling through the trees, the walk took much longer. Gytha had an unsettling sense that she was being watched, and she looked for eyes among the trees and brush. Wolves prowled the woods, along with enormous brown bears, wolverines, lynxes, and even foxes, though it would be strange indeed for a fox to stalk a human. Gytha kept a tight grip on her walking stick; it was not much of a weapon, but she was skilled with it.

The feeling of being watched did not fade until she reached the little village, but she saw no sight of any predator. Hunger fogged her mind and dragged at her limbs, and she was exhausted before she reached the village.

Few people offered any work, for they had little food or money to spare. Gytha had almost lost hope when Hildr Hilmarsson, the widowed younger sister of Torvald, took pity on her and offered her a little embroidery work.

The wind cut through Gytha's coat as she trudged home. If a predator watched her, she did not perceive it. Perhaps she was too tired to notice.

For a week, Gytha sat near the stove hunched over the work. A vague sense of crawling unease snuck over her, and it took a full day before she identified the sensation as a fever. Her skin tingled but her bones were cold, and she could not sleep at night. Nevertheless, she had work, and she was grateful for it.

When she presented the tunic to Hildr, the woman paid with a whole chicken, five potatoes, an onion, and a little salt.

"Thank you!" exclaimed Gytha. Her eyes filled with tears of gratitude.

Hildr pressed the bag into her hands. "I have a jacket, if you'd like to do it?" She smiled warmly.

"Yes. Thank you."

The walk home was frigid. The wind picked up and swirled snow around her feet in sparkling whorls. Gytha's stomach felt sour and empty, but it was foolish to think too much of it. Focusing on the discomfort, on the trembling weakness in her knees and the way her heart skipped unevenly sometimes when she strode too quickly up a hill, only made her fearful. It was better to think of courage and strength, of her father's great love for them and the quiet generosity of her mother.

Hunger had stolen the strength of their bodies, but it had not weakened their love.

When she looked up from the snow, she sucked in a sudden breath. Mere steps ahead of her stood an enormous white bear. It stared into her blue eyes with its huge black ones.

Her heart thumped wildly in her chest. She trembled, cold to her bones. The wind cut through her thin coat and snuck through the seams of her worn boots.

The bear took a step toward her, and she closed her eyes. Perhaps she would die now. Perhaps it would eat her and get a thin, bony meal from her body.

Without her, there would be enough food for her father and mother to eat every day. Not much, but enough to survive the winter.

Eight children! Was it any wonder winter was hard?

When she opened her eyes, the bear was gone.

She stumbled into the lodge and presented her earnings to her mother.

"Are you all right?" her mother asked, frowning worriedly.

"I'm just a little dizzy." Gytha blinked as her mother wavered before her. "I'm sorry, Mamma."

"Go lie down. Thank you for this, Gytha. Get a little rest. Your father will be back soon." Her mother kissed her forehead and said, "You're burning up!"

Gytha stumbled to the bed in the corner that she shared with Sigrid and Solveig and drifted into a feverish darkness.

She woke to her mother's cool hand on her cheek. "Eat a little, darling."

"I'm not hungry," she mumbled, and she turned her back to her mother's worried face.

She slept until noon the next day.

"I need to work." She sat up and the room danced and spun.

"Eat, Gytha." Her father held up a bowl of soup. "Can you hold it or shall I feed you?"

She blinked at him. "You should eat it." The dim firelight caught the sharp lines of his cheekbones and the shadows under his tired eyes.

His eyes burned with emotion. "Eat it, Gytha. It's my job to worry about the family, not yours. Your job is to get better. That's all. So eat it."

The soup was thin but flavorful, and she managed a few bites before the dizziness and fatigue were too overwhelming. "I just want to sleep," she whispered. "Please eat, Pabbi."

He brushed at his eyes. "One more bite, Honeycake."

She leaned her forehead against his and closed her eyes. The spoon touched her lips and she managed to swallow the bite before she fell asleep again.

The fever receded and rose again in waves. When she could sit up, she moved to the fire and worked on Hildr's jacket; each time, she saw that her mother had worked on it while she slept.

Finally the jacket was done, Gytha's own fine stitches indistinguishable from her mother's. "I'll take it back to Hildr," she said.

"Do you feel up to it?" Her mother looked at her worriedly. "Why don't you stay here? I'll walk it back."

Gytha smiled reassuringly. "I feel better, Mama." The fever lurked, but she could see the fatigue in her mother's face.

Her father was nowhere to be seen. "I'll take the jacket," Gytha said again. "Where is Pabbi?"

Her mother looked away. "Checking the traps. He'll be all right." Her voice shook.

Gytha licked her lips. "Is he sick too?"

Her mother nodded once. "Take Solveig with you." The woman focused on the mending in front of her. Her fingers were trembling, and her cheeks were flushed.

The little ones were sitting quietly on the floor not far away; Sigrid, the second eldest, was teaching them simple words by writing them in water on a small blackboard which they had been given many years ago. They had run out of chalk long ago, but water worked quite well, and the heat of the stove dried the surface quickly when they wanted to write something new. The elder six children had learned to read this way.

"You're sick, too," breathed Gytha, realizing that the flush in her mother's cheeks was not solely from the heat of the fire. "I'll be back soon."

She pulled on her threadbare coat and waited while Solveig, third eldest of the children at thirteen, pulled on her own coat and picked up the basket with Hildr's jacket. Then they hurried outside.

The afternoon was so clear and bright that Gytha squeezed her eyes shut for a moment against the brilliant sunshine reflecting off the snow.

Solveig tugged on her arm, and they started off together toward town. "We were really worried about you." The girl's voice quavered.

"I'm all right." Gytha smiled reassuringly down at her sister, ignoring the faint, feverish tingle of sweat across her back.

They tramped through thick snow on the trail, following their father's footprints until his track left the path and turned into the forest to the north of town, where one might find deer, elk, hares, and grouse. Game was scarce this far into winter, but there was little use in sitting around the lodge growing weaker from hunger. The children needed to eat, even if Ivarr went hungry. He had snares set in a hundred places, and they knew he would check them all before turning toward the river.

Soon Gytha and Solveig reached the first of the many paths used by the townsfolk. Packed snow indicated that many men had already made their way to the river and to the lake for ice fishing.

The exercise had her blood pumping, and she breathed out clouds of white fog that glittered in the brilliant sun. By the time she reached Hildr's house, she was out of breath and nearly stumbling with fatigue. Her cheeks were flushed and sweat crusted her hairline with salt, frozen as quickly as it rose.

Again, Hildr was generous, and again Gytha thanked her with tears in her eyes.

"Would you…" Gytha swallowed. "I think I misjudged your brother. I see the kindness in him. I would be honored to accept him, if he will still have me."

Beside her, Solveig's mouth dropped open in surprise. "But…"

Hildr bit her lip, her blue eyes gentle. "He has already sworn to marry a widow from Langaholt, closer to his own age. He asked her just after he heard of your refusal."

An icy wind gusted, and Gytha swayed. "I didn't refuse him." Not exactly.

Hildr's expression softened. "He took it as refusal. Anyway, he understood; he is old for you. Here." She produced a small bag of flour and wrapped Gytha's hands around the top of it, her own fingers warm against Gytha's icy ones. "It isn't much, but it is all we can spare. I'm sorry."

"Thank you." Gytha felt numb, both stomach and mind empty of all hope.

"If the sled from Langaholt brings supplies, Torvald will bring you something."

"Thank you," Gytha said again. She curtseyed a little and turned away. Hildr was kind, and she would have been a good sister-by-marriage, even if Torvald was too old. Gytha might have done worse.

She had done worse. What would they do now? She had condemned her family to a tragic winter of starvation and illness and slow death.

The walk toward home was a blur of icy wind and despairing thoughts. What could she do? Her skin tingled with fever. Her feet were heavy and her head was light, as if she would be borne away in the next frigid gust.

Solveig took the little bag of flour from her and tucked it into the larger sack with the chicken, which she slung over her shoulder. She gripped the end of the sack with one hand and tucked her other hand in Gytha's.

The wind gusted so hard that Gytha staggered and fell, nearly pulling Solveig down with her. She remained on hands and knees for a moment, staring at the snow, and then slowly clambered to her feet.

When she looked up from the path, there was an enormous white bear.

CHAPTER 2

Gytha froze, trembling with cold and fear and fever. Though she wished to run, she could not make her feet move, and so she stood still.

The bear stepped forward, each great white paw nearly as wide as her body.

"Gytha," Solveig's whisper was panicked. "What do we do?" Her fingers gripped Gytha's sleeve.

"Don't run." Gytha clenched her jaw and raised her chin, too tired and feverish to think of anything else to do.

No one else was on the path. The trees rustled overhead.

The chicken! Gytha grabbed the bag from her sister and held it out as if the bear would be distracted by it. As if a scrawny chicken would satisfy a beastly hunger.

The colossal creature took another step forward, and another, each movement slow and steady.

The bear stepped so close that his nose nearly touched Gytha's, ignoring the chicken entirely. His soft breaths warmed her face.

She tried to stand firm, as if she were brave, but her heart was thudding so hard that she could barely hear Solveig murmuring prayers beside her.

The bear's thick fur rippled in the breeze. Its head was huge, and though she could not see its teeth, she imagined them long and white, just inches from her face.

It stared at her silently, huge black eyes intent on hers.

Gytha was so cold she felt faint and distant from her body. Perhaps the bear meant to eat her. Perhaps it didn't.

She ventured a quavery, "Hello."

She was so cold that she barely cared if it ate her. Perhaps it was all a fever dream.

The bear snuffed softly into her face and took another step forward. It sniffed curiously at Solveig's woolen hat and then her shoulder, and then turned his attention to Gytha. The warm air of its breath tickled her neck, and she trembled, imagining huge teeth crushing her throat.

A voice as distant and faint as a memory said, "Are you afraid?"

"Yes." Her voice shook.

There was a sound like a soft, grieved sigh. "I mean you no harm." The bear's huge, dark eyes held hers as its body curved around them, blocking the wind.

"You're a bear." Gytha's voice cracked, the sound somewhere between a shriek and a sob.

"You are troubled by many things, not only your fear of me. Will you tell me of your griefs?"

Solveig's huge, terrified eyes were filled with tears. "It's going to eat us," she whispered.

Perhaps it was the fever that loosened her tongue, or perhaps it was that she felt that talking could not make the situation any more hopeless than it already was. "My father and mother are sick, and we've run out of food."

The bear merely looked at her, as if it expected more, and its patience, or what she took to be patience, shattered what little control she still had.

"The whole family is starving! My father hasn't eaten anything but half a bowl of porridge in over two weeks, and even with the chicken from Hildr we have barely enough for the little ones for a day or two, and Brinja and Halvard cry at night because they're so hungry. And Randulf says he's fine because he's realized that Pabbi and Mamma are giving their food to the littlest ones, and he wants to be brave, and he's too young to have to worry like that! And it's my fault because Torvald was going to marry me and then he'd share his food with us but now he won't."

The bear tilted his head. "There is food enough in the village, and they won't share?"

Gytha shook her head. "No, no, it isn't that they're stingy. But we had a terrible harvest and so did the rest of the village. Everyone is struggling but us most of all because of the hens the lynx killed. We lost all the hens right at the beginning of winter. And Torvald has his wife's family to take care of now. He doesn't have any food to spare."

The bear snuffed softly, as if to himself. "I will walk you home," he said at last. "But put your hands in my fur to warm a little." He turned to Solveig and said, "You, too, little sister."

Hesitantly, Gytha put one hand and then the other on the bear's neck. There were a few snowflakes on the long outer coat, but the underfur was even thicker and warmer than she had imagined, and without stopping to think how dangerous it was, she burrowed her hands deeper until she felt not only the bear's trapped body heat but the quivering skin of the beast itself.

She pressed her face into the fur, breathing deeply. The creature smelled of ice and pine and something warm and reassuring, a little like the scent of a new, clean lamb. An animal scent, but that of the animal itself, fresh and clean, not dung or sweat or filth.

From the bear there emanated a soft, growly sort of rumble that made her bones shiver, and she drew back, suddenly frightened.

"Little sister," the bear said again. "Do not be afraid." He leaned his great head over Solveig's shoulder so that she was nearly enveloped in the immensity of him.

Solveig stood stiffly for a moment before apparently accepting that there was nothing to be done. She put the bag with the food on the snowy ground and dug her hands into his fur with a muffled whimper.

The bear gave another grumbling murmur.

Their fear had subsided when he said, "Now, will you let me walk you home?"

Gytha felt a strange little flutter inside her, something like hope, or the memory of hope, at the gentleness of his voice. "Yes, Master Bear," she said. "Thank you."

He snuffed a soft laugh. "I am no master. I would hope to be a friend, if you will let me."

Solveig picked up the sack with the food and they set off, one on each side of the great creature with a hand buried in his thick fur. He kept his steps slow and steady to match their smaller strides. By the time they approached the lodge, the shadows were long and the forest around them whispered in the wind.

"Go ahead," Gytha said to Solveig. "Do you want help with the food?"

"I can carry it." Solveig looked at the bear and gave an awkward little curtsey. "Thank you."

In a moment, Gytha and the great bear were alone under the last faint hint of sunset. The moon was new and still below the distant mountain peaks, so the darkness was broken only by starlight reflected on the snow. The bear was an enormous, pale shadow beside Gytha.

"Thank you," Gytha said, her voice tremulous with cold and fever. "You've been very kind to us. Thank you for not eating my sister or me."

A soft, rumbling that made Gytha feel suddenly warmer came from the bear. "I have a favor to ask, and I wanted you to trust me first."

"A favor?" The girl caught her breath on a sob. "I have nothing to offer. Not even enough food for my little sisters and brothers."

"You are cold. Go inside now." The bear's great nose gave her a gentle shove toward the door.

She stumbled up the path and turned to look back once, just before she opened the door to the lodge. If the bear still stood there, she could not pick out his bulk among the shadows.

Inside, Ivarr and Hlif lay on their bed; Hlif had her back to the room, and Ivarr had wrapped one thin arm over her. Sigrid had begun cleaning the chicken and Solveig was cutting up the potatoes. Ashild, one of the twins and ten years old, was mixing flour with water and the last of the precious butter to make dumplings.

Brinja, the youngest at only three, clambered over Ivarr to nestle herself next to her mother in the bed. Neither of the parents moved.

Slowly, the lodge filled with the rich scents of the chicken and potatoes and the dried herbs Sigrid had sprinkled over them. They even had a few onions, though onions alone would hardly fuel a body for long.

At last, Sigrid pulled the pan from the oven and said, "Come eat, everyone!" Everyone scrambled to the table, but Ivarr and Hlif did not move.

Gytha crossed the room and touched her father's shoulder. "Pabbi, come eat."

Without opening his eyes, he shook his wife's shoulder gently. "Hlif, my love, there's chicken for dinner. Go eat."

Hlif sighed softly. "I'm not hungry."

Ivarr levered himself up to see her face. "My love," he said hoarsely. "Get up. I'll help you. Go eat a little."

"And take it out of the mouths of my own children? I would rather die." Hlif sat up, the movements betraying her weakness, and sat with her back against the tapestry hanging on the wall of the lodge. Her eyes were sunken and feverish, and she whispered to her husband, "They need you to survive the winter. Go eat."

At this moment, there was a muffled thud against the door.

"What was that?" Ivarr straightened, his tired eyes suddenly sharp. He strode across the room, gaunt and grim, only stumbling once. He took up his axe in one hand before he wrenched open the door.

An elk lay across the doorway, its neck broken. The body was still warm.

"What is this?" Ivarr knelt to examine the animal and suddenly fell back with a cry. The great bear loomed above him, immense and terrifying.

"It is a gift for you and your children. You are hungry. Eat."

Gytha heard the words clearly, but Ivarr did not seem to. He stared up at the enormous creature with both hands upon his axe.

"The bear is a friend," said Gytha, feeling shaky. "Thank you, Master Bear."

The bear dropped to all fours and disappeared into the night.

For some minutes Ivarr struggled to drag the elk around the house to the storeroom. The bear returned, took the elk's throat in his mouth, and dragged it easily around the lodge to the storeroom door. Then it disappeared again.

It took all of Ivarr's strength and the help of Sigrid and Solveig to drag the elk the last few feet to the rope. When the carcass was in position, Ivarr attached the rope of the block and tackle system, which was designed so that even a child could lift a great weight. He hauled on the rope until the elk was off the ground, tied off the rope, and then sank to his knees, dizzy with hunger and fever. When he could stand, he found his knives and methodically dressed the elk, saving everything. Solveig took some of the blood to make blood pudding, and the rest went into small bowls to be frozen for later. The organs would be eaten, and the intestines would be used to make sausage casings. And of course, the best was the meat, which would age in the frigid storeroom. Gytha and Sigrid helped with this familiar task. They put the bowls of entrails at the far outer corner of the storeroom with the bucket of blood to freeze. The rich organ meat would give them strength as they waited for the meat to age.

By the time they were finished with the elk, the blood pudding was ready. Hlif roused enough to eat, for now that there was food for tomorrow, she admitted she was a little hungry. They ate nearly all of Gytha's earnings, most of the meat of the chicken and many of the potatoes and old carrots. When they finished, Hlif and Gytha put the bones and scraps and the tops of the carrots into a pot to simmer to make a rich stock.

For the first time in weeks, Ivarr picked up his drum and played softly while the children scurried around making the lodge ready for sleep.

At last, the family slipped into their beds, and they slept with hope in their hearts and full bellies for the first time in months.

Gytha woke to her father and mother murmuring quietly to each other over the table, steaming mugs in front of them. She strained to hear their words.

"I don't know what possessed that bear to leave last night."

"I didn't see it at all." Hlif had been lost in a feverish doze when the bear disappeared. This morning, her face was terribly pale, with blotches of pink high on each gaunt cheek.

"I thought it meant to come inside and take me or one of the children." Ivarr spoke under his breath, more to himself than to his wife. "Perhaps it wasn't hungry. Wild animals are wild, you know, unpredictable."

Gytha sat up, feeling the edges of fever not yet passed. She swung her feet to the floor and found her sheepskin slippers. Shivering, she pulled her sweater over her head, tucked the blanket back around Solveig, and made her way to the table.

"What did you mean when you said the bear was a friend?" Her father's eyes were sunken and shadowed with hunger and fatigue, and they held a gleam of fever.

"He walked us home from Hildr's lodge," Gytha whispered. "He called Solveig 'little sister' and told us both to warm our hands in his fur."

"It can talk?" Her mother turned to her in surprise.

21

"You didn't hear it? Solveig and I both understood him."
Gytha bit her lip, feeling strangely shy.

Ivarr frowned thoughtfully. "Do you trust it? I have
never heard of a bear being safe. Especially not in winter."

Gytha nodded, and then, under her father's sharp
scrutiny, rose to pour herself a mug of steaming water and give
herself a moment to think. When she sat again, she said, "He had
a kind voice, Pabbi. I do trust him, even if it makes little sense."

The little ones began to stir in their beds, and Ivarr
pulled on his heavy work clothes. "I'll go process that elk," he
said. "I think we'll survive the winter after all." He put a hand on
Gytha's shoulder as he moved around the table.

They ate blood soup, liver soaked in milk and fried in
the elk's own fat, and boiled potatoes for lunch and dinner.
Solveig and Sigrid shredded carrots and made them into sweet
cakes with the last of their flour and honey.

These meals, and those in the following week, lent them
all much needed strength. Ivarr's cheeks were still gaunt, but
there was a little color in them, and his eyes were bright and full
of hope.

None of the little ones had gotten sick, but they had
grown weak and lethargic from hunger. The elk had given
the children new life, and they bounced around the lodge, eager
to help with chores and begging their older sisters for more
reading lessons.

Yet Hlif remained flushed with fever, and even after a
week, her hands trembled when she picked up needle and thread
to do the mending. She dropped the cloth four times, and then
she fell asleep with her head flopped awkwardly to the side, her
cheeks hot and red and her fingers icy.

"Come to bed, Mama," Gytha urged. Hlif could
barely be roused at all, and she stumbled to bed with an
inarticulate mumble.

The next day, Ivarr wrapped some of the elk meat in a clean cloth and took it to a nearby family he knew was also struggling. He was gone for nearly three hours, for even with snowshoes, the walk was slow. When he returned, the sky was streaked with the last hint of orange sunset.

Snow swirled through the door as he stepped inside, stopping to stomp the ice from his boots before he closed the door. "Storm coming," he said. "Going to be bad."

He leaned back against the wall of the lodge for balance as he pulled off his thick fur snow pants, revealing regular indoor clothes beneath, and exchanged his boots for indoor slippers. His clothes hung off his gaunt frame; he was still far thinner than Gytha could remember from any other winter. But he moved with something closer to his customary vigor, not the lethargy of starvation.

"They're not quite as bad off as we were," he said. He was still breathing hard; the fatigue of deprivation was not entirely passed. "They sent some acorn flour and eggs as thanks."

His gaze lingered on his wife, who slouched in the rocking chair near the stove. Gytha crouched beside her, one hand on her mother's forehead.

He stepped closer. "Hlif, my love, go rest."

Her eyes fluttered, but she did not wake.

"Her fever's higher," Gytha said. "I took her outside earlier to try to cool her, and it helped for a while. I can take her again."

Without a word, Ivarr stooped to take his wife in his arms. Weak as he still was, he might have struggled to lift her, but she was as frail and thin as a reed. Gytha pressed close, as if she could help her father, but her father grunted with effort and staggered toward the door. Little Randulf opened it for them, his eyes wide with worry.

The sky was low above them, iron gray and ominous, but only a little snow fell softly. Ivarr sank down to sit on the steps with Hlif on his lap. He leaned back against the wooden wall of the lodge and shifted his arms to hold her closer. Hlif rested her head on Ivarr's shoulder, mumbling a weak protest against the cold.

"I think Master Eyvindr has willow bark. I'll ask for some from him." Gytha met her father's gaze across Hlif's pale golden head.

"I don't want you out in the storm. I'll go."

Gytha shook her head. "Pabbi, the children are desperate to see you strong again, and I feel the edge of fever not quite gone. The walk will be good for me. It's not that far."

Ivarr frowned at her and put a hand on her forehead. "You stay. I'll go." His voice brooked no argument.

The sky was rapidly growing darker, and the icy wind cut through Gytha's coat. She shivered, and Hlif roused a little at the motion.

Gytha sat beside her father, and together they carefully shifted Hlif to sit between them, leaning against Gytha for support. Hlif murmured something neither of them could make out, and Ivarr's worried frown grew more grave. He retrieved a blanket from inside and wrapped it around them both. Hlif's fever needed to come down, but freezing was a real danger, too.

He looked up at the sky and then back to her. "Don't stay out too long. Once you're inside, don't open the door to strange sounds," he said. "Especially not the bear."

Then he strode away into the deepening shadows. The wind picked up, swirling snow in dizzying patterns.

Gytha could feel her fever rising like a pounding song in her head, and the pain of the cold upon her cheeks felt like the only thing keeping her mind lucid. She sweated and burned while her fingers and toes turned to ice. Darkness fell, and still she sat with her mother upon the doorstep, too dazed to remember that she was supposed to go inside. The whirling snow that whipped past her face, dancing and spinning, made it hard to remember which direction was up and which was down.

At last, Sigrid opened the door. "Gytha! You must be frozen! I thought you'd come in already!" She and Solveig helped Gytha and their mother inside. The girls had been busy feeding, watering, milking, and cleaning the stalls of the animals in the barn end of the lodge for some time, and had only just returned from these chores.

They got Hlif into a chair near the fire, with a blanket wrapped around her and the two youngest, Brinja and Halvard, tasked with holding her icy hands to warm them. Then they turned their attention to Gytha, who had sat down at the table.

"You're frozen, too, Gytha!" said Sigrid. "Come warm up."

"I'm fine!" Gytha ran her fingers through her blonde hair, and her fingertips felt like ice against her scalp. "Pabbi ought to be back soon." She felt dizzy with fever, exhausted and freezing and yet too restless to be comfortable in the heat of the lodge. She accepted a cup of hot broth from Dagney and drank it gratefully, feeling the warmth sit in her belly like a banked coal. She was hot and cold at the same time, sticky with sweat and shivering.

Little Halvard, sitting with his head against their mother's knee and her hand against his cheek, said, "Don't faint, Gytha."

She put a hand against the edge of the table, and the wood was solid and warm against her frozen fingers. Little Halvard's face, turned toward her with concern in his huge blue eyes, split into two wavering images.

"I'm hot," she gasped, and she stumbled across the lodge to the door. She wrenched it open and fell to hands and knees in the snow outside.

Solveig darted across the lodge and out to her, closing the door behind her. "Come, Gytha." She pulled at Gytha's arm.

"I can't. I'm so hot." Belying this, Gytha had begun to shiver and tremble. She could not decide whether she wanted to be wrapped in blankets and crawl into the fire or bury herself in the snow. Her skin was hot but she felt like there was ice inside her, skittering like fear through her burning skin and up her spine.

One hand slipped, and she fell on her face in the snow. With a groan, she curled onto her side.

Suddenly, the bear appeared out of the swirling, snow-filled darkness. He snuffled at Gytha's face.

"She smells of death." His voice rumbled so quietly that the girls barely heard him over the wind.

"Does that mean she will die?" Solveig looked up at the great beast.

The bear sighed. "I would..."

His soft words were cut off by a furious shout. Ivarr appeared out of the whirling snow and threw himself at the bear's face, beating at the creature's eyes. "Get away from them!" He tried to dig his fingers into the bear's eyes.

The bear gave a roar of pain and shook his head, dislodging Ivarr, who fell beside Gytha. Ivarr scrambled to his feet and stood protectively over the girls. "Get away!" he shouted, waving his arms and taking a step toward the bear.

The bear rose to his full height and looked down at the man. A deep scratch at the edge of one eye bled down his huge muzzle.

Sigrid opened the door, having heard the noise, and screamed.

Ivarr shouted again at the bear. Then he cried, "Get Gytha inside! And give me my axe!"

Sigrid tossed the axe into the snow near him and grabbed at Gytha's feet.

"Wait." The bear's voice rumbled as deep as thunder.

Ivarr caught up the axe and advanced on the bear. "Get away from my daughters."

The great bear shook his head, and drops of red scattered across the snow. "I mean your daughters no harm. Nor you, either."

Ivarr heard only roaring, and his eyes widened with fear. Yet still he advanced, putting himself between his daughters and the bear.

Behind him, Gytha shoved herself to hands and knees. "I'm fine," she whispered. "Just a little dizzy."

"I can help you." The bear's voice rumbled like distant thunder, deep and wild and raw. "Tell your father I mean you no harm."

Gytha struggled to her feet, leaning hard on Sigrid, and gasped, "Pabbi, wait! He's a friend. Please."

"Get inside!" Ivarr's voice cracked. "*Please*, Gytha!"

The wind caught at Ivarr's coat so suddenly and so roughly that he staggered, and as he did so, the bear reached forward with one huge paw and knocked the axe from his hands. The beast shoved closer, crowding Ivarr back with his great shoulder.

Then the bear was face to face with Gytha. "You're dying," he said, the deep voice thick with grief. "Please let me help you."

"If you can help me, you can help my mother." The words tumbled from Gytha without forethought, and she stood straighter, one hand braced on Sigrid's shoulder.

"Of course." The bear ducked its huge head. "But please, will you trust me? I wish to ask a great favor of you, one that requires sacrifice from you. But I believe you are brave enough for it. I have seen you endure suffering with grace, and I have no one else to ask."

27

"I would do anything to save my mother." Gytha shifted her weight to her own two feet and her knees buckled. The bear shoved his head under her arm, so that she fell over his neck with her face buried in his thick fur. The warmth of him, pine-scented and wild, filled her lungs, and she felt a little more clear-headed. "Don't hurt my father. Please, Master Bear."

Ivarr was shoving desperately at the bear from the other side, unable to reach his axe or his daughters.

"He does not hear my voice, so he is frightened." The bear shifted again, presenting his broad side to Ivarr and his bleeding face to Gytha. "Tell your sisters to bring your mother, and any others who are sick, and I will do what I can for them."

"Bring Mamma outside, please." The words tasted strange in Gytha's mouth, full of fear and desperation. Sigrid's shadowed eyes widened, and Gytha whispered, "*Please*, Sigrid!"

Ivarr twisted beneath the bear's neck and reached Gytha. "Are you hurt?" His hands gripped her shoulders.

"No." Her vision blurred and refocused, and her ears roared in time with her pulse. "Pabbi, don't hurt the bear. Please."

At this moment, Solveig and Sigrid opened the door again, Hlif standing unsteadily between them. The bear turned to stand face to face with the older woman. He breathed into her face, and a growling rumble came from him.

Then Hlif stood straighter, and she cried, "A bear! Girls! Ivarr! Come inside before it eats you!"

The bear snuffled roughly and turned away, grumbling. He breathed into Gytha's face, his breath hot and fierce, and said, "Your mother is healed. But your fever will not go so easily. I will come again tomorrow morning. Rest well."

Finally able to move more freely, Ivarr caught up the axe again and swung it at the bear's head. The beast barely avoided the blow and retreated into the night, snuffling and shaking his head.

Moments later, they were all inside with the door securely locked behind them. Once he had assured himself that none of his daughters was hurt by the bear, Ivarr collapsed into a chair near the fire with his face buried in his hands. His hands shook; in fact, his whole body shook as the terror receded. For several minutes, the only sounds were those of the wood in the stove.

Hlif knelt beside Ivarr and wrapped her arms around him. "I'm all right, and so are the children," she murmured.

He gripped her shoulders with white fingers and pulled back to search her face. "Are you well, love? You're not hurt? And your fever?"

The woman's clear blue eyes were warm, and her thin lips curved in a soft smile. "Not the tiniest ache of fever. Feel." She put her forehead against his. "I feel tired but strong and healthy, Ivarr, like I do at the end of a good harvest."

She turned to look at the children, and he turned with her, his eyes gleaming with unshed tears. Sigrid sat with the little ones on the thick rug, helping Brinja change into her pajamas and glancing up at her parents at intervals. The twins, Ashild and Dagney, were making acorn flour flatcakes, trying not to look upset, and Randulf and Halvard were alternately practicing their handwriting with wet fingers on the chalkboard and looking at the adults. Solveig sat beside Gytha on their bed, talking quietly to her older sister.

"Look at them," Hlif said. "We're all whole."

Ivarr stared at them all in turn, drinking in their faces with renewed love and gratitude for their lives. "I don't understand." He shuddered. "The bear was growling like it meant to eat them all."

Dinner was rich and filling but quiet. Hlif seemed entirely well, though the fatigue of weeks of fever made her even quieter than usual. Ivarr looked down at his hands, lean and scarred, and the dried blood under his fingernails. He rubbed it away thoughtfully.

At last Sigrid spoke, looking from one sister to the other. "Solveig said you and her heard the bear speak. But I just heard growling and roaring."

Gytha took a deep, steadying breath. "Yes. He was kind to us. He said he healed Mamma, but my illness would not go so quickly."

"I just heard roaring," Ivarr said. But his eyes found his wife's gaze across the table, and her thin cheeks, now pink with health. "How do you feel, my love?"

"I have not felt better in years." Hlif smiled again. "I heard only animal growls and roars, but if the girls heard him speak, I believe them. I cannot even tell you how wretched I felt, my mind half-gone with fever. The breath of that creature on my face felt like life breathed into me, hot enough to burn away the illness itself. I don't know what magic it is, but that is not an ordinary bear."

Sigrid bit her lip and looked at Gytha. "But you're not well."

The eldest of the children looked down at her bowl. "No." She blinked, trying to ignore the shimmering black spots in her vision. "I feel less feverish, though." That was true; instead, she felt dizzy and weak and light-headed, as if the floor kept tilting beneath her.

When she went to bed, she fell asleep before she'd even pulled the blanket up against the chill. Solveig crawled into bed over her, pulling the blanket up over them both.

Gytha woke well before dawn, her pulse pounding in her ears. For several minutes, she lay silent and still, trying to calm her racing heart. There was no reason to be afraid. But the dark spun around her, and she closed her eyes against the dizziness. That only made her feel sick, so she slipped her feet into her slippers and pulled on her sweater before stepping closer to the stove. She drank a cup of water and then stared through the grate at the embers.

Every inch of her ached, and chills crawled up and down her spine, alternating with sweaty heat. She brushed her hair with trembling fingers and braided it over her shoulder. The pale gold strands gleamed in the dim light.

At last, restless with fever and churning thoughts, she walked to the door. She pulled on her boots, her coat, and a hat she thought was probably hers, though it was hard to tell in the shadows, and then opened the door and slipped out into the frigid darkness.

The night was utterly still. Every now and then a distant sound reached her ears, the quiet creak of cold wood or the soft hoot of an owl. The silence felt immense.

Gytha swung her arms back and forth in a futile attempt to warm herself. Then she sat on the flagstone, leaned back against the wall of the lodge, and sighed. The air was so cold it stung her lungs, but she felt oddly free and full of hope.

The sky above shimmered with green and pink, soft ribbons of color undulating across star-strewn expanse. The ethereal beauty of this silent display brought tears to her eyes. There might be no flowers visible in the frigid winter, but there was color and beauty even in the wild, inhospitable north.

Across the wide yard, a great shadow detached itself from the looming darkness of the forest and ambled closer. Soon she could see that it was the bear. The snowy white of its fur gleamed under the bright, clear starlight, and its dark eyes were impossible to read.

At last it loomed in front of her.

"Are you afraid of me?" it rumbled softly.

"No," Gytha said honestly. "You are a bear, and I know bears are dangerous, but I cannot fear you." She braced herself on the wall as she stood, for the dim world of snow and shadows danced before her eyes. When she could focus on the bear again, she bit her lip.

The pale light of the stars fell on an ugly, blood-crusted scratch from the inside corner of one eye down its great muzzle almost to its black nose.

She stepped forward, and when the bear did not move, she put one hand on his neck. The other hand traced a line down his muzzle beside the scratch. "Did my father do this?"

"Yes." The bear's answer was quiet. "He meant to protect you. He is a brave man, facing a bear without even his axe in hand to save his children."

"He is brave and good. All the same, I am sorry for it. You wouldn't hurt me, would you?" Gytha studied the bear's face. It was difficult to tell exactly how he spoke; his mouth was not made to form human speech, and yet it was not difficult to understand him. She felt sure he was a male bear.

His teeth were as long as her longest fingers and his head was nearly as long as her arm. She ought to have been terrified.

Instead, when she met his eyes, she felt only trust.

The bear held her gaze. "I would not harm you, no. But the great favor I must ask of you is not safe."

"What would you ask?" She laughed in quiet disbelief. "What can I have to offer you? You saved my family from starvation this winter. I owe you my life."

He withdrew just a little and shifted so that he breathed into her face again, his hot breath like a wash of summer sunshine that made her warm to her toes.

"There." He ducked his head and sighed heavily, as if he were suddenly exhausted. "I have no hold over you, no healing held back." He swayed on his feet.

The feverish chill in Gytha's bones was gone, replaced by a sense of warmth and comfort. The crawling restlessness in her stomach, sick and sour, was entirely vanished.

Gytha frowned and looked at him more closely. "Had you held back before? I feel entirely better. How did you heal my mother and me?"

The bear did not raise his head. "A little magic. All I have." After a moment, he said almost inaudibly, "I had not intended to withhold healing before. I found a little more strength in the night, and I wanted to spend it on you."

With a sudden rush of gratitude, Gytha put one hand atop his head and caressed the fur as if he were tame.

He flicked one ear, and she froze. "I'm sorry. I just…I felt safe, and I didn't think. I didn't mean to offend you."

A soft, tired rumble reached her ears like distant thunder. "I am not offended." He turned his head a little, as if hinting that she might rub his ear, so she did so.

Then he said nothing else. As she stood beside him, leaning against his great shoulder with her hand softly scratching around his ear, she began to perceive what she had not at first. The crushing fatigue that made his enormous body shiver and tremble, not from cold but from the effort of staying upright.

"What favor could a great creature like you, full of magic, have to ask of me?" Gytha said at last.

The bear sighed again. "I ought not ask. I have been selfish to think of it."

Gytha smiled. To think that this bear was dangerous! "Please ask, Master Bear. I would like to do you a favor after you have been so generous to my family."

"My name is Alexander." He lifted his head at last and met her eyes. In the darkness, she could not see their color, only the faint, reflected gleam of the cold light of the stars. "I would ask you to come away with me to the North for a long time. Far away from your family. I would not able to speak with you, but I would be with you. There are…others…there; they are not friendly, but they would not harm you."

The young woman's soft caress of his ear slowed. "And what would I do there?" she asked carefully.

The bear sighed and hesitated. At last he said, "You would be fed and housed and provided with entertainment of many sorts. But if you do not finish the task, I cannot ask another."

"What task?"

"A man must share your bed for the nights of a year and a day, and you must not look upon him or touch him." The bear's voice was so low that Gytha strained to hear his words. "Of course he would not touch you either, you understand."

Gytha frowned. "Will we talk, then? Much can be learned by honest conversation, and a man's looks are hardly the most interesting or important thing about him."

"You may talk as much as you like. He may not answer nor give any signal of agreement or disagreement."

"So we are to remain strangers, even in such an intimate setting." Gytha frowned. "Why would you ask such a favor?"

The bear turned to look at her again. "I cannot say." His dark eyes gleamed in the starlight. "Do not agree out of obligation. It is too much to ask of anyone."

"Why did you call Solveig 'little sister'?" Gytha asked, partly out of curiosity and partly to give herself time to think.

"I thought I would be proud to have such a sister, and clearly she is younger than you are." The bear hesitated and said, "I have given you my name, but I do not know yours. Will you give me your name, as if we are friends?"

The young woman blinked. "My name is Gytha," she said. "I am sorry. It was rude of me not to tell you earlier."

The bear's deep, rumbling chuckle set her mind at ease. "Gytha," he said, as if testing the sound of it. "It is a beautiful name."

"Why can Solveig understand you, too, but Papa and Sigrid only heard roaring?"

The bear sighed softly, as if grieved by this. "I have only a very little magic, and it is borrowed. It was an unexpected gift that she understood me. I thought only you would hear my words."

Gytha chewed her lip as she thought. The cold seeped through her coat and her boots, and she shivered. Without thinking, she leaned a little closer to the bear, letting her shoulder rest against his again.

"Let me talk to my family and I will tell you my decision tomorrow morning," she said at last. "But I think I want to say yes."

Alexander twisted his head around to look at her again. "What? Why?"

She took a deep breath. "Because you asked it."

CHAPTER 3

For hours, Gytha treasured that early morning conversation without sharing it with the others. She turned Alexander's words over in her mind, remembering the tone of his deep, rumbling laughter, the feel of his hot breath on her face, and the trembling, exhausted strength and solidity of his shoulder. The blood-crusted gouge down his long muzzle. When she had made her decision, she told her parents.

"You're out of your mind," Ivarr said firmly. "Absolutely not."

"Pabbi, please." She stood and walked around the table to kneel in front of him. She took his hand and put it to her forehead. "The fever is gone, and Alexander did it. He could have held healing over my head and bargained with me for it, but he didn't."

"But it's a bear!" Her father's voice rose. "Bears eat people!"

"His name is Alexander, and he didn't eat us. He gave us food and healed Mamma and me." Still holding his hand, she said, "You scratched his face pretty badly. He wasn't even angry. He said you were brave to face a bear to save your family."

Her father's blond eyebrows drew downward in disbelief. "How did it tell you that? Animals don't talk."

Solveig said, "I heard it speak, too, Pabbi. He has a nice voice, all rumbly and soft."

Ivarr looked from one girl to the other. "Sigrid? Have you heard it talk?"

The girl bit her lip and reluctantly shook her head. "No," she said. "Not in words. I only heard growling and rumbling. But I saw it breathe into Mamma's face and then she was well. It didn't growl at her or bite or anything. Just breathed at her."

She looked at Hlif for support, and Hlif reluctantly nodded. "I felt his breath on my face like a hot wind, and it felt like clean fire in my bones, burning away the fever. I can believe he is not an ordinary bear." Then she frowned. "But I agree that the task is not safe, and I would risk myself sooner than I would risk you, Gytha. Will he take me instead?"

"Mama!" Gytha said, shocked. "The little ones need you! Papa needs you!"

Hlif said sharply, "You are my child, Gytha! It is my right and duty to protect you."

"But I must do what is right!" Gytha cried.

The argument went for hours, until everyone had wept at least once. Even Halvard and Brinja cried, for they were not used to raised voices or disagreement of any sort.

In the end, Ivarr all but barred the door. "I won't keep you a prisoner, Gytha," he said at last. "But even if I believe that you hearing it talk wasn't the fever but the true words of the bear,

I cannot think it wise to go traipsing off to the wild north with a predator as your only companion. Whatever it wants, it can't be good for you."

"He has been kind to us, Pabbi, and I want to help him."

Ivarr stopped pacing and faced her. "No good can come of it, Gytha. Don't do it."

She stepped closer and put her arms around his waist and rested her head against his chest. His heartbeat in her ear felt like his steady, reliable strength. Even now, she was not tall enough to put her chin on his shoulder as Mamma did. He wrapped his arms around her, and she realized he was afraid.

She looked up at him. "I'm not frightened, Pabbi. If he meant to hurt me, or any of us, he has had so many chances. If I am hurt, then I know it will not be by his choice."

He sighed and tightened his arms around her, but he said nothing else.

Long after the lamps were blown out and everyone was in bed, she heard her parents talking in anguished whispers.

She woke long before dawn and dressed quietly. She wrapped some bread and cheese in a clean rag and stuffed them inside her coat. Then she peeked outside.

The bear stood at the edge of the trees, a shadow lost in the shadows until it took a step forward. Silently he strode to her until they stood face to face.

"You are brave. I did not think to see you." The rumbling words were so soft and low that Gytha barely heard them.

The young woman took a deep breath to steady her voice. "I will go with you and do as you asked."

The bear twitched in surprise and stared at her. "You will?"

"It means a lot to you, doesn't it?" she asked softly.

"It does." Alexander sighed. "But you are not bound by what binds me. You need not take on this hardship."

Gytha licked her lips, tempted by the opportunity to forget it all. A whole year without her family! But the bear—Alexander—had been generous to them. He had saved them from a cruel death.

Wouldn't it be wrong to refuse to help him in return?

The door opened suddenly, and Ivarr stepped outside holding a lamp, his eyes wide. "It's not growling," he said under his breath. "What strange creature is this?"

He held the lamp higher, so the light gleamed on the bear's glittering eyes and caught the blood dried dark on his muzzle. "What do you want with my daughter?"

Alexander said, "I have asked a great favor. I have not compelled her."

Ivarr's eyes widened, but he looked at Gytha. "Do you hear words? I only hear growling."

Gytha nodded. "He said he asked a favor, but he has not compelled me. It's true, Papa. He isn't forcing me."

"Why do you want her in particular? Couldn't anyone do what you need?" Ivarr addressed the bear and then looked to Gytha to understand the answering growls.

"It could be any maiden, unmarried and unpromised," Alexander answered. "But I had only enough magic to ask one. I chose you, Gytha, because I saw how courageously you bore your suffering, and because my time here in the south is short. I am bound tightly, and I will soon either return or die."

Gytha relayed this to Ivarr, who studied the bear with narrowed eyes.

"What will you do if she refuses?" he asked.

"I will die here. I will not return alone."

Gytha met her father's eyes.

"He told me not to agree out of obligation. He isn't forcing me at all. But have you not taught me to meet kindness with kindness? How much kindness has he already given our family? Mamma and I are healed, and we all have food enough to last the winter. Would it not be cruel to refuse him this?

Ivarr's eyes burned with emotion. "It is cruel to ask so much of you."

The bear dropped his head. "He is right. I should not have asked." His voice was nearly inaudible.

Gytha took a deep breath. "Even before I knew he faced death, I knew that I ought to go with him. I need to do this to stand upright before God and before you and Mama. I need to know I was brave enough to do the right thing."

"And the right thing is to go with him for a year and risk all manner of suffering for a bear?"

"Yes, it is." She raised her chin and met his eyes, keeping her gaze steady. "You taught me honor and compassion, and you taught me courage. I've seen you live it well, Papa. Let me follow your good example."

With one eye on the bear, Ivarr set the lamp down on the snow. He wrapped his arms around her again, heedless of the bear and the cold deep enough to freeze a man's blood in his veins. In the strength of his arms and the shuddering of his chest, she felt his grief and pride. "Don't leave without kissing Mama and your brothers and sisters."

"Of course not." She smiled up at him and stepped back inside. The others were stirring, even though it was far earlier than the little ones usually woke, and she embraced them one by one, kissing the little ones on the cheeks for good measure. "Be good for Mama and Papa while I'm gone," she said at last. "I'm not afraid, so there's no reason for you to be. I'm having an adventure!"

Sigrid looked at her doubtfully, but Solveig smiled back at her. "You'll be all right," she said, her voice only a little unsteady. "He's a nice bear."

Her mother went outside and talked quietly with her father for several minutes. Then she hugged Gytha tightly and whispered in her ear, "Are you sure, Honeycake? You don't have to do this."

"I'm sure, Mama."

When she stepped outside again, she had a pack full of hastily made flatcakes, some acorn flour, and cooked elk venison wrapped in cloth. The meat and flatcakes would freeze in the pack and be ready to warm and eat as she traveled, and the flour could be cooked when she arrived at their destination.

Her father still stared at Alexander, who stood like a great white mountain, motionless but for the faint rippling of his thick fur in the breeze. "Take good care of my daughter," Ivarr said, his voice rough with emotion. "Understand this: I love her, and if you hurt her, I'll hunt you to the end of the earth and beyond. Understand?"

Alexander bowed his head solemnly, and the man pressed his lips together.

The bear's rumbling voice reverberated in Gytha's bones, soft and deep. "The way is very long, and your legs will tire. Will you let me carry you?" She nodded, and he lowered himself. "Climb on my back, and hold on tight."

Her father watched in awe as she climbed up. The white fur was so thick that her legs sank into it, and she buried her hands in it, grabbing handfuls to steady herself. "Does it hurt when I hold on?"

The bear snuffled as if in soft laughter. "Not at all. Don't fall." Then he took off in a surging, ground-eating run that carried them into the forest in moments.

All day and night he ran without stopping, his powerful muscles working beneath Gytha's legs. She had never ridden a horse, but it must be easier than this! She rocked and swayed, and she might have fallen off except that she clamped her legs around the bear's ribs and gripped his fur with both hands. She kept her head down to avoid the lower branches of the spruces and firs, but the bear chose paths that did not have too many low-hanging branches, and he slowed when he approached them to give her time to duck.

Gytha's legs burned from the effort of holding on. In fact her whole body burned from the unfamiliar strain. Her face stung with the cold, and she feared that her nose had become frostbitten and fallen off. What if she returned to her family unrecognizable?

Exhaustion finally overcame her, and she lost her grip on Alexander's fur. She slipped sideways with a helpless sense of falling into darkness.

The scent of bear and an incongruous feeling of safety and warmth filled Gytha's senses as she woke slowly. She moved a little and then groaned; every muscle of her body ached fiercely.

"Are you hurt?" The bear's voice rumbled through her bones.

She pulled away, struggling to make sense of where she was. The bear shifted and the world moved.

"Oh!" She had been curled up, lying between the bear's front legs as it had laid its great head and neck over her. When she moved, snow slid off the bear's head and fell into her face.

Gytha brushed the snow hurriedly from her face and stood up. The world was blanketed in another layer of heavy snow, though only a few fat flakes still fell. The world was gray and silver, and Gytha couldn't tell whether it was dawn or dusk.

"Where are we?" She looked back at the bear.

He stood and shook the snow from his body in a great rush. "North."

She looked around again. Her stomach was empty, and the feeling was both familiar and discouraging. Had she made a terrible mistake? Without the bear's fur around her, her coat was too thin to protect her against the lethal cold.

"Is your food too frozen to eat?"

"Yes. But I will eat next time we stop." She put two of the flatcakes and some of the elk venison into an inner pocket, where it would warm next to her body.

On every side were tall, dignified evergreens, and the snow was so thick that much of the underbrush had been entirely covered. The stillness was almost eerie.

The bear's soft, rumbling voice broke into her thoughts. "Can you climb on again? We have a long way to go."

Gytha's legs buckled when she turned, and she fell to her knees, biting back a cry.

"What is wrong?"

"I'm terribly sore." She groaned as she struggled to stand, legs trembling. "Oh, everything hurts."

"Use me to steady yourself."

She hauled herself upright with handfuls of his thick fur. At last she stood, resting her forehead against his shoulder and trying not to let her trembling breaths turn into tears.

"How far north are we going?" she managed.

"The end of the world." Alexander's voice was low and, if she wasn't mistaken, grieved.

"Are there wolves here?"

The bear turned to look at her, his dark eyes grave. "There are wolves here, but we are going too far north even for them."

He lowered himself to a crouch, and it still took her two tries to climb onto his back. When she was on, he began to run in the same powerful, rippling gait that had taken them so far.

"Is it morning or night?" she said, and the wind of their speed whipped her words away.

"It is winter, so it is night here. The sun does not come back until summer, and that is very short, and many months away."

He ran for an hour before slowing. "Can you eat and ride?"

"Yes. Thank you." Gytha ate while he continued walking. Her eyebrows and eyelashes were crusted with frost, and her face felt frozen when she opened her mouth for each bite. When she was finished, she put the rest of the flatcakes and elk venison back into her coat to warm.

"I am finished. I should have asked you if you wanted some. I'm sorry. Are you hungry?"

"I will not take food from your mouth." He began to run again. He continued without ceasing for hours. Gytha's hands cramped in his fur, and she lay down with her head against his churning shoulders and dozed. She woke when he changed course. They crossed frozen streams and wound through ice-crusted canyons that gleamed in the moonlight.

Perhaps he ran for hours. Perhaps days.

At last he slowed to a walk. Gytha sat up, dizzy with hunger and fatigue. Her legs, buried deep in his fur, were as toasty warm as if she were sitting by the fire at home, but her body was cold, and she felt weak and strange.

"Thank you for your courage." Alexander's voice sounded strangely thin. "Remember, do not look at or touch the stranger in your bed. Do not be afraid."

Gytha frowned at his odd tone. "Are you all right? You sound ill."

The bear tripped and nearly fell, but caught himself before she lost her grip and fell headlong. "I can't think." He stopped and shook his head roughly. "I forgot my name for a long time," he said in a rush. "No one wanted it. No one remembered. Not even me. Only because I wanted you to trust me did I search through my mind for it." He brushed one great paw roughly over his face and shook it again before stumbling forward.

For several minutes he continued walking in silence before he said, "I cannot speak to you once we arrive. Not even a word. Remember what I said. Do not look at him. Do not touch. Do not be afraid."

"Don't look. Don't touch. Don't be afraid." Gytha murmured to herself. "Are you ill?"

"Tired."

The bear kept walking, but his steps became more uneven.

"You must be hungry," he said. "Eat if you want."

"Do you want some of the meat?"

"No. Thank you."

Still he pressed on without another word. He turned a little to the left and crested the low hill which he had been following for some time, then picked his way down the other side. The ice crust was heavy enough to hold his weight in most places, but sometimes his huge feet broke through and he went stumbling through the layers of ice and snow until he found better footing. They had passed out of the forest into rolling Yhills, and the world was white and gray and silver in the moonlight. To the west, the mountains were closer than Gytha had ever seen them.

To the east, the horizon was broken by low escarpments dividing this land from the higher tundra, and far behind them to the southeast, taller mountains reached for the stars.

"I didn't know there were mountains to the east," Gytha said. In the dim and sparkling night, they were only shadows, and she could not tell how far away they were nor any detail about them. "And I've never seen the ones to the west this close. We must have traveled more west than I realized."

"My home used to be on the other side of those mountains." The words were low and breathless.

"Are you all right?"

The bear shook his head again and snuffled his nose into the snow. "I am fine."

He pressed on, carrying her miles across the tundra, until they reached a wide crevasse, and he turned east and followed it for several miles until he reached a broken path that led deep into the shadowy hollow. His steps were nearly silent, but Gytha could hear his labored breathing. Above them the sky was a splash of stars, but the hollow itself was as black as pitch, and Gytha could not even see the bear's white head.

"How far down are we going?" she ventured.

"To the bottom and back up. Hold on."

In the interminable night, she could not see the bottom of the crevasse, and she was too frightened to keep her eyes open as they descended. She nearly catapulted over his head as he followed a steep, narrow path down the side of the gash in the world, but she gripped his sides with arms and legs and buried her face in the fur over his shoulders. She could not tell if it was ten minutes or several hours later that his gait shifted as he reached the narrow icy floor of the ravine and began to scramble up the other side. The climb was even steeper than the path down, and the way was uneven, slippery, and fraught with broken ice that crumbled under Alexander's great paws. More than once they nearly fell, but he always caught a better grip and surged upward.

By the time they lurched over the edge on the other side, Gytha had bitten back several screams of terror. The bear stood still for a moment, his sides heaving, before stumbling forward.

"I think you need a rest," Gytha said.

"I'm fine."

"Then say that I could use a rest. That was terrifying."

"Oh." Alexander stopped with his head hanging down.

Gytha slid down from his back. White fur strands stuck to her sweaty palms and between her fingers.

"You should eat again," Alexander said.

"I ate everything but the acorn flour, and that must be cooked."

"Oh." The bear swayed as if trying to hold his feet in a strong wind, but the air was still.

"Aren't you hungry?" Gytha said gently.

"I don't know."

Gytha rested her head against his shoulder and felt his exhaustion like a great abyss that would swallow them both whole.

Finally he said, his voice low and almost ashamed, "If you can withstand your hunger a little longer, I do not think I can face her tonight."

"Face who?"

The growl that answered was nearly inaudible, for all its restrained fury. His throat worked, but he did not answer her. Finally he managed, "The queen."

"The queen?"

He shuddered and nearly lost his footing.

Hunger curled in her belly, familiar and regrettable, but not intolerable. She was more tired than she could ever remember, and her legs trembled like those of a newborn lamb. "I am as tired as I am hungry. If you will keep me warm, I think a nap would do us both good."

Feeling bold and yet entirely safe, she curled up between his front legs, with her back against his chest. Carefully he lowered his head so his neck was a warm weight over her body.

"I am sorry." His low voice rumbled through her body. "I had hoped to carry you there safely before you had to suffer too much from hunger. Even if it is a prison for me, you will be safe there."

"A prison?" She twisted, trying to see his face, as if he were a person and she could read his expressions.

His throat worked and he grumbled something inarticulate. At last he managed, "I…I cannot say more."

When she said nothing else, he sighed heavily and relaxed. The weight of his head dropped, and she realized he had fallen into an exhausted sleep within seconds.

Despite her own fatigue, she lay awake for some time. Beneath her, the ice was frigid, and she shifted several times so that different parts of her rested against that life-stealing cold. Alexander might have been dead for how much he noticed her wiggling; his warm, solid weight was the most welcome shield against the cold and any other danger.

When she did drift into sleep, she dreamed strange, unsettling things. Fingers made of glittering ice snatched at her arms. Something howled behind her, and when she whirled in terror, a shriek came from another direction. Knives of ice spun in the air like snowflakes in a blizzard. A castle of ice loomed over her, and a voice hissed, "Foolish child!"

Gytha jerked awake with a gasp, and Alexander rumbled a soft question.

"I had a bad dream. I'm sorry." Gytha buried her face in his fur and tried to steady her breathing. He lay his great head over her back, and she whispered her thanks into his neck.

Her stomach growled.

"It is not far now." Alexander sighed, his head still low. "I am bound to silence in the palace. Remember the rules."

"Do not look. Do not touch. Do not be afraid." Gytha nodded, as if she were not terrified. "Do not expect you to answer."

48

The bear nodded. Then, slowly, he stood, not quite stifling a groan.

"Are you sore too?" Gytha smiled up at him. His face was quite handsome, now that she thought of him as a friend. His dark eyes were soft and limpid, with the light of intelligence in them. Even the livid red gash down his muzzle seemed only to remind her of his gentle nature.

She patted his cheek affectionately and then said, embarrassed, "I'm sorry! Was that too bold?"

Alexander's surprised chuckle caught her off guard. "Someone must be bold, and it cannot be me. Don't forget the rules, Gytha." He lowered himself to let her climb on. "Lie down on me. Your jacket is too thin for this place."

When they set off again, Gytha could feel his fatigue and reluctance in every step, but he did not falter. He climbed yet another low hill, and then crossed a long stretch of broken ice chunks.

"I've never seen land like this." Gytha sat up and looked around curiously. Her eyebrows were covered in frost, and every breath felt like it was burning her with ice from the inside out. Her eyeballs felt like they were freezing in their sockets. She shivered convulsively and leaned down to press her body into his fur, her eyes closed. Her back might freeze, but her face was full of the scent of clean, snowy bear.

He was safe.

Then there was a strange sound, like a rushing of wind and water and stone unlike anything she had ever heard before. His steps shifted and his body tilted, so that she felt she might slip forward if she did not hold on even more tightly.

She peeked through the rippling white fur. He was following a narrow, precarious path down a cliffside. To her left a steep rock face rose up above their heads. To her right, she could not see the ground, and the strange rushing sound came from far below.

"Remember, Gytha. Trust me, if you can, and be brave." The bear's words were almost inaudible.

Gytha took a deep, shaky breath and stretched a little farther.

Enormous chunks of ice surged atop the water, like the layer of ice atop a bucket that had been broken but not melted. The icebergs crunched against each other with the force of the ocean waves below. Bits of froth were visible at intervals between the sharp edges as the ice chunks broke apart and crashed together again.

As far as she could see, the starlight glinted on a vast, broken, shifting sheet of ice.

This was the edge of the world.

CHAPTER 4

After many minutes, the steep path widened onto a small promontory, an ice-crusted and precarious outcropping with the salt wind whipping up in their faces. Alexander turned left into a cave and an even deeper darkness.

The path was level, and for some distance he did not turn to either side. Gytha kept herself flat on his back, both for warmth and for fear of bashing her head on some unseen rock. The darkness was absolute.

Soon the rushing of the waves grew distant and Alexander turned downward on a long, sloping path. At last there was a faint light around a corner. When they reached it, Gytha could see that they were in a long, rough hallway carved of stone, and at the end there was a set of softly glowing doors.

When they drew closer, Gytha saw that the doors were made of ice or some translucent crystal, for the pattern on them was intricate but hard to discern. The refracted light gleamed and glittered on many carved surfaces, so that the doors were like two enormous jewels.

The doors swung outwards, and a strange little man nodded them inside. Alexander and Gytha passed through a short hallway into a great hall, which was lit with myriad lamps. She looked at the little man, but after so long in darkness, her eyes were dazzled, and she could not tell what about him had struck her as so strange.

The hall was a marvel! The ceiling rose far overhead, carved of smooth stone and vaulted in elegant lines. Great columns marched up each side of the room. The floor was polished stone, but over it were thick carpets of unusual colors, colors Gytha had only seen in small, expensive bundles of embroidery thread. So many rugs of such fine thread was almost unimaginable!

On every wall hung tapestries of equally fine make, and near one corner there was a desk, beside which there were several baskets containing a few skeins of wool, and knitting needles. The room was cold. The bear walked through it as though it were familiar and uninteresting, but Gytha craned her neck to see it all.

Alexander continued through the center of the room and turned into another corridor which led to another room of similar size, with different tapestries and carpets, and then another room, smaller, with a fireplace, and another room with a pool of water beneath a waterfall, and another like the first. Then another hall and more rooms, great hall after great hall, all luxurious and unique and deserted. At last, after another corridor, the bear turned through an open door into a room smaller than the rest but still quite spacious, about the size of her family's lodge, including the side that housed the animals and the storeroom.

On one wall there was a fireplace, cold now but with logs cut and kindling ready. There was a low pallet of thick woolen blankets and piles of furs, enough to be comfortable even without sisters to help warm it. The ceiling was not as high as in the other rooms, nor was it smooth; the stone had been intricately carved to depict flowers and vines, the delicate petals coming out of the stone in gorgeous relief.

Alexander crouched, and Gytha slid off his back with a groan. Her sore legs buckled, and she fell in an ungainly heap to the floor. The bear lowered his head in what appeared to be sympathy.

Without rising, Gytha looked around, noting the washing basin carved into the wall. Next to it was a wooden table with a lovely alabaster pitcher. The room was lit by several lamps on small tables throughout the room. The light was warm and friendly, picking out the red accents in the thick rugs layered in front of the fire.

On another wall, several low wooden shelves held books! Even the rich merchants in town only had a dozen or so books, and these shelves held several hundred. The books were large, with neatly lettered titles painted in gold on the spines. The leather covers looked old, well-used but well-kept. There was something tall in the corner covered with a white cloth that draped all the way to the flagstone floor.

By the sleeping pallet, there was a pair of lambskin slippers and a robe of heavy silk.

"Is this where you live?" Gytha turned to Alexander, who lowered his head and stared at her wordlessly.

No, that could not be right. Everything except the books looked new, yet Gytha had the feeling this was a very old place. Old, and full of stories. Full of sorrows.

Besides, bears did not sleep in beds, nor did they need layers of wool or lambskin slippers to stay warm. What a strange thought. This room was obviously intended to be hers.

Gytha got to hands and knees, grimacing as her sore legs protested, and slowly made her way to her feet. The room spun for a moment, and she wondered why she was dizzy again.

It must be the hunger. She had been so cold and so nervous about this strange world that she had forgotten she had not eaten in quite some time. Had it been many hours or days? How many days? It was hard to tell, since there was no dawn or dusk. Only night.

Suddenly Alexander gave a low, almost inaudible growl. He rose, the motion smooth and silent, and took two steps, putting himself between Gytha and the door.

Then a beautiful woman appeared in the doorway. She was captivating, enchanting, so beautiful it hurt to look at her, yet Gytha could not look away. Her hair was as black as night, her skin white as ice, and her lips like ripe berries. She wore a green velvet dress, low-cut and tight-waisted, with sleeves that fluttered away from her shapely white arms. Gytha's mouth fell open.

This was a fairy queen! Gytha knew it without any doubt. No human had ever looked so regal and terrifying, so cold and sharp and dangerous, so untroubled by the deadly chill of this place. If a bear could talk, any story of magic and wonder could be true, though Gytha could not immediately recall a story of a fairy queen. Her thoughts raced.

The woman's ebony hair was caught up in loops by a hundred pins topped with pearls and sparkling crystals, and more glittering gems adorned her neck and ears. Her bare shoulders shone pale in the lamplight.

When she caught sight of Gytha, she laughed and strode past Alexander, catching the girl's face between her long, elegant hands.

"Oh, bear! You've brought me a girl! How perfectly sweet of you! She's so beautiful!" Her laugh was like bells tinkling, a crystalline beauty that rang and glittered in the air. She caught a little bell from her skirt and rang it, the sound less lovely than her voice. "Servants! Come! You have a task!"

Gytha blinked and tried not to recoil too obviously.

The woman pinched her cheek with one hand, and her fingers were icy cold. She turned Gytha's face one way and then the other, and then stepped back and looked at her from head to toe. "Oh, she's beautiful! Too skinny, of course, but that can be fixed. How marvelous! Oh, excellent work!"

The girl's heart sank, though she could not have said exactly why. A little coil of fear twisted in her empty stomach. She tried to catch a glimpse of the bear's face.

The bear had withdrawn to the darkest corner of the room and stood there motionless. Gytha could not read his expression; all her thought earlier of how she could see the kindness in his eyes seemed foolish. His face was impossible to read, and if he thought of anything at all, she could not tell.

The beautiful woman continued to talk, her voice like bells and her hands as strong as iron as she turned Gytha this way and that. She seemed pleasant enough, but Gytha was so exhausted that she could not keep track of what the woman was saying.

Without the bear's warmth against her body, the room was frigid. Gytha began to shiver.

A servant slipped into the room without a sound, ducking her head as the woman gave her instructions. Wordlessly she stripped Gytha of her worn, thin clothes and pulled a long silk chemise and then a new dress over her head. All blue velvet and intricate silver embroidery, the dress was exquisite, but Gytha was too dazed to appreciate it much until she realized that it was warmer than her old clothes. At any other time she would have been amazed by its beauty, but she was so tired and cold and hungry that she could barely keep her eyes open.

She did wonder briefly whether it was strange for the bear to see her without her clothes, but when she caught a glimpse of his face, his head was on the floor and his eyes were closed. He looked asleep.

The servant was strange, and even up close, Gytha had a hard time figuring out why. It was a puzzle for another day, perhaps, because as soon as she was dressed to the queen's satisfaction, with warm silken trousers on beneath the dress, silken stockings and sheepskin slippers on her feet, the queen whisked her down the hall to yet another hall.

Alexander heaved himself to his feet and followed, padding softly behind them. Gytha imagined he was as exhausted as she was; his steps sounded heavy and slow.

The next room was a banquet hall, with a long table and many seats. Dozens of the strange servants stood along the walls, as if there were dozens of guests, but there were none. The queen sat at the head of the table and directed Gytha to sit on her left. The bear stood in the corner, watching silently.

The servants brought the food in courses; Gytha had never eaten a meal in multiple courses other than when the soup wasn't finished when the children were hungry and so her mother gave them bread first. This was intentional.

The food was strange to her, but delicious. Dumplings in beef broth, pastries with mushrooms and pheasant and strange herbs, and vegetables Gytha had never seen before came in succession. There were meats she couldn't identify and cheeses unlike anything she had ever imagined.

She nearly fell asleep sitting up. With her belly full and her exhausted body finally warm, it was all she could do to pretend to pay attention. But she thought suddenly of Alexander.

"Isn't he hungry too?" She motioned toward the bear standing silently near the door.

The woman's laughter was like crackling ice. "Oh, no! Bears don't eat as humans do, you know." She waved a hand dismissively, and Alexander lowered his head.

Gytha could feel his eyes on her, unreadable.

The woman kept talking, about balls and festivals and all sorts of nonsense that Gytha assumed had little to do with her. Besides, she seemed to be having some sort of problem with her hearing. When she wasn't intently focused on listening with her full concentration, the queen's voice seemed to break into pieces individually beautiful but together signifying nothing. A bell-like tone, a crackle, a shriek like the wind, but no words unless Gytha tried very hard to listen to her and nothing else.

Gytha assumed this strange difficulty in deciphering the queen's words was because she was so tired. She nearly fell asleep at the table, and finally someone, either Alexander or the queen or perhaps one of the servants, realized that she was no use at all. The servant hustled her back to her room, undressed her like a doll, and stuffed her under the covers.

The room was silent when Gytha woke except for the soft crackle of the fire. She might have slept for an hour or a week; she could not tell, other than that she was hungry again. The lamps were out save one turned down low on a nearby table.

Her old clothes were gone, but there was a neatly folded stack on an upholstered chair by the fire. She did not remember the chair being there the night before. There was a matching footstool in front of it, which she also did not recall. Had she merely been so dazed that she had not noticed the furniture, or had someone brought in furniture while she was sleeping?

What a disconcerting thought!

Gytha lay in the bed for some time, turning everything over in her mind.

There was a small desk in one corner of the room with a wooden chair with a velvet-covered seat and delicately turned spindles on the back. Atop the desk were several crystal tumblers which held quill pens, ink, and drawing charcoals, as well as a stack of paper. This extravagance made her thoughts whirl uneasily.

What sort of place was this? It was far too rich to feel comfortable. She would have to be cautious.

As far as she could remember from the direction of their travel, they had traveled almost due north from her family's house. A little west, but mostly north. She tried to remember a map. What was north of the northlands? She couldn't picture it. This strange, underground place must be near the north end of the world.

The silk sheets and many layers of woolen blankets had kept her cozy. She had apparently kicked off several layers of fur, and they lay on the floor beside her in a jumble. The fire had kept the air relatively warm, but the stone wall beside her was frigid.

She slipped from the bed and hurriedly pulled the wool dress on over the silk trousers and silk chemise, and then pulled on the slippers. The clothes were surprisingly good armor against the chill, especially when she wrapped one of the smaller blankets around her like a shawl.

She turned up the lamp and explored the room more carefully. The books were strange; some of them appeared to have been written in runes she had never even seen before. Others were in her own language, and a few were written with letters she recognized in an unfamiliar language.

Shifting her focus, she turned to the far corner and the enormous object that loomed there beneath the cloth. Cautiously she pulled the cloth off to reveal a mirror. It was a massive thing, clear glass in a heavy wooden frame that tilted easily when she moved it and stayed in place when she let go. This was perhaps even more expensive than the collection of books.

The girl held up the lantern, her weakened muscles straining, and met her own eyes. Her hair was terribly mussed; half of it had come out of her braid and floated in a pale, disordered fluff around her gaunt face. She had seen herself in the mirror on the wall of the shop in the village and in her mother's polished copper kettle. But it had been months since she had been to the shop, and the kettle hardly showed her face with much clarity, not to mention that the colors were never this vivid.

Her eyes were huge and bright, though sunken, and her lips and skin were pale. She looked like a younger version of her mother, with the same high cheekbones made sharp by hunger and the same delicate lips. The lovely dress hung on her, far too loose, but she thought it would be close to the right size if she were well-fed and healthy.

After a moment, she covered the mirror again and walked to the door. She hesitated. She was not sure if she was ready to meet anyone other than Alexander.

Gytha listened at the closed door for a moment but heard nothing. Finally she opened it a crack. There was no sound from the hall, so she peeked out and almost shrieked.

A servant was standing against the wall across from the door. He must have been in darkness and silence until she opened the door and let the lamplight out. He smiled coolly at her when she pressed a hand to her pounding heart.

Gytha swallowed hard and tried to smile. He was strange, with his silent, close-mouthed smile and his cold, courtly gesture toward the hallway. Apparently she was welcome to wander as she chose, at least for now. She stepped out into the hall and looked from one side to the other. To her left, both sides of the hall were broken by wooden doors with rounded tops, and the hall curved away to one side. To the other, soft light came from around a corner not far away. Both sides of the hall had long strings of carvings just above her eye level. Perhaps they were meant to be words, but she did not recognize the language.

The first room was mostly bare. There was a dark fireplace, tapestries on the walls, and a table with a chair, but no other furnishings.

The servant followed almost on her heels, and Gytha snuck surreptitious glances at him at intervals. He was less shy; every time she looked at him, he was watching her.

At first she thought the strange look of his skin was a trick of the light.

Then, when she turned from examining one tapestry to look at the next, she caught a glimpse of his ear. It was distinctly pointed at the top, as if someone had pinched it very hard when he was a baby. The pointed top was nearly hidden beneath his iron-gray hair.

That was strange too; he did not look old enough to have a head full of gray, with no hint of gold. His cold, slanted eyes were a light, silvery blue-gray. His skin was pale steel gray, like an ominous winter sky, and his features were as sharp as cut glass. Not a single wrinkle softened his brow.

The more cautious glances she snuck at him, the more she wondered whether he was human at all. She wondered if his skin were struck with a metal rod, if the metal would ring as if it had struck stone.

At last, when she could not bear his silent scrutiny any longer, she turned abruptly and said, "Hello! My name is Gytha. What is your name?"

His eyes widened in surprise, and then he bowed.

"You won't tell me your name?"

He shook his head, his eyes fixed on hers.

"You won't speak at all?"

He shook his head again.

"Oh." Gytha swallowed and bit her lip.

The servant gestured politely to the door, and she continued her exploration.

The next two rooms were much the same, though the tapestries were all unique. Then she found a kitchen with an attached store room for food.

Another servant stood at a long stone table chopping vegetables. The two servants nodded to each other without a word, and the one chopping vegetables smiled coolly at Gytha, with her lips closed. She felt as though they had communicated something about her.

Their dispassionate silence was distinctly disheartening, and she tried not to be too discouraged. She had not anticipated having friends while she was here, other than perhaps Alexander, so it should not discourage her that these servants were unfriendly.

The servant in the kitchen turned back to her work. Gytha was not entirely certain at first this was a female, but she thought so. Her hair was a gray similar to that of the other servant, and her pointed ears peeked through the straight, smooth strands. Gytha thought this might be the one who had undressed her the previous night; it relieved her that it had been another woman, whatever sort of woman she might be.

"Hello," Gytha ventured. "I'm Gytha."

The servant looked up and nodded politely. The angles of her face and lips seemed ever so slightly softer than those of the other servant, and Gytha grew slightly more confident that it was a female. The emptiness in her stomach was familiar, but it was more difficult to ignore with the sight of food in front of her. Would it be rude to ask for food? She did not want to let her current hunger make the rest of the stay here more challenging by offending her hosts.

The female servant glanced at her again and turned away. She pulled a plate from a cabinet and cut several fat slices of golden cheese, which she arranged in a neat curve. She added purple carrots, which contrasted beautifully with the rich cheese and the smooth white of the plate. The servant pulled a steaming loaf of bread from an oven Gytha had not noticed, sliced an enormous piece from the end, and put it on the already-full plate. She pushed it toward Gytha without a word.

"Thank you," the girl said, sincerity filling her voice.

The servant's gray eyes flicked over her face, as if she were vaguely startled, and then she nodded. She pointed to a small wooden table for two and chairs in the corner. Gytha sat and ate. Her escort folded his arms and stood near her, watching the other servant return to her work.

"Thank you," Gytha said again when she had finished eating. "May I know your name?"

The servant shook her head and did not look up.

"Well, thank you for the food." It felt silly to keep saying the same thing, but it was always better to be overly polite than not polite enough. Even, or perhaps especially, to magical beings who might be dangerous.

Gytha continued her exploration of the underground palace, for it was more expansive and varied than any palace or castle she had ever imagined. There was a great hall with a vaulted ceiling that soared so high above her head she could not pick out the details of it at all, except to see that it glowed a soft blue that permeated the room with a cold, clear light. The walls gleamed with rough crystal.

Another room was entirely given over to painting. Three easels of different types stood in a row, and one of these held a half-finished painting of a small village that seemed familiar. Gytha stopped, puzzled, before she realized that it was her village as it might appear from one of the hillsides to the north, looking south over the little valley where the houses nestled among the snowy trees. She had never stood in that exact spot, but she had walked lower on the same hillside.

The narrow street in the center of town looked more crooked, and the lodges more jumbled together, from this perspective. There weren't enough buildings for even a child to get lost. She found her own lodge among the trees some distance from town, and then the paths to the river, barely discernible as shadowy trails in the white snow beneath the trees.

As she moved the lantern closer to the canvas, the exquisite detail astonished her. There was Fastulfr with his thick fur cloak, striding up the path to his lodge with a brace of hares dangling from one hand. There was Tryggvi with his draught horse that he hired out sometimes.

Gytha blinked and drew back. The painting was beautiful, but it wasn't real. Her family's lodge looked comfortable and cozy, which it was, but the painting seemed to depict some imaginary time in which her family had not been plagued by bad harvests, bad hunting, hunger, and illness. All the pain and sorrow were gone from the picture, leaving only the joy.

Forgetting the servant, she stepped past the easel to look at the other canvases stacked against the wall. There were dozens of them, with more piled in an alcove she had not previously noticed. The next painting was very different, showing a breathtaking panorama of mountains, valleys, and rivers. Green trees, crystalline lakes, grass, ferns, rocks, cliffs, and snow were all painted with loving attention to detail. Every color was exact, every curl of every blade of grass was both realistic and unrealistically perfect, as if no pain or sorrow ever touched this magnificent land. Only after admiring it for some time did Gytha notice a tiny figure in the bottom right corner. A small white bear stood with his head down staring into a lake. Though the mountains and clouds above were reflected, there was no reflection of the bear.

Another painting, and another, and another. One showed a youth with short, dark brown hair and a crimson cloak standing on the balcony of a palace built into a steep cliff face overlooking choppy, sunlit water, rich with turquoise and indigo hues that stood out with startling clarity. In the distance, the water met the sky, as if the water would reach to the end of the world. The youth's face was turned away, so that the painting mostly showed his dark hair and very edge of his jaw as he looked toward the horizon. Who was he?

The paintings, despite their undeniable skill and beauty, had a melancholic, lonely feel. Gytha glanced at the servant and almost asked him who the artist was, but she could not bring herself to speak.

The servant had vertical pupils like a cat. His silence was unnerving.

She flipped several canvases forward to look at those farther back. A youth, perhaps the same as before but without the cloak, brandished a narrow sword at a figure that looked like the servant beside her.

Gytha looked over her shoulder at the servant and back at the picture, trying not to show that she had noticed the similarity. The servant grabbed her arm and pulled her away, pushing the canvas back among the others with his other hand.

"Ow!" she cried.

The servant smiled placatingly, not showing his teeth, and edged between her and the finished paintings in the alcove. He gestured toward the room and bowed slightly, somehow both humbly agreeable and menacing.

Gytha sidled away from him, trying to keep her heart from pounding. His hand was as cold and hard as ice, and his touch had sent a chill of fear through her whole body.

He followed her into the hall and to another door.

"Where is the bear?" she asked.

There was no answer, and when she looked back at him, he ducked his head politely and said nothing. So she swept on, trying to be brave. She found another empty room.

Then at last she found a room that might have been lived in. It was larger than hers, but not by much. There was a bed, a well-used fireplace, a desk and parchment, and a separate bathing chamber with an enormous tub set into the stone floor.

"Where is the bear?" she repeated, and received only silence as her answer. She turned back to the corridor and started toward her own room.

Then she felt the bear's presence behind them and stopped so suddenly the servant bumped into her. He stepped back, ducked his head, and said nothing, neither a word of anger nor an apology.

The corridor was scarcely wide enough for the bear to pass by her, but he hardly glanced at her as he passed. Gytha felt it like a sting, a slap in the face, and she was angry.

Tears filled her eyes, and she swallowed. The anger passed, and then she became afraid, for if the bear was not her friend in this place, then she had no friends at all.

But he was the reason she had come, and the anger returned, and she was both afraid and angry. She stuffed both feelings down in her heart and lifted her chin in a rush of proud determination not to show her fear.

She followed the bear down the hall, though she could feel his disapproval with every step. He turned down another corridor, and at last the narrow space opened to another spacious hall. The room was golden, with gold inlaid on every visible stone surface, and tapestries of green and gold and scarlet covered the walls. The floor was covered in thick carpets of blue and green with many glittering golden threads. Light filled the room, spilling from crystal and gold lamps like liquid sunlight. Far overhead sparkling chandeliers lit the vaulted ceiling.

The room was dazzling, and Gytha breathed a sigh of relief. She had not realized until then how oppressive the darkness felt, as if the whole crust of the earth pressed upon her.

The bear stood some distance away looking toward her, and when she met his gaze, he growled softly, so low that she could barely hear him.

Over the low menace of his growl was the sound of bells and ice cracking, and the queen swept toward her. Her face glittered in the light, and her slender hands were as strong as steel and cold as ice when she touched Gytha's cheek.

"So beautiful! She's so warm, bear. You are right!" She smiled triumphantly.

Her teeth were pointed!

Gytha tried to be brave, but she felt her heart pounding again.

The queen swept her toward a dais at the far end of the room. So many other objects and surfaces glittered that Gytha only now noticed the gilded throne upon the dais. The seat and back were upholstered in short, dark fur which Gytha did not recognize, and the arms and legs gleamed gold. Below the throne were steps hewn of the pale stone, with a decorative edge carved into the front of each one.

The queen dropped Gytha's arm as she sailed up the steps. She flung herself into the chair with a sigh and crossed her long legs. "Sit there!" Her voice was hard and sharp.

She pointed at the steps in front of her, and Gytha sank to sit on the second step from the top, careful not to sit on the queen's robes.

There was another chair beside her throne, slightly plainer but still glittering with gold. Gytha wondered whether it was for her king and whether she would meet him. The thought set her heart racing again, and she twisted her hands together in her lap.

The queen's robes splayed out across the chair and down the steps, many layers of silk and fur. None of the layers were wool, and the fur seemed to be only for ornamentation, not warmth; the dress left her long arms and her throat bare. She did not seem to mind the cold.

"Sit still!" She jabbed at Gytha with the point of one sharp shoe, and Gytha swallowed her protest.

"Bear!" The queen's voice rang out like shattering glass. "Dance for me!"

The bear shuffled forward and stood heavily in the middle of the room on all fours. His head hung down, and Gytha thought he looked terribly sad.

"Dance!" the woman cried. Several servants, all with that strange gray complexion, filed in through the far door and stood silently watching.

Then there was music, though Gytha could not see where it came from. The bear rose up on his hind legs and shuffled forward and then back. Side to side.

The music was quick and sharp, but his movements were slow. Was he resentful? Sad? Furious? Or merely exhausted? Gytha couldn't tell.

The show, such as it was, went on for what felt like hours. The bear continued his sad dance, and Gytha watched him awkwardly. She listened for his voice, but he said nothing. His eyes never met hers.

At last, when Gytha's eyes had filled with sympathetic tears, the queen cried abruptly, "That's enough! I am tired of this poor entertainment. Go away, bear!"

The bear dropped to all fours again and shuffled to the side, where he lay down with his sad, dark eyes on Gytha's face.

"Prepare food for my guest!" cried the queen to the servants. The servants hurried away, and the queen turned her full attention to Gytha.

Her eyes were a cold, silvery gray, and even in the warm light of the many lanterns and chandeliers, her skin had a gray-blue tone much like that of the servants. Had she been that color before? Gytha was sure she had been alabaster-pale before, a more human tone.

"Do you know who I am?" she asked.

"No." Gytha shook her head.

The woman shot a poisonous look toward the bear before looking back at Gytha. "I am Javethai, Queen of the North! Shall I assume you know the rules of your stay here?"

Gytha hesitated. "He told me, but I would like to hear them from you, too, if you don't mind," she said carefully.

Queen Javethai laughed, and the sound was sharp and brittle. "Clever girl! For a year and a day, you will stay here in my palace. Food and drink and entertainment will be provided for you, and no danger will trouble you.

"A man will come to your bed in the dark for a year and a day's worth of nights. He will neither speak to you nor touch you, and you must neither look at him nor touch him.

"I shall assume the bear told you that if you persevere, he will be rewarded with something he desperately wants, and you will be allowed to go home safely."

Gytha nodded. "Yes, more or less."

The queen laughed again mockingly. "You are an innocent, aren't you! Let us assume the man has no ill intentions, shall we?"

Increasingly uneasy, Gytha nodded again. She knew it sounded ridiculous. But Alexander could be trusted, couldn't he? He would not have asked her to do it if he thought the man had bad intentions.

"Let us also assume that for so many nights, you are able to resist your curiosity about the man who shares your bed." She raised her eyebrows in challenge. "No touching, no looking, no word of reassurance from a stranger in the dark. You must be a brave soul!

"At the end of the year, what reward do you think an enormous white bear would want?"

The girl's eyes turned involuntarily to the bear, who lay with his head on his paws and his eyes locked on her face. "I hadn't really thought about it," she admitted.

"Well, first he will eat you, of course," said the queen carelessly. "But beyond that. What do you think an intelligent predator might desire?"

"Why would he eat me?" Gytha's voice cracked.

Queen Javethai laughed, a bright, tinkling sound like ice crystals. "He's a bear! Of course he wants to eat you. But he wants you fattened up first."

"But you're feeding me."

The queen's red lips pulled back from her sharp, pointed teeth. "Far be it from me to prevent you from making your own foolish choices." She lowered her voice conspiratorially. "The bear and I have made something of a bargain or a wager. A contest of wills, you might say.

"If I win, I will make you my heir, bequeathing you all my extensive lands with their snowy beauty, and all my servants with their skills in the working of metal and stone. I am not human, as you are, so I will live many human lifetimes, but if you like, I can give you long life too, so that you live long enough to enjoy it as ruler, not merely heir. I will make you a princess with magic in your fingertips and ice in your heart, strong and cold and powerful." The queen's eyes gleamed. "Of course you will also be treated as befits a princess even while I rule."

Gytha swallowed. "That is a kind offer," she said carefully. "May I ask what exactly the terms of the bargain are?"

The bear's gaze still rested on her face, and she wondered what he thought of the queen's words.

"The bear thinks you will be able to resist the fear and uncertainty of a man sharing your bed for the nights of an entire year and a day. If you do so, he will take my throne and much of my magic, and he will try to defeat me, to usurp my rightful place as queen. If he succeeds in that, which of course he will not, he will rule with an iron fist, mistreating my people and causing much trouble for the humans in the south." The queen's lips twisted in anger. "Of course he would eat you before you saw your family overrun by ice goblins or the great wolves or even other white bears. You wouldn't have to worry about seeing the devastation you caused."

Gytha frowned. "And if I do not resist the fear and uncertainty? What happens if I look?"

"Then you will see that he is a handsome prince!" The woman smiled at her, sharp teeth gleaming. "A conniving, silver-tongued liar prince, with no mercy in his heart for my people. If you look, you will see the truth, and *I* will win the bargain, and I will enact justice upon the bear prince as I see fit."

"So if I don't look, the bear wins and he rules your people and kills mine, and if I do look, I see that he's a handsome but treacherous prince who lied to me about the bargain?"

"Exactly." Queen Javethai nodded, her eyes flashing.

Gytha bit her lip and snuck a glance at the bear. "Why did you consent to the bargain?"

The queen shot another murderous look at the bear before composing herself. "We have been at odds for two and a half centuries, and I was tired of waiting for him to give in. I am the queen! He has no right to hold out so long against me."

The bear's gaze felt like a weight on Gytha's face, and she wondered what he thought of the queen's words. The queen's voice had a sharp air of impatience and annoyance, and Gytha had the feeling she ought not push too far with these inquiries.

Queen Javethai said abruptly, "You must be hungry! The food!" She clapped her hands, and one of servants hurried back into the room. The servant bowed and motioned toward the door. The bear remained motionless, his dark eyes inscrutable.

With a quick, imperious wave of her hand, the queen bid Gytha rise and led her through the corridors to the dining hall. The queen threw herself into the chair at the head of the table with an air of careless power and authority.

Cautiously, Gytha asked, "This is a grand room. Do you often have banquets here?"

The queen's eyes flashed. "Not often. I will host no banquets until this contest with the beast is decided. I do not wish for interference in the game."

Servants brought food for them in many courses. The queen ate in silence. Every motion was graceful, but she had a dangerous, mercurial air, as if she might explode into fury at any moment.

Gytha did not speak. The food was delicious, if strange, and she had been so hungry for so long that the feeling of fullness was odd and heavy. Soon her head was nodding.

"Wake up, child," the queen said. "If you understand the rules of the game, we will begin tonight."

With a start, Gytha woke and tried to gather her scattered, fuzzy thoughts. "Neither you nor the bear will pressure me to make a decision?"

"The bargain requires a free choice," said the queen with stern dignity.

"What if...what if I can't sleep because it's unsettling to have a stranger in my bed?"

The queen's lips curled in annoyance. "If you pass the night without looking or touching, then it counts for the purposes of the magic."

"Can I talk to him, even if he can't answer?"

Her eyes narrowed, and she hesitated a fraction of a second before saying, "That is permitted."

Gytha turned everything over in her mind. "Thank you," she said at last. "I am rather tired. Will I see you every day?"

The queen gave her a cool smile. "Not every day, but as often as I wish."

Drowsiness pressed upon Gytha, and she nodded again. "Thank you."

At the queen's gesture, the servants bustled Gytha out of the great hall, down the hall, and into her room. She let them stir the fire but protested their help getting undressed. She finally shooed them from the room so she could change in privacy.

She found the soft silk night shirt and silk trousers from the night before and pulled them on before slipping into the covers. She lay on the very edge of the pallet, nearly touching the wall.

Then she waited.

Nervous tension curled in her stomach, but she was too tired for it to keep her awake for long.

CHAPTER 5

A slight shift in the pallet woke Gytha. She hadn't slept alone since Sigrid was born, when Gytha had been barely two years old, and her sister's movements had never kept her awake. Somehow this stranger merely lowering himself to the bed brought her to sudden, wary alertness.

The stranger froze, apparently having perceived that she had woken. The fire had died to low embers, and the room was far too dark to see anything, not even a darker shadow among the shadows. Gytha stared upward, not looking in his direction but not looking away, either.

"Good evening," Gytha whispered cautiously. She clenched the covers, trying not to tremble.

What had possessed her to do this? Surely there was an easier way to repay Alexander for his kindness! What purpose could this ridiculous bargain serve?

The queen's words turned over in her mind.

He'll eat you, of course, but he wants you fattened first.

He could have eaten her earlier.

Gytha did not trust the queen.

But here, in the dark with a strange man, she was not sure if she trusted him, either. Was he handsome prince? If so, was he a silver-tongued liar, deceiving her for his own gain?

After some time, when Gytha said nothing else, the visitor lay down, every movement slow and cautious, at the very far edge of the pallet.

Gytha twisted to face away from him. If she looked toward him, even in darkness too deep to see anything, would that break the bargain? She was not willing to risk it. He probably faced away from her, too.

Without meaning to, she let her eyes close, and she drifted into sleep again.

When she woke again, she was alone, and she felt as though it must be well past dawn, if the sun had dared peek above ground so far north. She dressed and sat in front of the fire.

She needed some sort of schedule for her days, because in the darkness, it was impossible to guess how much time had elapsed. She wanted to know how many days and nights had passed, and how many still had to pass before she could return home.

Moreover, she did not want to drift into some sort of strange, disordered rhythm in which she stayed up or slept too long out of loneliness or boredom. She would be diligent in some way, even if she didn't know how yet. There must be a way to help her family, even from here, and even if her help could not reach them yet.

She stood and strode to the door, picking up the lantern on the way.

The same servant was waiting there, his gray eyes and gray skin blending with the stone walls even with the lantern light on his face.

"Is there a way I can know whether it is night or day? I feel disoriented already." She smiled at him, hoping he would smile back.

He shook his head.

"There isn't?"

He shook his head again.

"Does the queen call it a night when I sleep and a day when I wake?"

He pressed his lips together and shrugged one shoulder.

"How will I even know when it has been a year?" Her voice rose with fear.

He turned and began to walk down the hall, motioning for her to follow him. He led her to the room with paints and canvases and pointed at a book on a table near the fireplace.

The book was open. The pages were blank, and a quill and inkwell sat to one side.

"Am I allowed to write in it?" Gytha asked. The very idea of a book to write in was so extravagant that it was difficult to believe.

The servant nodded.

"Do you have a name?" She turned to look at him, holding up the light.

He nodded once, and if she was not mistaken, there was a faint, reluctant light of amusement in his gray eyes.

"Will you tell me what it is?"

He shook his head.

"May I give you a name, just so I have something to use?" He stared at her, and she rushed on, "Magni? It's a good, strong name. Is that all right?"

He blinked several times, his gaze flicked away and then back, and finally he nodded once, decisively, as if this was some sort of momentous decision.

Gytha smiled, trying to be friendly and cheerful. "Are you sure it is all right if I write in the book?"

The servant nodded once and gestured broadly to the room.

"I'm allowed to use it all?"

He nodded again and gestured yet more broadly, as if to encompass the entire, mysterious palace.

"May I ask for more things?"

He nodded again, apparently satisfied with her understanding.

"May I have cloth and thread for sewing? I would like to do some embroidery." She frowned. "I would need more light, though."

He nodded and strode away, leaving the lamp with her as if the utter darkness of the halls did not trouble him at all.

Gytha set the lamp on the table and examined the book more closely. The cover was leather, and the pages were smooth, creamy paper, bound together with waxed thread. She had never seen such an expensive thing; even the few books Torvald undoubtedly owned were not like this. Certainly they were not intended for poor peasant girls to write in!

With steps as soft as a whisper, the bear stepped into the room and came up beside her.

"Hello." Gytha looked at him thoughtfully. "Do not look. Do not touch. Do not be afraid. I haven't forgotten."

Even down on all fours, the bear was tall enough that his eyes were level with hers. He ought to have been terrifying, with his enormous shoulders and long teeth and claws. It was strange to see him here, inside, where the scale of him was more obvious. The table looked small, and the quill pen ridiculously delicate beside his great head. She had never seen another white bear, but he was quite a big larger than the largest brown bear she had seen. The skull in the general store on the wall was as long as her arm from elbow to fingertips. Alexander's skull was half again as long, and the rest of his enormous body matched this size.

Hesitantly, she reached out a hand and put it on his neck. She ran her fingers gently through the luxuriant fur.

He turned with a growl so low that she felt it in her bones without really hearing it. She froze, her fingers still entwined in his thick fur. The servant sidled in, eyeing the bear cautiously. He put a large basket and another lamp on the nearest table and withdrew to stand just inside the door. Alexander sighed and put his head down.

"Thank you, Magni." Gytha smiled at him and turned to the basket.

She found a great quantity of finely woven wool and more than a hundred skeins of fine silk thread in many colors, along with needles and a small pair of sharp scissors. She looked up at the servant in surprise. "Thank you! This is just what I would have asked for, but I didn't even think to be so bold!"

Magni inclined his head with a polite smile.

"Is it all right if I turn up the lamps? Oil is expensive."

Magni nodded again.

Gytha arranged the lamps so they would spill their golden light over her and settled down in the chair. She laid out the colors of the thread on her lap and thought about her design for some time before threading a needle.

It was strange not to have chores or work. It was strange not to have her little sisters and brothers laughing or crying or shouting, or all of them at once, in the background.

A moss campion took shape slowly, first the tiny green leaves in a mound and then the delicate pink flower.

She brushed tears from her cheek with the back of her hand. There was no use crying. Tears couldn't make the time pass faster.

Every day she would add a flower to the work, and she could count the flowers to know how many days she had been underground. No, how many nights had passed. A year was three hundred sixty-five days, and one more was three hundred sixty-six. There was plenty of room on this cloth for that many flowers.

She took a deep breath and let it out slowly and put the cloth aside. The next piece she would embroider for sale, and that would be useful for her family when she saw them again. A year from now, good thread work would still fetch a good price, and that money would help her family get through another winter.

The bear lay nearby, his eyes on her face.

She blinked the tears away and focused on her work.

Her stomach growled, and she ignored it, partly because she was engrossed in the embroidery and partly because it was a familiar sort of discomfort, not worthy of fully attending. A short time later, Magni brought her a tray covered with a silver lid. When she lifted it, she saw a bowl of rich brown broth with many fat dumplings in it. There was also a sweet roll, hot from the oven, with a little pot of berry preserves.

"Thank you!"

The servant nodded silently and withdrew to the door.

When Gytha bit into the first dumpling, she was surprised and pleased to find that they contained meat! This was another extravagance she had not expected.

"Do you want a dumpling?" she asked Alexander impulsively.

After a moment, he heaved himself to his feet, as if he were exhausted, and moved closer to her.

She held a dumpling up toward him, but he pulled away, his eyes on hers.

"What's wrong?"

He looked toward Magni and lay down heavily with his head near her feet.

Gytha pondered that. Had she offended Alexander in some way? Or did he merely want her to eat everything? He knew a little of how badly her family had suffered, and she was still weak from their long deprivation. Perhaps he meant only to care for her.

She reached down and put a hand on his head for a moment. "I don't mind sharing, but thank you."

He huffed softly.

Some hours later, Magni brought her another meal of thick stew with many flavorful pieces of elk meat among the carrots and potatoes. A little bowl of fresh berries, small and tart, was another extravagance. Surely no berries could be obtained this far north! Someone must have traveled to find these.

She ate gratefully. Slowly, with food and sleep, strength would return to her limbs. She would also have to work; it would not do to sit around and embroider for an entire year!

Was her family all right? Did they have enough to eat? Her heart twisted and turned within her. The elk was enough; it ought to be enough. Not to be strong or healthy, perhaps, but they would not die. But fish and carrots and potatoes and berries would help keep their strength up, too, and they had very little of these.

But they would live.

Guilt and grief and relief and gratitude warred in her, until she could not have said what she felt even if someone had asked.

Not that anyone did.

The bear lay quietly on the floor near her. She offered him a piece of the meat from her stew, and he eyed her with a strange look in his eyes and did not take it.

"Bears eat meat!" she exclaimed. "I think they plan to feed me here, so I don't think you have to worry about me starving. Don't you want it?"

He looked away and put his head on the floor.

When she went to bed that night, she managed to stay awake until her visitor came. Even with the embers in the grate faintly glowing, it was far too dark to see anything, even if she had looked, and her eyes were closed.

His steps were nearly silent as he crept across the floor, and she guessed his feet were bare. Again he lay on the very edge of the pallet, as if he were more afraid of touching her than she was of him.

For she had come to believe Alexander's word that this man, whoever he was, would not touch or harm her in any way. His movements were careful, and he kept as much distance as possible between them.

A faint tremor caught her attention, and she tried to identify it.

He was shivering.

"You can use one of the blankets," she whispered. "There's plenty."

Of course there was no answer. She sat up and pulled one of the heavy furs from the end of the pallet and pushed it between them.

He flinched away, and she froze.

"I was just giving you a blanket. It's here now and you can take it. I'll be on my side so you don't accidentally touch me."

She withdrew and waited, hoping to feel him move.

After a long time, the fur lying bunched between them shifted, and she thought he might have pulled it over his shoulder.

Still, his shivering did not entirely fade away.

CHAPTER 6

When Gytha awoke, her guest was gone. Either he had stirred the fire for her before he left, or a servant had done it, because the flames crackled merrily and the room was relatively warm. She still needed all her layers, but at least her fingers weren't stiff with chill.

She added a tiny yellow northern poppy to her sampler and then continued work on the embroidery to sell. The intricate pattern was taking shape well, and she imagined the piece as the collar of a rich man's coat.

Meals came at intervals; for breakfast there was tea and a warm, flaky, buttery biscuit beside some berries, and lunch and dinner were hot meals. There was goat milk and hot tea and broth to drink.

When she was tired, she went to bed.

Her nighttime visitor came again, and again he accepted only the barest corner of the fur that she had put between them. Perhaps he was afraid of touching her, or perhaps he was merely being chivalrous.

But his silent shivering tugged at her heart.

She added a tundra rose to her sampler and asked Magni, "Is it too bold to ask for some more blankets for my bed? And a drop spindle and a carding brush? I'd like to make yarn."

He inclined his head politely and disappeared into the hall.

Soon Magni returned with the familiar tools, along with two thick wool blankets over his shoulder.

"Thank you! May I have some more light, too?" She bit her lip.

He brought her more lanterns, and soon the room was brighter than she had thought possible. Magni retreated to stand at the door.

"You're guarding me, aren't you?" she said at last. "You're always watching."

Something in his eyes flickered, and he nodded slightly.

She sighed. It wasn't pleasant to be watched all the time, but she supposed he wasn't doing it for his own amusement. He must have been given the job by the queen.

She stood and hauled one of the comfortable chairs over to him. "Are you allowed to sit while you watch me? It makes me feel guilty that you're standing there all day long just watching." Then she frowned. "Don't you get hungry? I've never seen you eat."

He blinked. Then he shrugged one shoulder.

Gytha wasn't sure exactly what that meant.

When he brought her lunch, she offered him one of the puffy, meat-stuffed pastries. He shook his head, but there was a sudden gleam in his eye.

"Don't you want it?" she asked.

His sharp features tensed just a little, and he gave a faint, reluctant nod.

"Are you not allowed to have it?"

He twitched his head sideways.

Gytha frowned. "Well, I don't want to get you in trouble," she said at last. "But you may have it if you want. It's your decision."

His stony eyes flicked up to meet hers, and perhaps they were a little softer than before.

"Anyway, there's no need for you to stand all day. I'm not going anywhere. Sit down if you want."

He did sit, one lean leg crossed over the other and his arms folded across his chest.

Alexander stood and loomed over him, and he shrank back into the chair, his eyes wide. Then the bear turned away and flung himself to the floor beside Gytha's chair. He sighed heavily.

"What's gotten into you?" Gytha frowned at him and then knelt before him. "Don't tell me you're jealous." She smiled teasingly and ran her hands over the bear's huge head until he lifted it and stared at her. She scratched under his chin and behind his rounded ear.

She bent closer and murmured, "I'm doing this for you, you know. Because you were kind to my family and me. Because you saved them, all of us, from starvation and fever and death."

The white fur beneath her fingers was so thick and warm! She hesitated and then said, "My nighttime visitor is cold. May I have some of your fur to make night clothes for him?"

His dark eyes held hers, and she rubbed softly down his

great muzzle. The scratch her father had given him had become a deep red scar from the inside corner of his eye down almost to his black nose. She ran a finger down his muzzle next to it, not touching the tender red skin in case it hurt, and then, impulsively, kissed him on the top of the head. "Thank you."

She began combing Alexander's fur. It was so thick that it took only a few minutes for her to produce an enormous pile of fluff. It wasn't enough for her plan but it was enough for a start.

The carding brush was a great help, but she still picked through the fibers to separate the long outer coat strands from the shorter, softer strands from the undercoat. She set the outer coat aside and considered the soft fur that remained. These fibers would make a much softer, warmer fabric than the outer coat would.

She twisted the fibers between her fingers and threaded it through the top of the spindle. The spinning motion was rhythmic and soothing, and she had produced a great length of fine white thread before too long. She wound it into a ball and hesitated. A fine, thin fabric would be more comfortable, but a thicker fabric would be warmer. She spun this fine thread into a two-ply yarn. It was still quite fine and soft.

In the basket with all the embroidery supplies she found knitting needles, so she set to work. She started with one leg of the trousers, and by the time she had used half the ball of yarn, her fingers were tired and her eyes were bleary.

When she looked up, Magni had put a tray on the nearby table.

"Oh, thank you." She stretched her arms and shoulders and felt a rush of dizziness. Her fever had been gone for days, but the weakness would take longer to vanish.

She ate slowly, savoring the rich flavors. Again, she offered a piece to Alexander and this time, at her encouragement, he took it delicately from her fingertips. His huge teeth did not even touch her fingers.

She reminded herself that he was not, in fact, an extremely large, gentle dog, but a *bear*. A wild bear, with his own thoughts and plans, even if he couldn't speak them now. But it was difficult to imagine him as anything other than gentle and patient. He endured her combing, her questions, and the boredom of their confinement with the mute patience of an animal.

But as she sipped her tea sleepily, she thought that she had never heard of an animal who could talk before. Not really. There were children's stories, of course, but nothing anyone had taken seriously. What sort of magic could give such an intelligent mind to an animal, and what did it mean?

Gytha turned the lamps down low and brushed her hair with her eyes closed. As much as she loved her little sisters and brothers, not to mention her parents, she had often wished for a little more privacy and quiet in the lodge. But after only a few days here, she longed for the overlapping voices, the happy laughter, the squirming hugs of the children. She missed her mother singing under her breath while she kneaded bread, and her father teaching the children the many rhythms of old songs. She missed her father's stomp on the doorstep as he kicked snow from his boots.

The tears slid down her cheeks and she brushed them away. She washed her face in the basin and piled the extra blankets on the pallet where her visitor was sure to find them.

Again Gytha was asleep when her night time visitor entered, and she woke only to the slight shift in the covers.

"I got extra blankets for you. You don't have to be cold, and you don't have to feel guilty about taking my blankets. I have plenty."

There was careful movement, a soft shudder, and then nothing.

More than half asleep, Gytha realized that she felt the same sense of safety with this stranger as she did with Alexander. The thought flashed through her mind, as quick and unexpected as a flash of summer lightning, that she had kissed the unseen stranger on the top of the head and asked him for his own fur to make clothes for him. Of course he would not mind her taking his fur!

Was Alexander really a prince? Was he truly a man or a bear? What was he really like?

She tried to remember the sound of his voice.

"Goodnight, Alexander," she mumbled.

Of course, he did not answer.

In the following days Gytha added bell heather, snow buttercups, mountain avens, purple saxifrage, yellow marsh saxifrage, northern willow, reindeer moss, diamond leaf willow, cotton grass, and snowdrops to her sampler. She combed more fur from the bear's coat and spun it into more fine, soft yarn, with which she finished the pair of soft trousers and then knitted a long shirt.

She tried to imagine how big the stranger was. She didn't want the clothes to be too small. So she added the clever way of tightening the waist that her mother had taught her, with buttons and tabs on the waistband. She made the shirt large, because extra fabric would only make him warmer once he was under the blankets.

The work took well over a month, though she spent nearly every waking minute on it. Not only was it a time-consuming project in concept, even her two-ply yarn was very fine, which meant many stitches were required to make even a small swatch of cloth.

At least her visitor no longer shivered each night. He accepted the blankets she pushed toward him, and though she never looked at him, she imagined that he smiled as he did so.

She did not look in the mirror often; it felt vain to examine herself as if her appearance mattered to anyone. But every five or six days, sometimes seven if she forgot, she would pull the cloth off and examine herself to see what had changed.

As the days passed, the sharp edges of her bones were covered by a little softness, and the sunken, desperate look in her eyes had faded to a kind of cautious resignation. Her hands looked more like hands ought to look, and her skin was smoother over her cheeks. She smiled at herself in the mirror sometimes to remember what it felt like, and to imagine whom she might smile at.

When Alexander saw her smile, did he interpret it as kindness or pity or happiness or something else? Did he know what human expressions meant? Magni seemed to understand, at least some, but it was almost as hard to read his face as it was to read the bear's.

When she put the last stitch in the soft collar of the shirt, she sighed and stretched. She rubbed her hands over her face and slouched far down in the chair. Aside from Magni, she was alone, and she wished Alexander had been there. He had contributed all the fur, after all.

Alexander was an interesting name, one she had only heard in foreign stories. If his home really was on the other side of the western mountains, maybe he knew the truth of some of those stories. There was a dark myth about an evil fairy woman who cursed those who stumbled on her cottage made of bones. There were stories about the great wolves in the forests, wolves nearly as big as horses, who in long-past winters had come into towns and pulled down men, women, and children in the very paths between lodges. They had even come into the larger cities to hunt one cold winter, when they were hungry and the elk and deer and mink could not be found.

In the dark, it was hard not to believe all the stories she had once discounted. It was clear to her that Magni, with his pointed ears and iron-gray skin, and his apparent indifference to the cold of this underground prison, was something inhuman. She suspected he was what her people called an ice goblin, but the name seemed ugly. He had not been unkind to her, and "ice goblin" had a nasty sound to it. Surely his people did not call themselves ice goblins.

She lay back in the chair and closed her eyes.

A touch on her shoulder brought her to sudden alertness. Magni took a step back and bowed slightly, his eyes flickering to meet hers for a moment before he looked away.

"Is it night? I should go to bed."

He nodded and gave his strange, closed-lips smile. Gytha rubbed her hands over her face and stood. She caught up the pajamas and carried them with her to the bedchamber.

She folded them neatly and left them on top of the blankets on her visitor's side of the bed.

Was it night? It was so hard to tell. What did "night" even mean, if it was dark all the time? Meals came at intervals, but she really had little way to tell if they were regular other than by how hungry she felt, and with little exercise and long practice at ignoring hunger, she did not trust her body to correctly apprehend time.

When she blew out the lanterns it was night. When she lit them, it was morning. But what was the truth?

The truth was something real, even if she couldn't see it. Far away, past the icy tundra and rolling, snow-covered hills and white-blanketed forest, was her family sleeping too?

She fell asleep with tears on her cheeks.

CHAPTER 7

I n the morning, the shirt and trousers were neatly folded again, but not how Gytha had left them. She must have slept through the stranger's visit entirely.

Well. That was something. It was a strange thought, but she must have felt safe enough to not be on tenterhooks while she waited for him to enter.

Now that the pajamas were finished, she felt it reasonable to give her eyes a rest from the close work. She read one of the books for a time, but she found it difficult to focus; the stories made little sense, and there were many words she had never learned.

By now she had added many small flowers to her sampler and explored all the rooms she could find. Neither of the servants spoke to her, and she had been too shy to press them much.

After nearly two months in this place, she felt bolder. The queen, with her flashing eyes and pointed teeth, had not come again, and Gytha was glad of it. The two ice goblin servants seemed to be the only ones in this place, aside from the bear and herself.

Having made her decision, she strode down the hall with Magni behind her. She entered the kitchen and found the woman crushing spices in a mortar and pestle.

"May I help you?" Gytha asked, smiling.

The woman's gray eyes widened and she looked at Magni and then back at the girl. She pressed her gray lips together.

"I don't want to get you in trouble," Gytha said, when the woman still hesitated. "But I know how to make bread and soup and other things. But you've made many things I've never learned. I'd like to learn from you."

The woman's eyes focused on Magni again, and they seemed to be having a whole conversation without saying a word. At last the woman gave a tiny shrug.

She pulled an empty bowl from a cabinet and put flour, oil, a scoop of sourdough starter, and salt into a bowl without measuring and pushed it toward Gytha. She pantomimed squishing the mixture with her hands. Soon she took the bowl from Gytha and put a cutting board in front of her, with a pile of fresh herbs cut from a little line of pots on a shelf in the corner. Despite the lack of natural light, the herbs looked healthy. Gytha could not identify them all, but she recognized chives, sorrel, and parsley.

Under the woman's silent but agreeable instruction, Gytha put some of the herbs into the bread dough and formed it into a round loaf, while other herbs went into a pot of bubbling soup. Magni looked on with a strange, tense expression. The bread was apparently for dinner, because the woman left it rising and began to prepare a tray for Gytha's lunch.

When the tray was ready, the woman pointed her out the door, and Magni carried the tray for her as they went back to her bed chamber.

"Thank you!"

It was her birthday, and there was no one to tell.

Month by month, more flowers were added to her sampler. She embroidered every flower she could remember from the world above ground, and when she had exhausted her memory, she created new and extraordinary flowers, great pink frilly things, tiny yellow bonnets, deep blue cups with bright scarlet centers, and even more fantastical shapes.

She spent the rest of her time on the embroidered collar to sell, but eventually she finished that, too.

When she clipped the last bits of thread from the collar and put it aside, she picked up another piece of cloth.

No. She needed a walk, some exercise of body and mind, something different to look at. Again she explored all the rooms, examining each tapestry in turn. The images were strange. One depicted a tall palace made of ice or crystal, and a crowd of ice goblins kneeling with their faces to the icy ground while a tall figure stood on the sweeping steps with arms raised. The standing figure might have been the queen Gytha had met, or perhaps some past queen; the intricate weaving did not have enough detail to identify individuals. Gytha found the image disquieting, and she turned to Magni.

"Is this the queen?"

He gave a short, sharp nod.

"Is she a good queen?" Gytha tilted her head and tried to read his expression.

His lips gave what was probably supposed to be his closed-mouth smile, but there was a strange light in his eyes that made it seem more like a grimace. He shrugged one shoulder.

Gytha sighed. She walked laps around the great, empty hall she had seen first until her calves burned and her feet were sore. Magni followed her at first, until she told him she was just going in circles, and then he stood in the middle of the room and watched her.

For well over two weeks Alexander had been nowhere to be seen. Gytha entertained herself by doing as much physical exercise as she could endure. She ran from one end of the great hall to the other until she was out of breath, and then tried to stand on her hands balanced against the wall. Her muscles burned from the exertion, and she relished the burn because it felt like strength finally returning to her limbs. Perhaps her body was weak, but the combination of good meals and exercise made her feel stronger by the day. Not that she had any real idea how to prepare her body for a physical challenge. She knew only that the exercise felt like it was doing her good by working out the last of the exhaustion of illness. When she went to sleep at night, she slept deeply and well.

Magni watched her activity without a word.

One day she ran laps around the great hall, and when she became too tired, she walked backwards. Then she turned around and began to walk, thoroughly tired and bored. Just at the moment when she decided she could not walk another step, the great bear stalked into the room.

"Where have you been?" Gytha asked. She crossed to him and put her hand out, but hesitated when he made a strange, growling nose in his throat.

She stared at him, and he lowered his head and turned away. But he didn't walk away; he just stood there with his head down.

"Don't be grumpy at me," she said at last. "Where have you been?"

Alexander gave a heavy sigh and turned a little toward her.

"Well, if you won't accept a pet on the head, at least keep me company. I'm going to try painting. I've never done it before." She walked down the hall, aware of the bear's silent, looming presence behind her.

"May I paint?" she asked Magni belatedly. She had assumed she was allowed.

He gave slight nod. She turned all the lanterns up and examined her materials. She was bored almost to tears, and the boredom made the loneliness worse.

This was a trial she had undertaken voluntarily, and she wanted to endure it with grace. Even with gratitude, for when in her life had she been able to eat such costly, exotic foods? When had she had such unfettered access to luxurious threads, not to mention paint and canvas and even oil for lamps? Much of this strange prison was luxurious.

But she missed her parents and her little sisters and brothers. She missed their bright eyes and endless questions. She missed Sigrid's quiet competence with the little ones and Solveig's thoughtfulness. She missed the way her parents looked at each other, with trust and camaraderie as well as love, because they were a team together against any threat.

In all the hunger and suffering and despair, she had never been alone. The love that surrounded her had been so powerful that she was like a fish swimming in water; the love supported her and filled her lungs, even though half the time she didn't remember it was there at all. Being known and loved was such a natural state of existence that now, isolated, with only wordless strangers for company, she felt the loneliness like a physical loss.

Gytha painted a mountain first, because in her imagination it was easy. Gray here, darker gray here, brown there for tree trunks, green pine needles, a blue sky. None of the shapes or colors were quite right, and she grew frustrated, painting over her crooked trees and unrealistic mountain surrounded by an improbable, flat plain. She lost track of time.

A deep sigh startled her, and she spun around. The bear was lying on the floor with his head upon his paws like a dog, sad or sleepy or bored, staring at her with mournful eyes. Magni was leaning against the wall, his eyes half-closed. He must be bored. She wasn't very entertaining.

"What? You think you can do better?" she asked the bear morosely. He sighed again, and she rolled her eyes in frustration.

He stood silently and stepped forward, towering over her, and bent his face so that they were cheek to cheek. His hot breath brushed her neck, and she closed her eyes, trying to remember his kind voice. His warmth, his looming presence, comforted her for a moment.

Then she opened her eyes, and the feeling was gone. Magni was staring at them, his eyes glittering with some unreadable emotion. The bear looked at her painting, sighed, and turned around to lie on the floor as before.

Gytha scowled at him. "I didn't think so." She huffed and turned back to the painting. It looked childish and awkward, despite her efforts, and she glared at it too. Finally she washed the brushes and put the paints back where she had found them. Her creative urge was quashed.

She went back to her room and cried.

Several days later, she went back to try again. She painted the entire canvas gray and stared at it, planning her painting before she touched brush to paint. The mountain was shades of gray. The sky was gray. The trees were gray-green, the river gray-blue. The colors felt accurate; she felt that the world had turned gray. The excitement of this adventure in the frozen north with her ice goblin prison guard and the gentle-hearted bear was entirely gone.

Neither the colors nor the forms were appealing, but it fit her mood. Her eyes welled with angry, discouraged tears. She rinsed the brushes quickly and rushed from the room.

That night she woke when her visitor slipped silently into bed. It almost didn't seem strange any more. "Did you see my painting?"

He froze.

"It's not any good. I wanted to make something beautiful because I want to redeem this time, so it doesn't feel like I'm in prison. But I just made something ugly.

"I don't want my time here to be ugly and worthless. I agreed to do this because I wanted to do something beautiful for the bear, because he was kind to my family and me. But nothing about my painting is beautiful."

In the chill darkness, there was no answer, but Gytha had a strange sense that the man was listening sympathetically. She didn't know what else to say, though, and he could give no word of comfort.

A flash of fear passed through her mind. What if her nighttime visitor wasn't Alexander after all, but a different stranger? She shifted away from him and shuddered. How could she know him if he would not talk? How could she endure such loneliness? She felt fragmented and unmoored from the love she had known all her life.

When Gytha ventured to the room with paints again, she was surprised to find that the painting was subtly different. The grey was tinged with a little blue there, a hint of cream there. Not so much that one would notice at first, but enough. The picture was more alive, more sad, more real. The crooked trees were transformed from awkwardly misshapen to mangled by the wind yet somehow dignified. The mountain looked foreboding rather than simply overlarge, and the flat plain now had the texture of wind-whipped snow and ice, with a hint of flakes eddying just above the ground.

She glanced at the bear, who had followed her in from the hall. He blinked silently and lay down. The paints she had left drying on the palette and the brushes she hadn't fully cleaned were all neatly washed and dried and put back where they belonged. Gytha felt ashamed of her childish messiness.

CHAPTER 8

Most nights she slept dreamlessly. The darkness surrounded her, edging in around the light of the lamps and candles, creeping close in the corridor. At night, when she blew out the lamps, she felt it like a thick weight. Day by day, it grew more impossible to even guess the passage of time with any certainty, and she felt this not as freedom, but as an unmooring from reality. She slept when she was tired and woke when she was rested. She painted. She embroidered another rich collar for her mother to sell.

She read one of the books, a book of fairy tales and legends, but the others were too obscure and written in a hand that was difficult and frustrating to decipher. She sat hour by hour curled in a chair by the fire. Sometimes she fell asleep and woke to the same firelight. It might have been moments, or might have been days that she had been asleep. She could guess only by how much she ached from the awkward position.

Magni's clothes were simple, only one layer of decent fabric, not nearly warm enough for the chilly cave palace. This was what finally convinced her that he was not human. The ears, the teeth…perhaps human people from the far north were different. She knew little of different peoples except that their differences were said to be shocking. Designs tattooed on faces, dark skin, even dark hair! Traders from distant lands told of many things a girl from a small town might never see. But all humans would shiver in this cold, would eventually get sick and die without proper clothes. Cold like this was inevitable death without the fires in the grate. Magni never seemed to feel the cold at all. He did not draw close to the fireplace, did not wear layers, did not shiver.

The darkness and the silence wore upon Gytha until she wept. Then her heart steadied, and she resolved that she must go home and see her family. She had lost count with her flowers; she was sure she must have embroidered flowers when she had only napped and the stranger had not entered the room at all, and had also missed embroidering some flowers when he had definitely been there. But there were over two hundred tiny flowers of dozens of species, of colors both realistic and fantastical, and she could barely remember the sound of the bear's voice.

She felt like she was going mad. The long winters had always tested the ability of humans to endure confinement and darkness. But never had she been so alone, with no sound of a human voice, for so long. Talking would not ease the gnawing in her mind.

Gytha carefully folded the embroidered collars on which she had spent so many hours and put them in the largest pocket of her trousers. She added to this her cloth of embroidered flowers by which she had counted the days and as many skeins of fine thread as she could reasonably fit in the pocket without it coming open as she walked.

She dressed in every layer she could find, with the thick fur cloak wrapped around her and three layers of socks stuffed into her warm fur slippers. She strode into the kitchen as if she owned it, but the servant who was so often there was not even present to be impressed by Gytha's confidence. She wrapped bread and cheese and dry sausage links with cloth and stuffed bundles into the other pockets of the trousers.

Finally she was ready, or as ready as she could be. She picked up the lantern and walked resolutely down the long hall she thought led to the outdoors.

Magni and the bear followed her silently.

She passed through the darkness with her head high.

At last she reached a set of dark wood doors. When she placed a hand on the handle, it was so cold her skin stuck to it for a moment. It opened with a crack of ice, and the air beyond was so cold that each breath stung her lungs.

Magni caught her sleeve between two fingers and shook his head in protest, drawing her back toward the relative warmth.

"No. I want to go home, just for a visit." Gytha bit her lip and held up the lantern to see his face better.

His eyes were wide, and the light gleamed in his irises as if she were looking into a pale gem. He shook his head emphatically and tugged on her sleeve again.

Gytha hesitated. Would it break the terms of the magic? It would be a shame to waste all the time she had already spent here.

Her reasons for wanting to help Alexander had not changed just because time had passed and she was stir-crazy and desperately lonely. The truth was still the truth. Right was still right and not wrong, even if it had grown more uncomfortable.

But she felt that she was going mad, lost in isolation so that her thoughts spiraled and flitted like snowflakes on the wind, dark and hopeless. If she could visit her family and regain a little perspective, it would do both her and Alexander good. Wouldn't it?

"If I come back, will the bargain have been broken?"

Magni bowed his head and sighed. Then he shook his head.

"If I go, then I can come back, right? I can come back to finish the nights of a year and a day."

Magni stared at the ground.

"I can come back, right?" Gytha repeated, wanting some kind of response. The air was frigid but deathly still around her, and she felt that it had always smelled of stone and ice. Could she even remember the smell of pine? Of spruce? Of good clean frost in the morning on green spring grass? Of her mother's soap and new lambs? The soft, sweet-salty smell of her little brothers and sisters after a long day playing outside?

A fox might gnaw off its foot to escape a trap. She felt like that fox, ready to suffer any pain to escape this prison.

Magni nodded.

"I'll just go for a visit. I'll come back."

The goblin tugged at her sleeve gently, urging her back toward the living quarters in the interior of the caves.

She pulled away. "I wasn't asking. I'll walk if I have to." Gytha yanked her sleeve out of his grip and strode away with her head high.

He followed, his steps quick, but he did not touch her again.

The darkness of the tunnel grew gray, and the rock floor slanted upward until at last she turned another corner and sunlight spilled down the corridor, bright and dazzling.

Gytha set the lantern down on the floor. She pulled the hood of her cloak over her hair and cinched it down as well as she could. She pulled on her gloves and set off. The chill of the air struck her like a physical force.

The nearer she got to the entrance to the cave, the more ice and snow clung to the walls and in the uneven spots in the stone floor.

The tunnel opened abruptly to the small outcropping she barely remembered through the haze of fever and exhaustion when she had ridden Alexander so many months earlier. The flat area was nearly as large as her family's lodge, scoured smooth of snow by the frigid wind that whipped up from the sea far below.

Gytha crept carefully to the edge and looked down.

The cliffside was just as steep as she had feared, and just as tall. Several hundred feet below, the sea thundered and hissed against the sheer rock face. The water showed a deep, cold turquoise as it frothed, and Gytha drank in the color for a moment before turning her attention to the path.

The way up to the top of the cliff was not quite twice as wide as her shoulders, and terrifyingly steep. It was a wonder that Alexander had been able to descend it without falling into the seething sea below.

The bear gave a low, menacing growl when she turned toward the path.

Gytha rounded on him, her pent-up frustration and grief overflowing in sudden anger. "I need to see my family! Do you understand that? I love them, and I miss them! I need to know they're all right."

She stared him down, her bright blue eyes against his dark, unreadable gaze. Then she turned her back on him, deliberately rude, and set off up the path.

She climbed until her legs burned, her eyes brimming with tears. She ignored the tears, letting the wind freeze them on her cheeks.

Her muscles protested the unusual exercise, and soon she was huffing and puffing her way up the hill. Each breath burned her lungs like cold fire, and her face felt like a frozen mask. Her eyebrows grew thick with frost.

At last she reached the top of the cliff, and she turned to look out at the vast sea. This was the very end of the world, an immensity beyond sense and logic. There was no sympathy or humanity here, only endless cold and water.

With the wind pulling at her cloak and sneaking between the layers of her clothes, the cold was like a living thing. It would freeze her from the inside as well as the outside, her face and her lungs at the same time.

She turned to look at the land. That was south. It looked just as endless as the sea, an immeasurable expanse of cold and ice, but if she could walk far enough, endure long enough, there was life. Family and love were there, somewhere beyond the snowy tundra.

With a deep, stinging breath, she set off.

Magni and the bear followed.

Hour upon hour, she strode over the ice. The wind died away for several hours, and the silence was broken only by the crunching of her feet upon the ice and snow. Her breath made clouds before her. The world was glittering ice, blinding white and pitiless, and she squinted and pulled her hood down to block as much of the light as she could. Snow-blindness was a real danger, and she had not thought to make goggles to prevent it. The light meant it was summer; this land must never thaw.

Where the ice was relatively clear of snow, the going was easy, though the breeze tugged at her as if to make her lose heart. Then the wind picked up, and snow began to fall, and the ice crust beneath her feet broke so that she stumbled through knee deep drifts until she found thicker ice.

Then the drifts were deeper, and the snow slithered into her boots before she could find a solid place to climb up again.

Again and again she fell through, and her breath came hard. The wind caught her hood and pulled it back so hard that the clasp in the front yanked on her throat.

She wept in frustration, and her tears froze on her face. Still she pressed on until the ice broke yet again, and she felt into snow as deep as her chest. Exhaustion pulled at her, and she forced her way through the snow until her heartbeat pounded in her ears louder than the howling wind.

Blinded by snow, she fought forward until her legs buckled and darkness threatened to overwhelm her entirely. She could make no headway against the snow and ice. The sweat of her exertion had turned to chills, and she shivered uncontrollably. She was half-buried in the snow, and she sank down until her head was beneath the surface.

Her shivers subsided a little and she had a strange sense of warmth. Perhaps she would not die of cold after all. She would take a nap and resume her trek.

A warning sounded in her mind. She *knew* the cold was death.

But she was so tired.

Did it matter if she died?

Magni's gray hand gripped the back of her jacket and hauled her up, so that she sprawled on the thin sheet of ice beneath the top layer of powdery snow. The wind blew right into her face, and she would have sobbed in frustration and despair if she'd had the energy.

Then the bear was in front of her, his great white body blocking the worst of the wind.

"Go away!" she screamed. "I want to go home!"

But he did not leave. Instead he lowered himself until the wind was again in her face. She clambered atop him, clumsy and weak with cold and exhaustion, and she clung to his back as he set off.

"How do I know you're not a liar?" she whispered into his fur. "How do I know they're alive? You told me this would help you but it feels like death. I'm alone and cold, trapped underground in a stone prison, and I'll never see anyone I love again. I want to go home."

The bear's steps did not falter, but there was a heaviness to them, and she thought there was a faint, low growl beneath her hands buried in his fur. She pressed her face into his fur and clung to him as she fell into an exhausted sleep.

For hours or perhaps days he ran, until the air grew warmer and his steps finally slowed. Magni was nowhere to be seen; perhaps he had decided not to come so far south, or perhaps he had merely fallen behind. Once Gytha realized he was not following them, she did not look up again. She did not want to see the tundra or the trees passing by. She did not want to know if Alexander was taking her home or if she would die somewhere out in the snow and ice. She did not care what happened to her, as long as the trial would end.

But when he began to stumble, she finally raised her head.

She sat up in surprise, ignoring the fatigue that nearly crushed her. They were at the hill just north of her village, and the houses were laid out before her just like in the painting. The air was frigid, but the wind was not biting. It was late autumn, not the dead of winter, and there was a hint of spruce and pine in the air, not only ice. It was later in summer than she had realized; the first snows had come already, but patches of green still showed through where the sun kissed the ground from dawn to dusk. Autumn would bring more frequent snow and shorter days.

The bear stumbled down the hill, his steps dragging as if he would fall on his face.

Finally she said, "Are you all right, Alexander?"

His voice was low and exhausted. "It does not matter. You are almost home."

"I can walk from here."

He did not stop to let her slide down, and instead carried her all the way to her family's lodge. A few feet from the door he pitched forward.

Gytha slid down and fell to her knees before she caught herself.

She turned to the bear. "Thank you."

His great face lay upon the ground with none of his usual dignity. The scarred side of his face was upturned.

Gytha's heart twisted in sudden sympathy. "Alexander," she said more softly. She scratched gently behind his ear, but he did not open his eyes. His breathing was labored.

"Alexander," she said again. Still he did not react. Worry fluttered in her heart, but she pressed her ear to his side. His heartbeat thudded beneath her ear. He must be exhausted. He had run for many miles.

He was strong. He needed rest, but he would be all right.

She had come to see her family.

She did not knock before she entered, so she startled them all.

"Gytha!" Their voices overlapped, shock and delight and excitement. In a moment she was engulfed in their hugs, their questions, and the warmth of their love.

Soon she was sitting at the table with Brinja in her lap, Halvard clinging to one leg, Sigrid braiding her hair, Solveig holding her hand, and her mother putting food in front of her as if there was no shortage.

She laughed and exclaimed over how much the little ones had grown. Ashild and Dagney were now nearly as tall as Solveig, Solveig had developed curves like the young lady she was, and Halvard was reading already. Randulf shoved a wooden carving nearly up Gytha's nose, begging her to admire the bear he had carved. "Look! See, it's your bear!"

Her parents sat across from her, their eyes full of questions they would not ask until the little ones were in bed. Dinner was long and slow and full of laughter. Their faces were full, with her mother's high cheekbones soft and lovely rather than sharp, and her father's shoulders thick with muscle from his work rather than mere bone and sinew.

"How far did you go? Where were you?" asked Halvard in his small, innocent voice.

"Where the land meets the sea to the north, at the very edge of the land. Beyond it, I think there is nothing but sea ice."

Halvard, Randulf, and Brinja looked at her with awe. Everyone had questions. She showed them her embroidery and gave the collars to her mother to sell; they would fetch a great deal of money, for her work was very fine and the thread was exceptionally vibrant. Hildr had been repaid for her generosity with a great deal of elk venison, but Hlif and Gytha agreed that she should also be given two of the skeins of thread which Gytha had brought.

When the little ones were put to bed, the older girls plied Gytha with more questions, and she assured them she was well. Finally Hlif and Ivarr sent them to bed too, sat Gytha in a chair by the stove with a cup of tea, and drew their own chairs close.

"You look well," Gytha said, her eyes searching their faces. "Are you?"

"Your bear brought us another elk and enough fish to feed the village," Ivarr said. "But it all means little if you've been badly treated. How are *you*, Honeycake?"

Gytha flushed and looked down at her hands in her lap. "I am well." But her voice caught, and she glanced at the door. She had hardly thought of Alexander in hours.

"Did he…did anyone hurt you?" Ivarr said. There was a tension in his voice, and she knew he did not want to pry, but he wanted to know if she needed him to avenge her. He would protect her against anything.

"No one hurt me." She bit her lip. "I was so lonely, I felt I was going mad. I wanted to come home."

"It hasn't been a year yet," said her father quietly. "He didn't touch you at all?"

"Not a touch or even a word." She looked down. "I wonder if Alexander is hungry. He was tired when he got here." Guilt twisted inside her, and she stood reluctantly.

"Is he outside?" Her father stood too. He caught up his axe, just in case, and followed her to the door.

The full moon smiled down on them, the light soft and bright, so the shadows seemed friendly and the snow glowed and glittered. The bear was a vast white bulk not far from the door. He had not moved in the hours since Gytha had gone inside.

She approached him cautiously, feeling that he had every right to be annoyed. "Alexander."

He gave no sign of having heard her.

Ivarr hefted his axe in one hand and edged closer. "Bear?"

A sudden twinge of worry sent Gytha to her knees beside the bear's great head. "Alexander," she said again. She ran her hand between his eyes, over the top of his head, and then around his ear, where she stopped and rubbed gently. "Are you all right?"

Still he did not move, and her worry grew. "Alexander!" she said more sharply. "Wake up, please. You're scaring me."

He gave a soft, almost inaudible grumble, and then twitched his ear. "What?" His deep, rumbly voice was so faint she bent closer to hear him.

"I was worried about you." Gytha sat back and frowned. "What's wrong?"

There was only silence for several breaths, until Gytha almost thought he had fallen asleep again. Finally he said, his voice low and hopeless, "I would rather die here with you than in that dark hole."

Gytha's eyes widened. "What do you mean?"

Her father knelt beside her and studied the bear. "Are you dying now?"

The bear took a deep, rattling breath. "Soon."

Gytha looked at her father. "Can you understand him now?"

"Yes." Her father had a strange, cautious tone. He put the axe aside and shifted to see the bear's face from another angle. "Can I touch your face?"

The bear answered without opening his eyes. "Do whatever you want."

Cautiously Ivarr touched the bear's muzzle. When the beast did not react, Ivarr stroked his fur gently and then, with careful fingers, examined the deep scar that ran down the bear's muzzle. The livid red had faded to dark pink, puckered a little at the edge of the bear's eye. Ivarr hesitated, and then moved his head closer to listen to the bear's breathing.

"You're sick, aren't you?" he said at last.

The bear was apparently lost in sleep and gave no more response, even when Gytha gripped his fur and shook his shoulder.

"There is nothing I know to do for him," said Ivarr at last. "I don't know what kind of sicknesses bears suffer, but we can feed him a little if he wakes."

Gytha wrapped her arms around the bear's great head and buried her face in his fur. "I'm sorry," she said into his neck. "I'll go back, if that's what it takes. I don't want you to die."

But he did not wake.

CHAPTER 9

That night, Gytha dreamed of an endless horde of ice goblins running over the great tundra toward her, holding all manner of weapons made of ice. The sound of their steps was like ice crashing against stone, and the sound of their screaming was like broken glass, magnified into a crescendo of noise so great and terrifying that she woke with her heart in her throat.

Sigrid murmured sleepily, "What's wrong?"

"Nothing. Just a dream." Gytha was trembling. She pulled on thick trousers, boots, her father's coat, and a hat, and stepped outside.

The bear still lay in the same spot, though he had shifted a little onto one side. Gytha nestled into his chest with one arm resting on his great shoulder. She threaded her fingers into the thick fur of his neck.

Neither her soft words nor her touch garnered any reaction, and her worry grew. She pulled her legs up and leaned into him, feeling the strength and solidity of his chest against her back.

Curled against him, she dozed with her head pillowed on his neck and her back warm against him. Only when the sun rose and spilled bright and golden across her face did she blink back to wakefulness.

"Alexander."

A soft, growly sort of groan met her ears.

"You're awake!" She knelt again by his face. "Are you sick?"

He blinked. "No."

"Then what's wrong?"

He closed his eyes again. "It doesn't matter. You're home."

"What's wrong? Last night you said something about dying."

The door opened behind her, but she didn't look to see who it was.

Alexander's voice was so low and quiet that she barely heard him, and she bent closer. "If you will not finish the bargain...it is better for me to die here...with the light upon my face." His great furry sides heaved with effort. "If I can dare to call you a friend, I am content."

Ivarr knelt beside Gytha. "Bear, what can we do to help?" He did not have his axe. "Do you need to eat? You have given us fish and meat; it is only fair that we share with you whatever you need."

The bear chuckled, low and rough and hopeless. "That was for you. I need Gytha to finish the bargain, or I die. But I do not ask it."

"Why not?" Gytha said, appalled. "I didn't know you would die if I left that place. Why didn't you tell me before we got all the way here?"

He took several deep, shuddering breaths, and Gytha wrapped her arms around his neck. With her hand in the fur beneath his jaw, she could feel his heart thudding raggedly.

"It must be a free choice. But now I cannot ask, because…you have what I want." He stopped, his sides heaving. "For two centuries and more I have wanted…love like this. I would not take you from your family."

"You can't ask, or you won't?" Ivarr said quietly.

The bear growled low in his throat. "I must not. It is wrong to put my wants before yours."

Gytha did not realize tears were slipping down her cheeks until her father handed her his handkerchief. She wiped them and buried her face in Alexander's neck, but he was lost in sleep or something deeper, and he did not react. His breaths were shallow and unsteady, and she felt the guilt like a heavy knot in her stomach.

For an hour, she paced back and forth across the yard, but she could come to no other answer that satisfied her. She must return north; both honor and compassion demanded it. Besides, she had said she would. Or at least she had implied it, if not outright promised.

Sigrid said hesitantly, "Is it possible he is not entirely honest with you? That he is perhaps acting a little more ill than he is, to tug on your heart?"

Gytha chewed her lip. "It is possible. But I do not believe he is. He has been only kind to me. If he wanted to keep me there, he could have. He gave me the freedom to choose by bringing me home."

Her father said quietly, "I heard him this time. Not just rumbling and growling, but I heard words." His eyes searched her face. "How about you, Gytha? Do you believe him?"

"I do." She closed her eyes against his compassionate gaze. "I do believe him, and I cannot let him die because I was lonely. I am glad to know you are well. I was worried."

Ivarr nodded reluctantly and put out his arm. She flung her arms around him and buried her face in his chest. His arm around her shoulders was strong, not thin and weak, and his hand cupped the back of her head, as he had done when she was a small girl. His voice was soft. "It grieves me to let you go again, but I think you are right. His voice is kind, and he spent a great deal of time hunting for us in winter and spring. The little ones, and your mother, perhaps all of us, live because of the meat he brought. We had enough to share with others, too; there are many in the village who might have lost someone in their lodge if not for him."

She nodded without looking up, letting the comfort of his embrace give her courage.

"I am proud of you, Gytha." His arms tightened around her. "I know it is hard, but you are brave. You can do hard things because they are worth doing."

"Thank you, Pabbi." She gave him her fiercest hug and then straightened to look him in the eyes. "You and Mother are good examples of courage. I will be brave, because you have shown me how." She swallowed hard and then said, "I had better say goodbye."

Tears stood out in Ivarr's eyes, but he nodded sharply. He kept an arm around her shoulders as they strode inside together.

The explanations and goodbyes were both too long and too short, and soon Gytha was shaking Alexander's shoulder.

"Wake up, please. I will go back with you."

It took some time to rouse him, and finally the thing that brought him fully awake was Brinja clambering atop his head and speaking directly into his ear. "Wake up, bear! Please wake up! Gytha is crying!"

He snuffled and grumbled and finally rumbled, "Don't fall off, little sister."

Brinja slid down his jaw and tumbled cheerfully to the ground. She thrust her small hands into the fur of his neck and patted him as confidently as if he were a lamb.

But his breathing was labored, and he did not rise.

Gytha said, "I don't want you to die, Alexander. Can you get up? I will go back with you to finish the bargain."

He swiveled an ear toward her. "I do not ask it of you."

"No, but I want to do it anyway. I said I would, and I want to keep my word. Especially since you have been so good to my family."

Still he lay, his sides heaving with ragged breaths, his eyes staring at the side of the lodge.

"Come on," Gytha prompted. "I can't carry you, so you will have to get up. But I can walk at first, if it will help."

Halvard and Randulf began pushing and shoving at the bear's great bulk, producing nothing but an exhausted, hopeless huff of laughter from Alexander. But at last he struggled to his feet and stood, trembling.

"I do not ask you," he said, looking down at Gytha with his dark eyes. "But if you will do it, I will take you."

She put a hand on his shoulder as if she could give him strength. "I will go with you."

After yet another round of hugs and kisses on the little ones' cheeks, they were almost ready to go. Ivarr said to Alexander, "Keep her safe."

The bear blinked his dark eyes and said softly, "I will protect her with my life."

Brinja and Halvard hugged the bear's great legs, and Solveig stepped forward to caress his neck. "Thank you," she said. "You have been kind to us."

Alexander huffed softly and said, "Thank *you*, Little Sister, for smiling at me. You have cheered a despondent heart."

At this, Solveig flung her arms around his neck and her face into his fur. She must have said something, for Alexander rumbled agreement.

When they set off at last, Gytha paced beside the bear with a pack of food from her mother on her back. Alexander's steps soon grew slow with exhaustion, and he stumbled blindly forward, his head swaying with each step.

CHAPTER 10

Mile after mile they walked, until Gytha felt sweaty and chilled and her legs burned with effort.

"I need a rest," she said reluctantly.

The bear collapsed where he stood, and he made no sound as she snuggled into him. She fell asleep without eating anything.

The journey north was like an exhausted fever dream. When they woke, Alexander waited for her to eat. Then he insisted that Gytha climb on his back, and he began to run. At times his feet stumbled, and the heaving of his sides told her he was nearly dead on his feet, but he pressed on, driven by desperation and magic, until again they entered the underground palace.

Alexander carried her all the way to her room, which was just as she had left it. She slid down his shoulder, and he collapsed to the floor.

"Thank you." Her knees nearly buckled as she knelt beside him.

He said nothing, and indeed he seemed to be barely breathing.

She changed into her nightclothes in the dark, slid beneath the covers, and fell into an exhausted sleep.

Not long after, she woke because her unseen visitor fell into the bed with unusual clumsiness. She felt a rush of gratitude toward him; he had spent his strength to bring her home and back safely. But it was too strange to think of him as a man; it was easier to speak to a bear.

Sleep claimed her again before she could think of anything to say to him.

CHAPTER 11

Lamplight filtered through Gytha's closed eyelids and woke her slowly. The lamps were all bright, and her nighttime visitor was gone. The fire was built up, and Magni stood by the door.

"Hello," she said. She slid from the covers and put her slippers on. Her chemise, overdress, and silk night trousers were as modest as any outerwear, and the room was plenty warm, so she did not bother to even pull on a robe.

His strange gray eyes flicked over her face, bright and curious, but he merely bowed his head in acknowledgment.

Her breakfast sat on the table near the fire.

"Where is the bear?" she asked.

A flicker of some unpleasant emotion flickered over his face, and he shook his head.

"Is he all right?" Gytha felt a sudden rush of worry.

Magni shrugged one shoulder. He pointed at the table.

The fatigue of travel lingered. Gytha ate slowly, savoring the flavor without thinking much of anything. Her muscles ached, and her mind felt fuzzy and sluggish.

She put her head on the table and drifted into a doze.

Without any warning at all, the queen swept into the room and announced in a ringing voice, "Come, child! I am bored! There will be a banquet tonight!"

Gytha jolted to her feet, startled. "Yes, ma'am."

The queen looked down her nose at the girl. "You should say, 'Yes, Your Majesty,' ignorant girl." Her voice was icy.

"Yes, Your Majesty." Gytha's voice shook.

"Come along!" The queen swept out of the room, her cloak swirling in her wake.

Her heart thudding, Gytha hurried after her, and Magni followed. The bear joined them a few moments later, padding silently along behind them in the shadowy corridor.

The banquet hall was transformed; rows of tables filled the center of the room while a longer table stood on a low dais at one end of the room. Several dozen servants stood against the walls while other figures found their seats. It was strange to see so many of the ice goblins; for months, Gytha had only seen Magni and the one female servant who prepared her food.

Gytha hesitated at the doorway, and the queen caught her by one wrist and pulled her toward the dais with an iron grip. The girl felt like a leaf on a fast-flowing stream, moving along without any say in where she went, and likely with an unpleasant, tumultuous drop soon.

So many figures moving in utter silence felt like a strange, unpleasant magic, and Gytha's stomach churned with nerves. The whole room was full of cold, crackling energy, like the feeling of standing on ice that was too thin.

One might plunge into lethal waters with no warning.

The queen nearly threw Gytha into a seat at the table, not the seat of honor but the one next to it. Gytha was still in her nightdress, and this belated realization only made her more uneasy. The dress was warm and modest enough, but surely it was not appropriate for whatever the queen planned. Still, Gytha did not dare mention it, nor voice any other protest.

"Sit." The queen's voice rang out like a crack of lightning, and the milling figures all sat hurriedly.

Gytha's eyes widened as she got a better look at them. All the upturned faces were pale gray or the palest ice blue, with sharp features and clear gray-blue eyes. Their hair was anything from iron gray to white, and some of them had *things* coming from their heads.

Antlers? Some were so small they looked like the nubs young deer and elk sported in the spring. But others…one near the front of the room had a rack as wide and tall as his arms spread wide, and each point was as sharp as an awl.

Their eyes all fixed on Gytha with sudden interest.

The queen said, "Eat and be filled!" Then she said other things, and Gytha looked up at her in sudden confusion. She felt she ought to understand, but the words were a jumble of sharp sounds that would not resolve into meaning, like bits of broken glass scattered upon snow.

With a clap of her hands, the queen ended her soliloquy, and the feast began. Servants brought course after course of food, and Gytha was served at the queen's table, as if she were a guest of honor.

The bear stood in one corner, silent and motionless, as if he hoped to become invisible by his stillness. Magni stood not far away.

Gytha felt terribly alone on the dais beside the queen, with her cold eyes and her broken-glass voice. She smiled tentatively at Magni.

His eyes flicked away, and he did not smile back.

The queen followed her gaze.

"Why do you smile at a servant?" The queen's voice was honey sweet, but so cold that Gytha trembled in sudden fear.

"I…I just wanted to be nice," she stammered.

"To a servant?" Queen Javethai laughed incredulously, the sound bouncing off the walls. "He is nothing! You will be a princess!" She tapped Gytha under the chin with one cold finger and smiled down at her. Her eyes glittered with anger. "You are a princess," she repeated, "and should pay no attention to a servant."

"I'm sorry," Gytha murmured.

But she wasn't sorry. Shouldn't one be kind, regardless of one's station? Hildr Hilmarsson had given her mending and embroidery to do, when she could easily have done it herself. She knew how desperately Gytha's family had needed what food she could spare, and she knew they would prefer to earn it rather than accept charity. She had paid generously for the work, too, more generously than was reasonable. There was kindness in that, and it was nothing to despise or regret. Alexander had been kind, too, especially if he really was a prince.

Suddenly the queen's voice rang out, as harsh and sharp and clear as crystal in the cold air. "Beat him. Now." She turned on Gytha, her voice filled with unveiled hostility. "Let him and the others learn from this, and let you take this as a lesson in comportment, child."

Four of the other servants took Magni by the arms. He cried out, his voice rough, and the queen roared, "SILENCE!"

And there was silence, except for the sound of Magni's uneven breathing.

The other servants forced him to kneel facing the queen with his face pressed to the floor. Another servant, larger than the others, stepped forward from the far wall. He carried a thick staff.

Gytha's mouth hung open, and her breath came short with terror.

The servant stood behind Magni.

The first blow fell upon his back with a sickening crack. Magni let out a harsh, guttural breath but said nothing. The second blow was as brutal as the first. Again the staff fell, and Magni made no sound. Another blow, and another, and another, and Gytha was weeping. The tears streamed down her face, and the blows continued. Magni slumped forward, and the servant did not stop.

Gytha sobbed and caught at the queen's sleeve, but the queen shook her off, barely even noticing her distress.

Queen Javethai stood, apparently to gain a better vantage point to enjoy the display. Her chin rose in pride, and her lips curled up with cruel amusement.

There was no blood, but the sound of each blow, sharp and echoing, was horrifying.

Magni lay without any sign of life.

Finally the big servant stopped and looked up at the queen. She stepped down from the dais and strode toward Magni, her cloak swirling behind her.

Magni did not move.

Queen Javethai kicked him in the face with one foot and his head snapped sideways, limp. She smiled. "It is enough." She turned back to the dais and strode up the stairs again, saying carelessly over her shoulder, "Take him away."

Gytha was trembling, tears sticky on her face. Was Magni dead? Was it her fault?

The queen spoke lightly of many things, but Gytha could not pay attention. There was to be another banquet soon. Did she enjoy her painting? Did she want anything? A loom had been made and would be in the room where she painted, along with many exquisite colors of wool for her to enjoy.

How could the queen talk of trivialities now? Gytha was numb as her mind replayed the scene over and over. Had she caused it? What had she done wrong? Was it because she had smiled? She felt sick with guilt.

Alexander still stood silently in one corner. When the queen took her last bite, she called him to dance. He shuffled to the center of the room and stood where Magni had been beaten.

"Dance!" Queen Javethai cried.

The bear's head drooped.

"Dance, bear." The queen's voice was as sharp and hard as a knife blade.

The bear shuffled from side to side without a sound.

Tears sprang to Gytha's eyes again. "Please stop," she whispered.

The queen glanced down at her and sneered. "Foolish child." She waved an imperious hand, and the bear continued to dance.

Over three hundred flowers adorned Gytha's cloth. It had been almost a year. Soon something would happen. Something would change.

She did not see Magni for many days. No one guarded her now. The cook sometimes peeked in the room, but there was no real need to guard her. She could no longer find the corridor that led to the surface.

Gytha felt so alone. The bear joined her sometimes as she embroidered and painted, but she was afraid to speak to him now. She did not want to see him beaten, too. Only when she was sure they were alone did she try to speak, and then only very softly.

She never heard him speak. She had not expected him to speak. She had known he would not. Still, she felt his silence keenly, and she clung to the memory of his voice when the loneliness tormented her most acutely.

Sometimes he felt more distant, sometimes irritable or even hostile, and once he growled suddenly at her, his eyes gleaming with feral hunger, before he shook himself and rushed from the room.

Once, when she was growing tired of reading by the fire, she asked him, "Was it my fault?"

He looked up at her, his eyes wide and blank.

"The servant. Was it my fault he was beaten?" Her voice trembled, and she watched his face.

He blinked slowly and then looked away. She could not interpret this. She tried to tell herself that it meant he did not blame her. But she blamed herself.

Her visitor still came at night. His footfalls were nearly silent, and he kept his distance from her as before. She wanted to talk to him, to either give or receive some comfort, but she did not know what to say. She was no longer certain that it was Alexander in his human form; she thought it was, but she was not sure. She felt unsure of many things. Did the world outside this dark underground prison still exist? Would she ever again see the faces of those she knew and loved? Would anyone know, or care, if she died in her sleep?

When Gytha, Sigrid, or Solveig had a bad dream, the other sisters would sleepily turn and snuggle closer, wrapping their arms around each other. Only in the depths of the worst winter had Gytha been fearful for long while surrounded by warmth and love. Even then, she had felt the comfort of her sisters sleeping by her side; no matter what happened, even if they all starved to death, they would go surrounded by love. Her mother and father would go first, and Gytha feared that far more than her own death.

This loneliness was alien and terrible. It would have been far easier to endure if she could at least hear the stranger's voice and be sure that it was Alexander. She did not need to touch him! But if he would speak to her, she would know that she was not alone with a stranger, but enduring a trial with a kind-hearted friend.

When Magni finally returned, she did not notice at first. He slipped in the room and stood against the wall beside the door. Eventually Gytha looked up, and her eyes widened. He looked the same as before, though a bit thinner, if that was possible. She wondered that she had ever been afraid of him. He was not large, and she stood straighter than when she had first stepped into these dark halls. She was fully as tall as he was, and heavier now that she had regular meals, though he was stronger. A beating like the one he had endured would have killed any human.

When she looked at him, his eyes darted away, glancing around the room quickly. Then he looked back at her and met her eyes.

She smiled tentatively, feeling suddenly tearful again. Though she thought him strange and unnerving, she was glad he was alive.

He glanced away again, and then looked back at her and smiled carefully.

"I'm sorry," Gytha whispered, her voice barely audible.

He blinked and then half-shrugged, a quick, awkward jerk of one shoulder. He didn't say anything, only leaned back against the wall and watched her.

She had thought he would look different somehow, if she ever saw him again. Suffering made one look different, didn't it? But he looked the same.

Still, somehow she read his expression differently. Perhaps that strange light in his eyes was sadness and resignation rather than cold hostility. Perhaps his attitude had changed, or perhaps she had changed.

Gytha smeared butter on the last piece of bread and slid the plate across the table toward him. "That's for you."

His gray eyes studied her face. He took a careful step forward and then stopped. She gestured at it again and then went to the basin to wash for bed, studiously ignoring him.

After a moment, he took another step forward, watching for her reaction. Gytha kept her back turned, noting his movement only out of the corner of his eye.

Finally he took up the bread and hesitated. At last he took a careful bite, his eyes on her. Once he decided to eat it, it was gone in moments; he barely chewed one bite before taking the next.

Still silent, he watched while she readied for bed, and turned his back to her when she slipped her dress over her head and exchanged it for the nightgown. His thin shirt pulled tight over his shoulders as he crossed his arms.

"I'm finished," she said.

He turned back around, his gray eyes sweeping up and down her again.

Gytha was not sure exactly how or why she was so certain that her nighttime visitor was the bear Alexander in human form. It was a strange thought, and she was not sure which was his natural form; was he a bear changed to a human form for the nights, or a human changed to bear form during the day? Why was he a bear during the entire visit with her family?

Still, something about him struck her as so familiar, perhaps even comfortable, and she did not have that feeling with anyone else here.

Not once had she thought that Magni was the one who visited at night. His presence was uneasy and vaguely threatening in a way that Alexander's had never been, even when he growled.

Besides, Magni had never shivered during the day, though his clothes were not warm. Not to mention that he was too small and light to be the body that shared her bed.

Finally she stepped closer to him, holding up the lantern to see his face better.

The gray color of his skin was not a trick of the light; he was gray from head to toe, and his skin was rougher than she had thought at first, almost like sandstone. His eyes were more lovely than she had realized. There was a pale ring of ice blue around his pupils that darkened to almost black around the outside edge.

"I am sorry," she whispered.

He blinked and then smiled, the expression a little sad and a little ironic. "You. Are. Sorry." The words sounded like they took effort, as if he wasn't sure if they were the right ones, or if he was saying them correctly. His voice sounded like stones grinding together, low and cold and sharp.

It had never been more clear that he was not human.

She nodded, biting her lip. Was he angry? Did he blame her?

His smile widened a little, and she could see sharp teeth behind his thin lips. Even his lips were gray. "You. You did not beat me." The words came out in a soft hiss, a snarl of cold fury masked in sardonic amusement. "The queen ordered it. The queen's servants held me down and wielded the staff."

"Aren't you one of her servants too?" The question sounded silly the moment it slipped out.

He licked his lips and smiled, showing his teeth. "Not anymore."

Gytha swallowed. "So you are not angry with me?"

He blinked twice, his gaze flicking over her face so quickly that she wondered what he was seeing. What decision he was making.

129

"I am angry," he said at last. "Angry enough to kill. Angry enough to die." His strange, pale eyes held hers. "But not with you."

When he volunteered nothing else, she said, "May I ask your real name? I guess it's not Magni."

His lips drew back in a faint smile, less bitter than the others. "My name is Eshkeshken."

Gytha repeated it carefully, testing the sound of it. It sounded like ice crystals scraping against stone, and the sound fit him.

"The bargain is finished in two nights. Do not betray your friend after all this time." His words were soft and serious. "What did he tell you?"

The bear appeared in the doorway at this moment, and he entered, his eyes fixed on Eshkeshken. He gave a low, rumbling growl.

"Do not look. Do not touch. Do not fear." Gytha's voice shook a little. She did not want to be afraid of Alexander, but the menace in his growl made her heart turn over.

The ice goblin turned to look at him, a thin, almost frail figure against the immense white bear, and then looked back at Gytha. "Good. Do not fear him. The *queen* lies." His lips twisted in fury and scorn as he spoke of the queen. Then he bowed and stepped out of the room. The bear looked at Gytha and then padded into the corridor too, leaving her alone.

Gytha found herself trembling, as if the ice goblin had threatened her. His fury was terrifying. But he had not threatened her at all; if anything, she felt that he was an ally in some conflict she did not understand.

She could not sleep, so she was intensely aware when the stranger crept in, his steps soft and his movements careful. He lay down with a groan that barely reached her ears, and in a matter of a minute or two, she heard his breathing slow as sleep claimed him. He sounded exhausted, like her father did when he'd been working on the trail for days, when merely breathing was an effort because every muscle ached.

"I don't know all of what's going on," she whispered. "But I did this because the bear asked me to. Are you Alexander, too?"

He did not answer, and his breathing did not change.

"I'm glad I did it, but I'm glad it's almost done. I'm lonely here. I wish you could answer me. It would be less lonely if I could hear another human voice."

Still he slept.

The next day she barely saw Alexander or Eshkeshken, and the female ice goblin was nowhere to be seen, either.

But at bed time, Eshkeshken appeared in her doorway. "Put on your coat and boots," he said in a low voice. "Hat, too. Gloves." He handed her a pair of lambskin gloves.

She blinked at him. "To sleep? I'll bake like a loaf of bread in an oven."

His gray eyes flickered, and he said, "You gave me bread as a kindness. Take this as a kindness from me."

She licked her lips and finally nodded.

He added softly, "In the morning, the year and day of nights will be done. You must be ready." He nodded to her and slipped out of the room in his usual silence.

Bundled up in thick layers, she struggled to get beneath the covers, and sleep did not come.

Her nighttime visitor crept in with his usual care. He slipped beneath the covers, staying far from her, and soon his breathing grew slow and even as he fell into sleep.

Gytha grew drowsy, despite the oppressive heat of her many layers. At last, she began to fall into dreams.

CHAPTER 12

A crack of thunder and a blinding light made her cry out in fright, and she sat up, flinging one hand up to keep the harsh light out of her eyes.

Her visitor was slower to wake, and as he blinked in exhausted incomprehension, she saw his face clearly. A deep pink scar puckered the skin at the inside corner of his left eye and dragged down the length of his nose. His long hair was as brown as elm wood, and his eyes were brown too.

The queen's sharp, grinding voice rang out in fury. "Foolish child!" Her eyes blazed. "Why did you not even look at him?"

With one gray hand, she reached out to Alexander, and he shrank back, keeping himself between the queen and Gytha.

He fought free of the blankets and furs and stood, though he had to get a little closer to her to put his feet on the ground. He extended one hand behind him, as if to keep Gytha away from the queen.

Light blazed from the queen's crown so brightly that he shielded his face with his other hand. Gytha squinted, but she could not help trying to see him. He was of about her father's height and terribly thin, and his brown hair fell in messy curls halfway down his back.

The queen cried, "I am tired of this foolish bargain! You will marry me within a fortnight, Alexander de Gracey, or I will rip out your heart and eat it in front of all my subjects."

The young man said hoarsely, "Your Majesty, you promised…"

"I lied!" The queen's voice cracked with fury. "Submit to me because of the bargain or submit because of my power. I care nothing for your reasons. But submit you will, and I will have you as my own." Her cold gray eyes flashed as she focused on Gytha. "Idiot human. I will honor this part of our bargain, Alexander: I will leave the human child here, unharmed. Now, come, and you will see the glory and might of my kingdom. Soon you will either rule with me or die in agony."

She caught the young man by the nape of his neck and lifted him nearly off his feet. Then she ripped a hole in the world and vanished.

The world collapsed around Gytha in a clap of thunder. She covered her ears and closed her eyes, and the last thing she remembered was rocks and ice falling upon her head.

Muffled sounds slowly brought Gytha back to awareness, but it took some time before she understood her situation. She was entirely buried in snow and ice, but someone was methodically digging somewhere above her head, producing the cold crunching of snow.

"Help!" she called, but her voice was weak. It was hard to breathe, even though there was a little space around her nose and mouth.

There was an answer, but with her hood muffling her ears and snow beyond that, she could not understand the words.

Eventually strong hands freed her head and arms and hauled her out of the snow. She staggered and would have fallen, for her legs felt weak, but Eshkeshken kept his hands on her arms, steadying her until she nodded.

"Thank you," she said gratefully.

His gray eyes swept over her and then he nodded and stepped back. His gaze flicked to behind her shoulder, and she turned to see the ice goblin cook.

The female bowed a little and said, "I am ready." She had a heavy pack over each shoulder, and she slung one of them off and handed it to Eshkeshken.

He nodded formally and looked back at Gytha. "Can you walk?"

"Yes." She looked around in wonder.

In three directions, starlight glinted on ice and snow. A short distance to the north, the vast icy tundra fell away to the sea, which shifted beneath a thick layer of broken sea ice. The tops of the icebergs were jagged and of uneven height, so that it was difficult to imagine how one might even attempt to cross them.

Broken chunks of ice formed a low ridge some distance away, and far in the distance, outlined against the black sky, mountain peaks glittered with snow. Besides the two ice goblins and Gytha herself, no sign of life was visible, and for all she knew, they had been transported to an entirely different world in which no life existed.

"Where are we?" she whispered. "What happened?"

The female said, "The queen put an end to her pretense of mercy."

Eshkeshken set off west, striding over the ice with utter confidence. "Come, Gytha, if you would rescue the bear prince."

"Yes. Yes, of course." Gytha hurried after him, feeling more at a loss than before.

The female goblin walked behind her.

"Um. My name is Gytha," the girl offered after a moment. She had introduced herself nearly a year ago, but not since then, and it was only reasonable to assume the goblin might have forgotten it. Anyway, it was better to be unnecessarily polite than unnecessarily rude.

"Dakjudr," the goblin said.

That was unlike any name Gytha had ever heard before. Gytha turned everything over in her mind, trying to keep from weeping as she did so. Tears would only freeze on her cheeks.

Her nighttime visitor had indeed been human, but his face had that distinctive scar. She had been right. Somehow, the human had been the bear, or the bear had been the human.

Now the queen held him prisoner and would either marry him or eat his heart. They were far from any shelter and far from wherever the queen was, as far as she could tell. What had happened to the underground prison with all the paintings and embroidery supplies and furs?

"What happened to the caves?"

"The queen unmade it," Eshkeshken said over his shoulder. "It was only a prison, not the real palace. We must get to the palace to find her."

"Where is it?"

He waved a hand in the air. "East of the sun, west of the moon, where only the winds can follow."

Gytha frowned and looked around. "Then where are we going?"

"To ask the winds for help." He turned around and walked backward for a moment, unconcerned with the cold or uncertain footing on the wind-swept ice. "You were kind to me," he said seriously, "when you did not know who I am. A prince repays his debts."

"A prince?" Gytha asked, her voice trembling.

"We go to rescue your bear prince, because you care for him, and we go to kill the queen, because I can no longer countenance her rule of my people."

"Your people?"

He smiled at her, his lips pulled back from his sharp teeth, and said softly, "My people." Then he turned around and began to walk again. "Are you warm enough to live?"

Gytha swallowed. "Yes. Thank you for making me wear all this."

He waved a hand in acknowledgment of her thanks, but said nothing else.

Hour after hour they walked, until Gytha was staggering with fatigue. The darkness never changed. The stars remained overhead and the sun never rose. At last Dakjudr said something that Gytha did not understand—it sounded like glass shattering —and Eshkeshken stopped. "We can rest here," he said.

In a few minutes, they had dug out a depression in the snow and ushered Gytha into it. "It will be warm enough for you to rest."

"What about you?" She glanced from one to the other. Their shirts were similar and fit loosely, so they fluttered in the wind, highlighting their thin, hard frames. They wore long sleeves, but their hands and faces were not flushed with cold, and they did not shiver.

"We do not suffer from the cold as you do," Eshkeshken said. "Rest now. There are miles yet to go."

She crawled into the hole, which was just big enough for her to be out of the wind. She pulled her hood close around her face and listened to the wind rush past. Eshkeshken and Dakjudr spoke together quietly in their strange, rough voices, and she tried to imagine what they might be saying. She dozed.

Sooner than she expected, one of them reached down and shook her shoulder gently. "Come."

She clambered out of her strange resting place.

Eshkeshken handed her a piece of yellow cheese. "Eat while you walk. You need strength."

"Thank you." Gytha turned everything over in her mind as they tramped through the snow. Alexander's face had been visible only for an instant, but the ugly scar down his nose was the same one that had marred the bear's face. Her midnight visitor, the man, was the bear who had taken her home expecting to pay for that generosity with his life. She had known this, but still it was difficult to understand. The bear who had promised the stranger would not touch her was the same man who had kept his distance, listening with sympathy when she wept from loneliness.

She wished she had bared her heart to him in the many hours they had spent in the dark. The darkness would have provided privacy for tears and an excuse for boldness. What ought she have said to him? She had not been brave enough.

"I know the bear is the man," she said at last. "But why did you say he was a prince?"

Eshkeshken looked back at her in apparent surprise. "You didn't know? The queen stole him from human lands two and a half centuries ago. She wants him for her own, because his face is handsome and his skin is warm."

"But he will not have her?" Gytha's voice carried a question, but she was beginning to understand.

Dakjudr said, "His heart is warm but as hard as stone toward her. How can love arise when coerced? Love must be given, not taken by force."

Her footsteps crunched on the snow, and Gytha turned to look at her in surprise.

"What sort of queen is she?" Gytha asked.

"A usurper," said Dakjudr darkly. "Eshkeshken has been denied his birthright for far too long."

Eshkeshken said in a low voice, as if justifying himself, "I would have let her keep the throne if she had not been so cruel."

"But you are the rightful ruler?" Gytha pressed.

"My mother was Javethai's older sister, and when she died soon after her father the king, the throne was meant to go to me. But Javethai is much older than I, and crueler, and I did not want to risk war for the sake of status." His steps were steady, but his voice grew quieter and rougher with emotion. "I should have intervened before now, when I learned of her cruel bargain with the human prince. He did not deserve these centuries enmagicked into a beast.

"But I thought her pride would not let her break her word as she has. I thought, if I let it play out, she would release the human.

"Now I see she has lost all semblance of honor, and I can no longer excuse my own cowardice. The time for patience and peacemaking is at an end."

They continued walking in silence.

Hour after hour they walked, and at long intervals the ice goblins handed Gytha bread and cheese and cold sausage to eat.

Finally, when she was so tired her steps were uneven again, Eshkeshken changed his path and clambered up a low ridge to the snow-swept top. Gytha followed, breathing hard, and found him standing at the very top, with the icy hill falling away before him.

When they were gathered, he called in a loud voice, "East Wind! Please hear me."

A voice rang out. "What do you ask of me, goblin?"

"My companions and I wish to go to the castle at the end of the world, east of the sun and west of the moon, where Queen Javethai rules in my place. I am Prince Eshkeshken of the ice goblins, and this is Dakjudr, my friend and ally."

The wind whirled and spun and the swirling dust of snow coalesced into a vague figure in front of them. Fine snowflakes caught the dim starlight, lending the translucent figure a strange, ethereal beauty. No clear features were discernible, but there was a sense that the figure was looking at them each in turn.

"And what will you give me for my help?" The voice hissed and sighed like a winter breeze over frost-covered stone.

"As the rightful king of the ice goblins, I will give you my gratitude." Eshkeshken bowed low and remained with his head lowered.

The snowy figure turned a little toward Gytha, its translucent shoulders wisping away and then reforming. "You have a human with you. It is strange for a human to travel with ice goblins." There was a question in this statement, but Gytha was not entirely sure what it was.

Eshkeshken straightened and put a hand on her shoulder in a way that seemed to Gytha to be somewhere between protective and possessive. In his low, cold voice, he said, "She is a friend and an ally against the usurping queen, at least as regards the bear prince. Will you carry us there, East Wind?"

The wind whispered against Gytha's cheeks. "What will *you* give me, human child?"

Gytha licked her lips. "I don't have much to offer," she said carefully. "But I will tell you of my family, if you would like to hear."

The wind laughed softly. "I have never been so far south. The lives of humans are of little interest to me, but I have no love for the goblin queen. Tell me of your family, child, and I will do you a favor of my choosing."

Gytha opened her mouth and Dakjudr put a restraining hand on her arm. Eshkeshken said, "A favor? Will you take us to the ice goblin palace?"

"No." The wind whipped briskly around them, throwing snow into a glittering cloud. "I will take you to my sister, the West Wind. She knows the mountains better than I do."

Eshkeshken bowed slightly. "Thank you." He looked at Gytha and said, "The East Wind is just and honorable. Speak without fear."

The snowflakes swirled so dizzyingly that for a moment Gytha entirely lost her bearings. She closed her eyes and felt the ice beneath her boots, the strength of Eshkeshken's grip on her shoulder, and the steady pull of gravity and fatigue on her body.

"My father is Ivarr Bjornsson, and my mother is his wife Hlif. I am the oldest of eight children. My little sisters and brothers are Sigrid, Solveig, the twins Ashild and Dagney, Randulf, Halvard, and Brinja. Halvard learned to read while I was in the queen's prison. The bear prince saved all our lives with healing magic and with elk and fish he brought my family to eat. He is—"

The wind spoke suddenly. "Healing magic? How did he come by that?"

Eshkeshken said, "I lent it to him to use in the south, for what purpose he chose. It was my personal magic. The queen has no such power of her own."

The wind sighed softly. "Have you any magic left, prince?"

"Very little." Eshkeshken straightened, his sharp face raised proudly. "When I take my rightful place, I will take the scepter from my aunt and regain the power that is mine by birthright."

The wind was silent for some time, though it swirled softly about their shoulders, tugging on Gytha's hood occasionally. Finally it murmured, "What of the goblin kingdom? What sort of king will you be, small prince?"

Eshkeshken said, "I have no quarrel with the human kingdoms. I will pursue no war that is not forced upon me."

The wind whispered, "The injustice of Queen Javethai has been an offense to me for long years. I will support your claim, Prince Eshkeshken. Hold still, and I will give you something that may be of use in your revolt."

The ice goblin prince stood even straighter, his spare frame erect and proud as his clothes whipped in the wind. Then he gasped and clutched at his chest with one hand. He hunched a little, his features contorted in pain. Then he straightened again, his face a ghastly shade of gray.

"Thank you, East Wind," he said hoarsely.

Then they were caught up in a whirlwind and the world spiraled into madness.

Snow and stars spun, and the wind whipped and pirouetted around them until Gytha had no sense of direction at all. In fact, very little sense of self remained.

When the wind finally dropped her on a snowy hillside, she lay face down in the frigid fluff, unable to even think of rising.

Snow stuck to her eyelashes, froze upon her cheeks, and filled her nostrils.

Strong hands turned her over, and she stared dizzily up at the star-strewn sky, dark and infinite. Dakjudr's face hovered over her. "Gytha, human child, do not die now. Your bear prince needs you."

She blinked snow from her vision and tried to think. "Yes. Yes, of course." She struggled to sit up, and Dakjudr's arm around her shoulder steadied her until she could sit on her own.

Gytha looked around.

Eshkeshken stood some distance away doubled over with his hands on his knees. He retched and coughed, then pressed one hand to his chest as he groaned.

"Your Highness," Dakjudr called. "The human child is awake."

The ice goblin prince coughed again, his thin shoulders hunched for a moment, before he straightened. He strode over to Gytha and offered her a hand.

She accepted his hand, feeling guilty for it but having the distinct feeling that he would have been deeply offended if she had refused his help.

"Are you all right?" she asked cautiously.

His striking gray eyes flashed. "I am angry, and I am strong. Do not worry about me, Gytha. Are you well enough to continue?"

She swallowed her fear and pretended it did not matter. "Yes."

"Then follow." He caught Dakjudr's eye and nodded, as if they understood each other, and then he led them upwards.

The mountain climbed toward the sky above, steep rock faces jumbled together with snow drifts and ice-crusted crevasses like cracks in the earth itself. Eshkeshken offered her his hand at the most challenging parts of the climb, and she felt, if not exactly safe, at least a little protected.

As they scrambled higher, Gytha's heartbeat thudded in her ears, and her breath came hard. The icy air stung her lungs painfully, and the wind whipping past felt like ice shards against her skin.

Her foot slipped, and Eshkeshken caught her arm and hauled her up the last few feet.

"Thank you," she gasped.

He extended his hand next to Dakjudr, who climbed behind Gytha.

All three stood atop a high, rocky promontory. The wind howled over the shoulder of the mountain some distance above, but where they stood, it was only a frigid caress.

Eshkeshken pressed a hand to his chest and grimaced.

The sky above was a blanket of stars, and above them in a great, sweeping curve, the air shone in a rippling ribbon of pink, green, purple, and blue. Gytha gazed up in wonder; she had seen the colors before, but never with such clarity or brilliance. The beauty felt like a gift and a reassurance that even if all their efforts fell to ruin, beauty was not entirely overcome.

The wind curled around Gytha's hood and murmured, "I have not seen a human in these lands for many long years. Where do you come from, child?"

Gytha glanced at the Eshkeshken, who nodded that she should reply. Her voice sounded thin in the immensity of the cold night. "My village is called Aoalvik, but it's so tiny no one knows it except for we who live there. Langaholt is not too far away; more people live there. Aoalvik and Langholt are far south of here."

A soft tickle wove between her hood and her hair, a cold whisper around the back of her neck beneath the layers of cloth and fur. Gytha shivered, and there was a soft answering shiver that felt like amusement.

Then the feeling died away, and Eshkeshken stood even straighter, as if the cold touch had startled him. A low murmur met Gytha's ears, but she could not understand what the wind said. She heard only Eshkeshken's reply.

"You know my claim is just, West Wind. I will take no vengeance upon your children for ignoring me these long years if you will aid us now."

The wind laughed softly, but it did not seem unkind. "Those seaside breezes? They had no power."

"I know." Eshkeshken sighed. "Please. You know Javethai is unjust, and it is a shame upon us all if her crimes are rewarded."

"What will you give me, goblin prince? I do not need your absolution or your mercy on the seaside breezes." The wind slipped cold fingers through Gytha's hair.

"What do you want?" Eshkeshken's face was stoic, but there was an edge of desperation in his voice.

"Human child, tell me of the southern trees. The South Wind tells me that they embrace her and scratch low upon her underside, turning her inside out and upside down in the summer, and that little songbirds and great birds of prey ride her shoulders. Is this true?"

Gytha glanced at Eshkeshken, who nodded. She swallowed. "The wind whispers through the trees in the summer, but I don't know what it would feel like for the wind. The sound is lovely and peaceful, and the breeze carries the scents of pine and spruce and the sound of the river, if you're close enough. If the wind is coming from the right direction, sometimes from our lodge I can hear the sound of children laughing where they play on the hillside."

The wind tugged at her thick coat, and she staggered. "And what do you think of this icy land?" it whispered.

Gytha said honestly, "I think it is beautiful, but far too cold for me. I never thought so much ice and snow could have such variation in color and texture, and the starlight on the snow glitters like nothing I have ever even imagined! But humans were not made for this cold, and I would have died already if not for Prince Eshkeshken and Dakjudr. They have been kind to me."

The wind swirled around them, only a hint of snowflakes in the air making the movement visible. For some time there was no sound at all, and Gytha almost thought the wind had left.

Then it whirled into their faces again, and she blinked snow out of her eyes.

"What do you ask of me, goblin prince?" The words were soft and curious.

"I ask for you to take us to the palace where Javethai rules in my rightful place, the ice goblin palace at the end of the world, east of the sun and west of the moon, where only the winds can follow."

"That is very far."

"You are strong, West Wind. Will you carry us there?"

"I cannot go that far."

Eshkeshken's eyes flickered in frustration, and his lips pressed together. Then he bowed politely. "Can you help us get closer, then? Time grows short for the bear prince, and my people have already suffered too long under Javethai's rule."

The wind hissed over the snow, the sound low and almost menacing. At last the voice said softly, "What of you, Dakjudr, the quiet, dutiful servant? Have you no desires of your own?"

The goblin woman stood up straight and smiled fiercely, her gray eyes shining. "I serve my prince, even if all others prove faithless."

"I did not ask what you would do. I asked what you wanted." The voice of the wind was soft and curious.

"I want to see the Eshkeshken upon his throne," Dakjudr said. "I want to see justice done for my brother, whom

Javethai murdered. If it can be done, I would also see the bear prince restored to his people. It is a stain on the honor of our people to keep a prisoner so unjustly."

Eshkeshken hissed between his teeth. "I cannot fault any man for not wanting to marry Javethai. A cruel wife she would be, indeed. His captivity is a dishonor upon us all."

The wind gave a little quiver that might have been a laugh. "For what reason do you serve your prince, Dakjudr? Justice?"

"And love and loyalty. For he was good to me when others proved cruel or apathetic. I would sacrifice much to see him on his rightful throne, not only because it is his and Javethai must fall, but because I wish for better for my people. He will teach them a different way."

"So selfless," murmured the wind. "As if love is all that matters."

"It is what matters to me," Dakjudr said.

For a moment there was only a desolate stillness, and then the wind whispered, "I will help you, goblin prince, because I bear no love for Javethai the Usurper. I will take you to my brother the North Wind. Tell him that I wish to hear of Javethai's fall, for I think it will entertain me for many long winters to come."

With no other warning than this, the swirling gusts caught them up like leaves in a blizzard, and they spun into a vortex of biting cold and glittering ice.

The silence brought Gytha to her senses. She lay curled in the snow, as if she had been taking a nap. For several minutes she did not move as she took stock of her many aches. Everything hurt, but nothing seemed too serious. Her lungs burned with each breath of frigid air.

A racking cough some distance away startled her, and she sat up.

Eshkeshken leaned over with one hand pressed to his chest, breathing heavily. He coughed again, and it seemed the force of it would tear him apart. He groaned and knelt with none of his usual grace, one thin hand pressed to his chest.

"A gift," whispered the wind.

"Thank you." The goblin prince bowed his head and gave another convulsive cough.

The wind disappeared, leaving them in a strange, expectant silence.

The ice beneath Gytha creaked, and she stood in alarm. "Where are we?"

Eshkeshken groaned something that she could not understand. The prince took several labored breaths before he looked up. Gytha clambered to her feet, and her eyes widened. The higher vantage point made it clear that they were not merely on a hill of ice, but on one of many enormous icebergs floating in a vast black sea. The starlight was too dim for her to see much detail, but the shifting colors of the northern lights gleamed on the ragged edges of the icebergs and luminesced overhead.

The iceberg's movement was so slight that Gytha could barely perceive it at all. Instead, she felt the movement as a sense of uneasiness in the pit of her stomach. To look out upon the vast, jagged, moving plain was to feel that the entire world was unsteady.

Eshkeshken still knelt in the snow with one hand pressed hard to his chest. His breaths sounded harsh in the immense stillness. Gytha stepped closer to the goblin prince and offered her hand. He stared up at her with his gray eyes as if he did not understand for a moment, and then, with a strange twist of his lips, he took her hand and let her pull him to his feet.

He swayed and then straightened and looked around. "Where is Dakjudr?"

Her voice came from behind an icy mound. "I am here." A moment later, she appeared a short distance away, brushing snow from her hair. "I did not think the West Wind would bring us this far."

"It was a harsh kindness, but I am grateful for it." Eshkeshken put his hands on his knees and took several rasping breaths.

Gytha's gloved hand hovered at his shoulder, not sure whether he would want the help or comfort. "Are you all right?" she asked cautiously.

He coughed and wiped his mouth with his sleeve. "Do not worry about me, human child," he said. His voice was as harsh as ice crystals, but when she caught his eye, she thought his expression was not entirely unappreciative. "Are you injured?" He looked between her and Dakjudr, his cold, beautiful eyes sweeping over them in turn.

"I am well," Dakjudr said, but her steps were a little unsteady as she joined them.

Gytha concurred.

The starlight glinted on the tops and the edges of the ice peaks against the velvet sky. A great distance away, one of the enormous icebergs shifted and rolled, shedding ice and snow in a cloud like an avalanche. The roar of it hitting the water reached them several seconds later, and the great, smooth peaks that had previously been under the water glittered under the northern lights. The motion settled, and the roar faded slowly as the waves subsided.

The air was so still and quiet that the groaning of the ice was like unearthly singing. Far below, she could hear the soft lapping of the water against the ice.

They did not walk far before Eshkeshken stopped and pressed a trembling hand to his chest. He stumbled forward a few more steps and then fell to his knees with a groan.

Dakjudr darted to him. "What is it?"

"Ice." He hissed through his teeth and bit back another groan. "North Wind, please hear me."

The answering gust of wind actually knocked Gytha off her feet, and she began sliding down the slick ice toward the water far below. Eshkeshken lunged at her and caught her by one wrist. He steadied her while she regained her footing, and then he slowly, painfully, stood upright.

"North Wind," he said hoarsely. "I am Prince Eshkeshken of the ice goblins, and I go to challenge Queen Javethai the Usurper who sits on my throne. Will you take my companions and me to the palace at the end of the world, east of the sun and west of the moon, where only the winds can go?"

The wind hissed and howled in a maelstrom of snow around them. "What will you give me in exchange for my help?" The words were a sibilant whisper that shivered Gytha's bones.

"My gratitude as the rightful king of the ice goblins." Eshkeshken stood straighter, though his face contorted for an instant with emotion or pain. "Also you will receive the satisfaction of knowing that justice was done in the north lands, as befits the greatest of the Four Winds."

"Flatterer," the wind murmured.

"It is true." Eshkeshken raised his sharp face to the sky, as if he studied the stars. "Pettiness and selfishness have ruled for too long in my kingdom. Will you aid me or not?"

"What will the human give me in return for my help?" The wind flicked a sudden burst of snow into Gytha's face, as if to startle her into some confession.

The girl bit her lip and looked at the goblin prince. "What would you like?" she asked.

"What does a Wind want?" the North Wind mused. "How should I know what I lack? Tell me something interesting, human child, and tell me why it interests me."

Gytha swallowed. "If you help us go to the palace, I will try to free the bear prince who has been captive for many years. It is unjust that he has been imprisoned for the queen's pride, and she means to either marry him by force or murder him. Prince Eshkeshken will be a much better ruler than Queen Javethai."

"I know all that, foolish child. Tell me something interesting that I *don't* know." The wind tugged playfully at the golden tendrils that had escaped her hood.

She took a deep breath. "I didn't know ice goblins existed outside of stories until just this last year, and I think they are quite interesting. I think it will be a grand story to tell my children someday, that I helped the rightful king take his place on the ice goblin throne, and it will be wonderful to say that he is my friend." She glanced at Eshkeshken as she said this; it felt bold somehow, even though he had already claimed her as a friend. As if she had been any help to him.

His eyes flickered, but he did not contradict her.

When the wind did not answer, she continued carefully, "I also did not know there was such a thing as magic strong enough to turn a human into an animal, so that is interesting to me. But it will be even more interesting to unmagic him, if we can do it, and then to know the bear prince as a man. He was kind to my family and me, and it would be good and honorable to help him in return."

The silence drew out, and the wind was so calm that Gytha wondered whether it had gone away entirely.

But at last it murmured, "You are very dutiful, human child. Tell me something selfish about your quest. Humans fascinate me; so few of you ever come so far north. I understand the ice goblins already."

Gytha frowned, considering and discarding answers one after the other. Finally she said, "The bear prince has a kind voice, and I wish to see him with his natural face. I wish to see him seeing me, so that I can know if he thinks I am lovely and kind, as I want to be. I think he is a good man, and I would like to know if he might admire me, as I already admire him."

The wind chuckled softly. "That *is* an amusing thought. Thank you, human child."

Then there was silence for several minutes. Eshkeshken swayed and gave a soft, painful cough once, but he remained upright.

"Is the wind gone?" Gytha whispered at last. "Is it not going to help us?"

"I believe it is thinking," the prince said.

Then, without any warning, the wind was back, swirling merrily around their faces. A long pole dropped into the snow in front of Eshkeshken. "My sisters have given you gifts already, but I will give you a greater one, goblin prince. Stand firm."

A moment later, Eshkeshken cried out in sudden pain and doubled over with his hand pressed to his heart. He gasped and gritted his teeth, his eyes closed tight against some unknown agony. "Thank you, North Wind," he managed. "Your generosity will be remembered." He groaned and tried to straighten but fell to his knees with his face to the ground.

Dakjudr and Gytha reached for him, but the wind said, "Don't forget the lance," and Gytha caught it up in one hand as they were whirled into the sky.

The air was colder than ice and as still as death. Gytha's breath trembled in her lungs, and her face and eyes felt like they were freezing.

She clambered to her feet, disoriented and exhausted nearly beyond thought. By some miracle, she had kept hold of the lance through their wild tumbling, and she leaned on it for a moment before she straightened.

Dakjudr lay some distance away on her back, breathing heavily but apparently no worse for wear. The ice goblin woman rose slowly, and the two of them looked for Eshkeshken.

In all directions, the world gleamed softly under the shifting lights of the aurora and the silver starlight. A thin layer of snow lay over ice as hard as stone, and every part of Gytha's body felt bruised by the landing, though she could not pinpoint any serious injury.

Dakjudr called out in the ice goblin language, but there was no response. Her gray eyebrows drew downward in worry, and she listened carefully. Still there was no sound. They searched for Eshkeshken, calling at intervals.

At last they found him not far away but separated from them by a low ridge of ice. They had landed and stood on a slightly higher plane, while he lay in the shadow below them and out of sight until they finally found the edge in the dim light.

They slid down to him, for he was not moving at all.

Dakjudr fell to her knees beside Eshhkeshken. "Your Highness." She took one of his hands in hers and then felt at his throat for his pulse. "He is alive." She examined him carefully without moving him. "I see no injury."

Wanting to help, but not knowing how, Gytha knelt beside the goblin prince. She pulled off one mitten and touched his forehead; both the air and his skin were cold enough to be exquisitely painful. The contrast of her warm hand against his frigid skin made him flinch and blink into a muzzy awareness.

He gripped her wrist with one cold hand and stared at her, his eyes wide and confused. "Gytha," he said, as if reminding himself who she was.

"Yes." She nodded. "And Dakjudr. I have the lance from the North Wind, too."

He grimaced and clutched at his chest with his other hand, letting her go. "Thank you." He struggled to his feet, not protesting when Gytha and Dakjudr helped him.

When he was more or less upright, Gytha offered him the lance.

He leaned on it and closed his eyes.

Gytha wondered whether he was going to faint. His normally impassive face was strangely pinched. "What are the winds doing to you?" Gytha whispered.

The goblin prince shook his head without opening his eyes. Dakjudr hesitated and then gripped his shoulder again with one strong hand, steadying him as he swayed.

At last he straightened with a grimace. "I think I know what to do." He met their eyes each in turn and said, "Thank you for your courage. When it is time, Dakjudr, I'll give you the lance. You must be brave enough for us both. Kill the queen and free our people."

Dakjudr hesitated and then nodded once, as if she understood more from these words than Gytha did. "Yes, Your Highness."

Far above, a sliver of moon gleamed bright silver among the uncounted stars. Eshkeshken looked up at the sky for a moment and took a deep breath. Then he set off across the snow-covered plain.

"Where are we going?" Gytha said to his back.

"The palace is not far." The prince's voice was strained, and he said nothing else.

For quite some time they walked without speaking. Gytha looked around. The ice beneath their feet was solid and nearly flat.

"Is this sea ice?" She had the odd sense that they ought to whisper; the world was so quiet and strange, with no wind or sounds of life other than their footsteps, that they ought not break the silence.

"Yes." Eshkeshken's voice was equally hushed. "We are nearly there." He strode on another hour before he stopped and faced them. "Are you ready?"

"What do I need to do?" Gytha whispered.

Eshkeshken studied her a moment and then tapped the lance against the side of her head gently. "I gave you a little magic." He grimaced and pressed a hand to his chest. "Almost everything I have left. You will be able to understand our language until the magic wears off."

His blue-gray eyes flicked to Dakjudr's, and he held her gaze for a moment. "Do what must be done, even if it kills me. You understand?"

Dakjudr bowed deeply to him. "Yes, Your Highness."

Eshkeshken turned and led them forward. Within three steps, he vanished. Gytha hesitated but followed him.

CHAPTER 13

The magic felt like walking through a thin film of water, a frigid rush of power from her head to her toes. She looked around in amazement. A great white city rose before them. Starlight glittered on a thousand spires that reached to the heavens. A thousand windows glowed with cool blue light.

Gytha had never seen anything so beautiful or so cold in her life.

Eshkeshken walked straight up to the towering wall and pulled open a door which Gytha had not even noticed. He strode through as if there were nothing to be afraid of at all, leaving the door standing wide open for Gytha and Dakjudr to follow.

He led them through many expansive halls and wide courtyards. The walls of the city and the buildings within it were made of gemstones, ice, packed white snow, and what appeared to be magic itself, gleaming with a pale light that made lanterns unnecessary. When they walked through empty halls, the ceiling glowed softly, like bright moonlight through ice, so that it was always light enough to see.

At last they approached a wide, open courtyard which was not empty. More ice goblins walked toward the end of the courtyard far off to the left, which they could not quite see from their position in the narrow alley. On both sides, the snowy walls glowed as if lit from within, and the floor of the alley glittered as if it were made of diamonds. There was not *much* light, to be sure, but what there was gleamed and sparkled on every surface.

Eshkeshken paused some distance from the end of the alley; the walls were close on both sides but above, the black sky above was scattered with thousands of bright stars. The courtyard was so wide that the details of the opposite wall were indistinct, but it rose high above their heads, dotted with windows.

He glanced back at them, his gray eyebrows drawn down in what Gytha took to be concern.

"I'm ready," she whispered. "Although I don't know what we're doing."

His gaze held hers for an instant and then flicked to Dakjudr's face. His jaw tightened, and he nodded to her.

"I understand," the goblin woman whispered.

For a moment more, he hesitated. Then he turned, raised his chin, and strode out into the throng with his head high.

They followed.

At first, no one seemed to notice them as they joined the rear of the gathering crowd. As they made their way to the front of the crowd, a few of the ice goblins began to take notice.

"Your Highness?" A goblin some inches taller and much older than Eshkeshken grabbed at the prince's arm.

The prince turned and his eyes widened. "Arenenak?"

The ice goblin dropped to one knee and bowed his head. "I thought you were dead." His voice rasped like stone grinding against stone.

"Not yet." Eshkeshken glanced up at the dais at the end of the courtyard. "Do me a favor?"

"Anything." The older goblin looked up at Eshkeshken, his gray eyes shining. "Iphreshken is here, too."

"Tell him and any others loyal to me that the bear is not to be harmed, and keep the queen away as much as you can. I will challenge her soon."

The goblin stood and looked down at the prince. "We are preparing now for the wedding. She plans to marry him in three days."

Gytha gasped, "That's too soon!"

The goblin glanced at her curiously but then looked back at Eshkeshken as if he could not look away. "The queen is not patient."

"He does not want to marry her, does he?" Her voice shook, and she took a deep, stinging breath.

Another goblin stopped and knelt before Eshkeshken. "Your Highness."

Eshkeshken put a hand on the goblin's gray head and smiled a little. "Wirkelshen. It is good to see you."

This goblin was younger, probably not much older than Eshkeshken himself. He had a pale gray scar that arced down his forehead, over one eye, and halfway down his cheek. The prince hesitated and then touched the scar where it crossed the goblin's eyebrow and said, "Javethai did this?"

Wirkelshen gave a sharp nod. "Didn't lose my eye, though."

The prince gripped his hand and pulled him to his feet, and then grimaced and doubled over, gasping.

From the end of the courtyard, the soft murmur of the growing crowd changed into a grumbling, grinding roar. It wasn't exactly a happy sound, but it was excited and expectant.

Dakjudr stood protectively beside Eshkeshken's shoulder as he took several shuddering breaths. His gray skin had taken on an even more alarming hue, white around his lips and with blue shadows around his eyes.

"Your Highness," whispered Arenenak. "What is wrong?"

The prince straightened, swaying, and said hoarsely, "I'm all right. In a few days, either the queen or I will be dead."

Then there was a roar of voices, and the queen stepped out of a glittering, ice-crusted doorway flanked by a dozen guards wielding crystalline spears and swords.

Behind the queen, more guards followed, surrounding the bear and poking at it repeatedly with their weapons. Bright red blood spotted the bear's white pelt and darkened the tips of the guards' spears.

"Brave goblins of the north, citizens of the lands of ice and snow, see my triumph!" The queen's voice rang out like the sound of an avalanche, jubilant and terrible. "The bear prince has seen the folly of his recalcitrance and has agreed to marry me. What an honor I bestow upon the unworthy creature! This is a sacrifice I make for the good of all our people.

"The old king's magic is caught up in the enchantment that maintains this beast in his current form. When he yields himself to me in marriage three days hence, I will reclaim that magic and rule as I should, in strength and beauty and dominion over the north lands.

"For many long years, our power has been limited by the old king's foolish decision to tie up so much of his magic in this enchantment. This limitation is soon to be at an end. Soon our strength will be restored!"

She gestured at the bear, who roared in protest. One of the guards jabbed his spear deep into the bear's side, and the bear spun and shot out a paw in response, swiping the guard off his feet and sending him tumbling off the dais and to the ground. Other guards retaliated with more jabs and stabs, and the bear growled and whirled, striking out blindly. Despite the speed of its powerful strikes, the bear tripped over its own feet and nearly fell before gathering itself again. It shook its head as if it were disoriented.

"Alexander is so gentle!" Gytha whispered in horror. "What must they have done to him to make him so angry?"

Eshkeshken murmured, "There is cruel magic on him, threading through his fur and into his ears and eyes. He can hear very little, and he's nearly blind with it. He feels the pain of the injuries but has very little way to fight back."

"I must help him." Gytha swallowed. "What do I do?"

The ice goblin prince hissed between his teeth. "Offer Javethai a bargain. It would help if he knew we were here. He might hold out a little longer if he knew he was not entirely alone."

Full of righteous anger, Gytha did not wait for more instruction. She shoved her way forward, leaving the goblin prince behind, and cried, "Your Majesty! Please! Wait!"

The queen's expression sharpened, and she stood still, her eyes searching the crowd for a moment before she focused on Gytha. "You!" Her gray brows lowered fiercely. "Foolish human! It is too cold for your kind here."

"I want the bear freed!" Gytha shouted. "It's not fair to force him into marriage! He should be able to choose his fate!"

The queen laughed aloud. "He *has* chosen! He chose me!" She smiled wickedly. The illusion she had used to make her lips red, her skin white, and her hair black was gone, and the gray of her face was as cold and merciless as stone. Her teeth were sharp and white, and this was no illusion.

159

"What alternative did you offer him?" Gytha asked, still working her way toward the front of the crowd. Most of the goblins had fallen silent and looked between her and the queen, and Gytha could not tell if they approved or disapproved of her argument. Perhaps they merely thought her foolish and expected to see her thrashed or killed in some entertaining way.

The queen's smile widened. "Does it matter? He has chosen me above all others."

"Did you even give him a choice at all?"

Javethai grinned wickedly. "How foolish he would be, to choose anyone but me!"

"What about me?" Gytha cried.

She could have bitten her tongue. What had possessed her to say such a ridiculous thing? She didn't want to marry the bear prince! Or at least, she wasn't sure she wanted to. Maybe she would someday, but not yet.

Still, Eshkeshken had suggested offering the queen a bargain. Gytha steadied her frayed nerves. "What about me?" she repeated, hoping her voice didn't shake too much. "If you say he has chosen you above all others, he must have other choices."

The queen sharp eyes scoured her like the cruelest winter wind. "You dare speak in my presence, foolish human? Silence, fool."

Gytha trembled at the menace in the goblin queen's tone, but said bravely, "How can you say he has chosen you when he has had no choice at all? Surely you are not afraid to let him see me?"

The queen opened her mouth to refuse, but Arenenak, the older goblin who had greeted Eshkeshken, spoke from just behind Gytha's shoulder. "Your Majesty," he said in a most courteous tone. "It would be most enjoyable to see the bear prince choose you publicly. I think you deserve that honor."

Another goblin, whom Gytha did not recognize, said, "Your Majesty, it would honor you in my eyes to see the bear prince revere and love you for your power rather than merely fear you. Perhaps you might offer him the girl as a much inferior alternative?"

Queen Javethai's eyes flashed dangerously, and she growled deep in her throat. The bear rumbled behind her, but as the guards had given him a little space, he did not strike out at anyone. He shifted uneasily.

"Three days, Your Majesty." Gytha smiled as sweetly and innocently as she could. "Give me three days to convince him to choose me publicly. Doesn't he have a human form? He should be in that form, so that he can speak clearly."

The queen frowned at her and then looked out at the crowd. The murmuring and whispering of the ice goblins sounded like gravel grinding together, and Gytha felt the menace in it. The crowd was volatile, dangerous both to her and to the queen.

The bear appeared to have heard, or least to have understood, nothing of this, for he swung his head from side to side, growling, as if to defend himself from unseen attackers.

"Three nights," the queen said at last. "For three nights, you may enter his bedchamber, and if he remembers you in the morning and asks for you, I will let him choose between us. If he cannot even remember you, then that is his choice, isn't it?" She smiled, and for a moment the illusion flickered again: berry red lips, ebony hair, and fiery eyes.

Gytha's heart sank. The queen's confidence, and the cruel light in her eyes, promised that this would not be as easy as it sounded.

Would the bear prince remember anything? It took courage indeed to resist such an enchanting woman, full of magic and beautiful beyond all others. But he knew her cruelty;

he had seen this illusion of her before! Gytha held tightly to her fragile hope.

The queen cried to the crowd, "Hear this now! After three nights, we will have a wedding here, in this very court! Come and see the wedding of the queen!" Then she smiled down at Gytha again, and said more softly, "Foolish child."

With a graceful motion, she dismissed the onlookers. She turned and barked an order at the guards, who poked and prodded the bear until he roared in frustration and bolted into the white castle.

Gytha cried out in frustration and tried to follow, but someone grabbed her arm. She flinched away before realizing that it was Arenenak, with Dakjudr not far behind him. She looked for Eshkeshken with wide eyes but did not see him among the many ice goblins. Their faces blurred together, gray skin and gray hair indistinct among the silver-tinted shadows.

Someone leaned close to whisper in her ear, "Foolish human child." She spun and could not identify who had said it; the crowd was still dense, though the goblins were dispersing among the many shadowed alleys and icy buildings.

"Follow me." Dakjudr caught her eye and waited until Gytha nodded before she led her into one of the buildings. Arenenak followed them, and shortly afterward they were joined by Eshkeshken and the scarred young goblin, Wirkelshen.

The ice goblin prince leaned back against the wall of ice and said, "We must get Gytha to the bear prince's quarters tonight."

"Your Highness?" Another goblin joined them, and Gytha gathered that this was Iphreshken, another ally who had apparently not known until now that the goblin prince was alive. From the quiet conversation and explanations, Gytha inferred that Eshkeshken had been missing for years, and most people thought the queen had murdered him. She had murdered many others with lesser claims to the throne. "I thought Javethai had had you murdered."

"She would have if she had known who I was," Eshkeshken said grimly. Gytha gathered that Eshkeshken had been in hiding and disguised for years.

After some discussion, it was determined that Eshkeshken and Dakjudr would rest in Arenenak's quarters. Gytha was a little startled by the prince's lack of argument about resting; he was usually the first to get up after a rest when they had been trekking over the ice. But now he looked decidedly ill.

Wirkelshen and Iphreshken were to escort Gytha to the bear's quarters and remain there to ensure that her efforts to convince the bear to marry her were not interrupted. Arenenak pressed a packet into Gytha's hands with a quick explanation before he turned his attention back to the prince. After another moment of conversation, they set off in different directions.

When Eshkeshken turned to follow Arenenak, he stumbled and would have fallen but for Dakjudr's grip on his arm. Gytha bit her lip and looked after him for a moment before starting after her guides.

For several minutes, as the two strange goblins led Gytha through shadowy hallways of ice and snow, she dared hope that everything would work out well. Her face was frozen, her stomach had been empty for so long she had almost forgotten she was hungry, and she was lost beyond the north end of the world.

But how hard could it be to convince a man to marry her, a kind-hearted, well-intentioned girl, rather than to marry the evil ice goblin queen who had imprisoned and tormented him for centuries?

It was not a difficult decision.

It should not have been a difficult decision.

Yet even this simple choice required that the man be awake to make it.

When they found the right door, there were guards in front of it. These halls were darker than the ones they had walked before meeting the queen, and Gytha could not see the faces of the guards clearly. The guards did not protest Gytha's entrance, but they did not allow Wirkelshen or Iphreshken in with her.

No matter; Alexander probably did not know or trust them anyway.

She stepped into the room alone.

The space was as dark as the underground palace, or prison, in which she had spent that strange year. No hint of light came through the walls nor any windows; perhaps it had no windows. There was no fireplace and no glowing embers from which to light a lamp.

She said softly, "Alexander?"

There was no answer.

"Alexander!" She raised her voice cautiously.

Still, only silence met her ears. The room was frigid. Gytha fumbled in her pocket for the packet Arenenak had given her. The thin sticks were made of stone, not wood, but the solidified droplets on the end would catch fire with friction much like matches would. The goblin had called them *jafliggi*.

Gytha felt around the room for some minutes before she found a low table with a lantern on it. She tried to light the jafliggi with her gloves on, but could not keep a good enough grip to get the thing to light. So she pulled off her gloves and lit the jafliggi quickly and carefully, feeling the cold numbing her fingers with every second that passed. She tried to keep her fingers steady as she held the tiny flame to the lantern wick. Fortunately the lamp was full of oil, and she turned it up as high as it would go before hurriedly pulling on her gloves.

The light made the situation all too clear. The room was windowless and nearly empty but for a pile of furs and blankets on the floor in one corner. Gytha carried the lamp closer and set it down on the floor.

"Alexander," she said, her voice soft. "Can you wake up?"

There was no movement from the pile of blankets. Gytha found what she thought was his shoulder and patted him softly, and then more vigorously as he did not move.

She pulled back one layer of fur and blankets, and then more, until he lay with only a thin, bloodstained shirt and ragged trousers between his skin and the terrible cold. These were not the clothes she had made him of his bear's fur.

Even now, at the cold air upon him, he did not wake. His face was turned upward, so that the scar down his nose was clearly visible, faded now with time and his overall pallor. His dark hair was long and messy.

"Alexander!" She shook his shoulder again with one gloved hand, and he gave no reaction at all.

He was not stiff enough to be dead, but otherwise there was very little sign of life. Gytha held up the lantern to see if his chest moved, and she sighed in relief when she saw that he did breathe after all, albeit far too slowly.

Perhaps he was too badly injured to wake. Fear tugged at her, and she pulled up his shirt to examine his injuries. There were more wounds than she had expected, and she winced in sympathy, feeling slightly queasy. The worst one was low on his left side, deep and still bleeding sluggishly. None of his wounds had been dressed or treated as far as she could tell. He was frightfully thin, and something about this made him look younger and more fragile than he must truly be. The voice she remembered, the bear's voice, was deep and strong.

She took off her gloves again and put her palms on his cheeks, feeling the icy chill of his skin sink into her palms. She leaned close and said loudly, "Alexander! Wake up!"

His eyelids did not even flicker. If anything, she grew more frightened. This was no natural sleep, and he was not comfortably warm beneath his covers. If she left him with the blankets off, he would freeze solid and die without ever waking.

She pulled his shirt back down and patted his shoulder, as if she could somehow comfort him. He had offered her comfort when he could not talk, and she wished he could feel her compassion now, when he could not hear. But he slept through this too without even a shift in his breathing.

Gytha pulled the blanket up over his shoulders and adjusted another fur so that it covered most of his head, leaving him a hole through which he could breathe without suffocating. Not that he was breathing much. Then she sat back on her heels and studied what she could see of his face.

She shouted at him several more times, despite her growing conviction that his sleep was magically maintained, and he would not wake. "What shall I do for you, Alexander? How can I help you?"

The cold pressed upon her like a weight, and the darkness in the corners of the room crept closer, like the quiet winter death that everyone in the north knew and feared. The cold slipped into a man's lungs and his mind. Gytha had even heard of men, lost in the snowy woods, who stripped down to their underclothes, for the death of cold was so deceptive that as their bodies chilled, they felt the snow upon their frostbitten faces as heat. They felt they were hot instead of cold, and with their minds muddled by the languor and delusion of hypothermia, hastened their own deaths. Her father had found one of these unfortunate souls after a long search for a missing man from a neighboring village. Ivarr had impressed upon his family most gravely the importance of not believing the delusion of warmth, no matter how convincing it seemed.

Gytha put her hand on Alexander's shoulder and took a trembling breath, letting the cold sting her lungs. She would not give up on him.

Someone knocked on the door and said, "Come out now."

She tucked the furs more carefully around Alexander and stepped into the hallway, leaving the lantern still glowing on the floor.

The lethal cold seemed to hit her anew as she followed Wirkelshen down the corridor, and she shivered convulsively. The walls glowed softly, but the light was so dim that it was still nearly impossible for her to follow the ice goblin until he reached back to take her gloved hand in his. Soon they had passed through several more corridors and a small, open courtyard. Wirkelshin knocked on a door made of ice.

It opened smoothly, and Arenenak ushered them in hurriedly. "The prince is sleeping," Dakjudr said, her voice like the whisper of snow sliding over rocks. She handed Gytha a plate of chunks of well-marbled red meat and fish, both raw, as well as cheese and bread.

"What is this?" Gytha asked in surprise.

"Seal and char. It is tasty raw." Dakjudr had a vague question in her eyes, as if evaluating whether Gytha would protest. "We don't use fire here often, and I do not want to court the queen's attention while the prince is ill."

Gytha bit her lip and looked toward the corner where Eshkeshken lay atop an enormous sealskin with one thin arm over his eyes. "What is wrong with him?" she asked. "Will he get better?"

"He is waiting for you to free the bear prince, if you can, before he challenges the queen openly. His vengeance can wait a little longer to ensure that the bear is fully freed of his enchantment."

Gytha set the plate down on the table and stepped closer to the prince's bed. She knelt beside him. "Are you awake?" she whispered. Her eyes were gritty with fatigue; it must be morning by now, as much as it was ever morning.

He coughed and turned on his side away from her, curling one arm under his head, without really waking up. His breathing rasped painfully.

Dakjudr said, "Eat, Gytha, so you can be strong for the challenge. Were you able to speak with the prince?"

"No." She choked down the strange, unpleasant meal and told the ice goblins of the bear prince's sleep that was almost death.

"What can I do?" she asked at last. "What can I do if he's kept sleeping by magic?"

The ice goblins conferred among themselves for some time in their own language so quietly that even with the prince's magic upon her, Gytha could catch only a few words. Finally, Dakjudr said, "They will try to understand the magic by tonight and devise some counter. For now, rest. You must be strong and brave for what comes." She led Gytha to a smaller room in the back where there was a pallet of blankets and a strange, crystalline cup of water that ought to have been frozen. "You can sleep here. I borrowed blankets for you. Will you be warm enough to live?"

"Yes. Thank you." Gytha settled down in the darkness and listened to Dakjudr slip quietly out of the room and close the door behind herself.

The whole world was cold and dark.

Would there ever be light and hope again?

For hours, Gytha drifted in and out of a restless sleep. The bear prince's voice was hard to remember now; she remembered how she'd felt when she heard it, but not the exact tones. It was difficult to remember her father's voice when he led the family in song, difficult to remember the laughter of the little ones. Brinja would be four years old now, almost five; she would be learning her letters and even embroidery. They had passed an entire summer without her, and it would be winter again at home. Did they have enough food for the long dark? Was Sigrid married already, since Gytha had not found a good husband who could help in time of need?

Gytha was not crying. But a few tears slipped down her cheeks and froze on the edge of her coat.

Too soon, Dakjudr woke Gytha with a hand on her shoulder. "Come eat. I am sorry it is not what you like, but it will keep your body strong."

The ice goblins were gathered around a table carved of ice in the common room. They sat on chairs made of enormous bones; Gytha could not imagine what animal they had come from, but it must have been monstrous.

Eshkeshken had woken and sat with his arms crossed over his chest, his expression distant and his meal untouched. The others had nearly finished eating, and even Gytha had managed to swallow most of the raw meat she had been given.

"Your Highness," said Wirkelshen at last. "You ought to eat. You will need your strength for what comes."

The ice goblin prince blinked and nodded. "Yes. You are right."

Gytha noted the deep shadows around his eyes and the white pallor around his lips. He looked even thinner and stranger than usual. She wanted to ask him if there was anything she could do, but he seemed to be focused inward, and she was not sure if he would welcome the question. Instead, she asked, "Did you find out anything about the magic?"

"Nothing useful. Try to wake him."

A sinking feeling of hopelessness pressed upon Gytha, but she nodded. Once again Wirkelshen and Iphreshken led her to the bear prince's chamber. The guards smiled coolly at them and allowed Gytha in alone, as before.

She found the lamp on the table again, so someone had moved it. Again she pulled off her gloves to light the jafliggi and then the lamp. The light was golden and bright, and the warmth of the flame flickered in sharp contrast to everything else about this strange world.

The bear prince was asleep in his pile of furs and blankets, and he did not react, much less wake, when Gytha spoke to him and shook his shoulder. Not even when she touched his icy cheeks with her warm hands. His skin was nearly as cold as Eshkeshken's had been, but it was not right for a human to be so cold. Ice goblins could thrive with bodies like ice, but humans were meant to be warm.

Kneeling by him, she wept in frustration and anger. How could he die now, when she and Eshkeshken and Dakjudr had come so far to rescue him?

His injuries were serious, but they were not enough to kill him. At least she was reasonably sure of that. She pulled up his shirt and found no new injuries, but neither did she see any indication that his wounds had been dressed or treated.

"How cruel they are to you!" she whispered furiously. "For the sin of refusing to marry a tyrant! She is beautiful, but that does not justify this. Not even for a queen."

She rested her bare palm on his forehead. The cold was like death. She caressed his dark hair. What a strange color! He must really be from far away, beyond the western mountains, because everyone she knew or had ever heard of had golden hair like hers, shading to silver as they aged. The thousand shades of gold, from the rich gold of summer sunlight to the palest gold of winter wheat, were lovely, and the silvers and grays that came with age signified wisdom and understanding. But dark hair! That was strange and exotic.

There was something in the color dear to her already, unusual as it was, because it fit his face. The scruff of beard upon her palm caught her attention; only now had she noticed he had shaved. Perhaps the queen required it, because none of the goblins had a beard. Even his eyebrows were brown. She ran a finger over them gently. Was it wrong to touch him while he slept? It felt simultaneously invasive and innocent; she wanted nothing from him but for him to live.

Her hand was too cold; she would lose her fingers soon. Gytha bit her lip and pulled her thick glove back on, her fingers tingling. She bent to speak into Alexander's ear.

"I haven't given up, Alexander, so you shouldn't either. Wake up, if you can."

His pale face remained as still as death, so she tucked the furs and blankets around him again and stood.

She strode out of the room with her head high. Again, Wirkelshen was waiting for her, his expression grave. His arms were folded over his chest, and he gave the guards a quick nod before he led Gytha away.

She didn't speak until they were back in the apartment with Eshkeshken, Dakjudr, and the others. The ice goblin prince sat on the floor with his gray head in his hands, and he looked up at her entrance.

"He didn't wake, did he?"

Gytha shook her head. "There is something unnatural in it. He's not well."

The prince nodded as if he had expected this. "The queen has enmagicked him in a different way than before. Perhaps his food or drink."

Wirkelshen nodded. "I spoke with the guards. One of them thinks it is the drink, and the other is sure it is the blankets.

I told them to tell the bear prince when he wakes that what they suspect, and if he will try to stay alert, we will do what we can for him."

A strange, fraught silence followed this. Eshkeshken's icy eyes flicked to Gytha and then back to Wirkelshen's hard features. "I am surprised," he said in a low voice. "I did not think you so trusting of the queen's servants."

"I wasn't." Wirkelshen bowed deeply in apology. "But the guard on the second shift, after Gytha entered the room, is my cousin, Karantikai; I hunted seal and fished with him a thousand times before he entered the king's service. Like many of us, he suspected Javethai in the king's death, if not your mother's. He never approved of the bargain with the bear prince, but he did not see any way to help the unfortunate prisoner. When I told him of the queen's new bargain with the bear prince, that the prisoner might be free if he chose Gytha publicly, Karantikai gave me what information he could."

The ice goblin bowed again, as if a little afraid of what Eshkeshken might say.

Eshkeshken's face contorted for a moment, and he pressed a hand to his chest, his breathing shallow and uneven.

"Your Highness?" Dakjudr asked.

"Don't worry about it." The prince's voice was rough. "The drink is easy to avoid, but he will freeze without the blankets. I imagine the queen has enchanted those to keep him insensible; even if he wishes to remain alert, he cannot do so and live."

Gytha said, "Can we get him other blankets? Where did mine come from?"

Eshkeshken looked at Arenenak, who answered, "Our people do not keep furs or blankets often, for we have little need of the warmth. These are borrowed from several friends around the city, and I know of no others."

"I can give him mine," Gytha said promptly. "My clothes are warm enough."

The ice goblin prince looked at her for a moment, his expression difficult to read. "Barely. You would risk death for him yet again? You hardly know him, and he cannot possibly repay you as you deserve."

Gytha's cheeks heated, and the feeling was exacerbated by the frigid air. She wondered how obvious her blushing was. "I know he is good and kind and brave, and that he saved my family from a miserable death. I'm not doing it because I want anything from him." She bit her lip and tried to hold Eshkeshken's steady gaze without looking away. "I want to save him from the evil queen because he has been captive for so long, and he must feel so lost and lonely and forgotten.

"No one should feel that their existence doesn't matter, least of all him. Out of his loneliness and despair, he still chose to be kind to me. How can I forget that and leave him in her power, knowing that I could have fought harder to free him?"

The ice goblin prince held her eyes a moment longer and then nodded, looking down at the floor of ice. He pressed a hand to his chest and coughed. "Sleep, then, if you can, and we will give him the blankets so that he may not freeze. If he keeps himself from the enchantment tonight, he may be able to speak and understand his peril and what he must do. For I wonder if she has not so enmagicked him that he remembers little or nothing of recent days other than the pain of the spears in his sides."

Gytha swallowed, feeling colder than ever. "What about a needle and thread? Or sinew? I can make some of the blankets into clothes for him. Anything would be better than what he has now."

Eshkeshken nodded and looked to Arenenak, who disappeared for some time into the city before returning with a small wooden box with a bone needle and a great quantity of fine thread.

Meanwhile, Dakjudr offered Gytha a plate of seal meat and whale blubber, both raw, with a faint crust of frost already forming over their surfaces. "Is this what the bear prince eats?" Gytha asked. Although she did not want to complain, the food was not to her taste in the slightest. Someday, she hoped, she would be able to make bread again with her sisters and teach them how to score the tops of the loaves to make lovely patterns. Warm, fresh bread with a good crust and butter melting into it was a homely delight.

Eshkeshken gave her a flat look. "I'd be surprised if she's fed him in days. She wants him weak and bewildered, not clear-headed, at least until she has gained his cooperation. Bring a plate of food for him tonight, and you might save his life."

Gytha nodded, feeling her heart twist with sympathy. Cold, raw meat and fat were unfamiliar and unpleasant, but they were kindly meant and generously offered.

"Your Highness," Dakjudr said gently. "Can you eat a little? Please?" She knelt before the prince and offered him a plate.

He nodded and took the plate with a tired smile. "Thank you." She bowed her head to him.

No one could find scissors, but Dakjudr lent Gytha a sharp knife. Gytha spent some time figuring out how she would turn the blankets into clothes that would be as warm as possible. Trousers were challenging, but she made them with several layers, a drawstring waist, and cinches around the ankles to keep out the cold air. The coat was also made of several layers of fabric and left very long, so that with a belt it might keep even the worst drafts out. She knew how to make clothes, of course, but she had never been in such a rush to make something warm before. These were rough and unlovely, but at least they would be better than what he had.

Her eyes were bleary and she was beginning to fall asleep when Eshkeshken touched her shoulder.

"Sleep," he said. "There will be time to work when you wake."

So she went to the other room to sleep. She lay on the ice with one arm under her head and stared at the darkness. It still seemed strange that the bear was a human prince. But the scar on his face was clear evidence.

What would he be like as a human? He had instinctively put himself between her and the queen's anger when the queen had come in a rage at the end of the bargain. His voice, at least his bear voice, was deep and calm, with quiet strength even when sorrowful. Would his human voice be as compelling as his bear voice, when it wasn't rough with sleep? Would he remember her at all?

What if he thought she meant to capture him the way the ice goblin queen had, and resented her for it?

The sound of the ice goblins talking softly in their own language in the other room was a low, grinding background to her whirling thoughts.

Eventually she drifted into an uneasy sleep.

CHAPTER 14

What was time, anyway? When Gytha awoke, she could not tell how much time had passed, or whether she was rested or exhausted. Everything was strange, and time felt like a strange, ephemeral thing, as insubstantial as the dust on a butterfly's wings and as mysterious as the northern lights. She ate and continued sewing. Her stitches were hurried and perhaps a little uneven, but they were close together, so the seams would be strong and tight. As she sewed, she listened to the goblins talking among themselves. Eshkeshken lay with his back to the room on a single blanket, untroubled by the cold but obviously deeply unwell.

"What is wrong with him?" Gytha whispered to Dakjudr.

"Ice."

Gytha felt this was not a clear answer, since there was ice everywhere for hundreds of miles in every direction, but she did not ask more.

At last, it was nearly time to go to the bear prince again. Eshkeshken was awake and alert, though he looked even worse than before. His eyes were deeply shadowed, and his lips were white. His straight, strong shoulders were hunched a little, and at times he pressed one hand to his heart, his eyes squeezed shut.

Dakjudr prepared a plate of raw meat for Gytha and another for the bear prince. When she offered Eshkeshken a similar plate, he muttered, "I can't stomach it."

Gytha hesitated and then, before she could talk herself out of it, put one hand on his shoulder. "I'm sorry you feel so bad."

His silvery eyes flicked up to hers. He gave a short huff of laughter and muttered, "You are too soft and warm for this land. Go to your bear prince, and don't worry about me."

He stood and offered her a hand, as if to reassure her that he was not yet at death's door.

The clothes were heavy, so Iphreshken carried them over one arm. Gytha had not used all the blankets for the clothes, so Dakjudr handed Wirkelshen the remaining blankets, which she had wrapped cleverly into an enormous bundle which he could sling over his shoulder. She gave Gytha the plate of food for the prince, piled high with raw meat, blubber, and fish.

Again, Gytha followed the ice goblins through the strange corridors of ice and snow. In some places, the walls were smooth panels of ice, as clear as glass, letting the light of the stars and the gibbous moon turn the hallway into pale shadows that skittered away in the light of the lantern. In other areas, the walls and ceiling were white ice or packed snow.

When they reached the bear prince's room, Wirkelshen nodded to the guards. They studied Gytha for a moment and then nodded her in. She stepped in and set the plate and lantern on the floor and then turned to accept the bundle of blankets and the clothes before closing the door.

A strangled sound made her turn hurriedly, her heart thudding with nerves.

On the far side of the room, well away from the door, Alexander stood shivering.

"You came," he said, half to himself.

"Hello," Gytha said. "Do you remember me?"

"A little." Shivering racked his whole body, and he did not approach her. His clothes were hardly warm enough for autumn in Gytha's village, and entirely insufficient for winter there, much less here in the frozen top end of the world. His shirt and trousers were thin and hung on his gaunt frame, and he wore old leather boots that might have been suited for long walks in the forest but not for the snow and ice that blanketed the world.

"Do you remember that my name is Gytha?" She held out the clothes. "I made these for you. They're not warm enough for this place, but they are better than what you have. You can have my coat if you want, too."

His dark eyes were wide and a little wild, darting from her to the door and back again. "You're the girl from the village," he said carefully. "The one I met as a bear."

"Yes." Gytha took a slow step forward. "Put these on. I'm sorry they're not better, but I didn't have much time."

He reached for the clothes, moving carefully, and Gytha wasn't sure if he was trying not to frighten her, or if he were frightened *of* her. He took off his boots and stood with his worn socks on the floor of ice, and she thought suddenly that he looked nothing at all like the great bear she had known. Of course his body was different, but the look in his eyes was also quite different.

He pulled on the thick, shapeless trousers over his old ones and stuck his feet back into his boots. He pulled the drawstring tight on his thin waist with trembling fingers. The coat was more like an enormous shirt with sleeves, for there was no opening in the front, and he had to pull it over his head. He accepted the belt and tied it around his waist and then tightened the straps on each wrist.

"You can have my gloves," Gytha said at last. "My coat has pockets, and I didn't have time to make pockets for you."

He looked up at her with a strange expression. "Why would you offer that?" He sounded absolutely mystified.

For a moment, Gytha was at a loss. How much of the past year did he remember at all? How much of his time as a bear did he remember? Did he even know where he was?

He straightened, still shivering. "Why are you here?"

"To rescue you."

His mouth dropped open. "What? Why?" He put his head in his hands, and his long, messy curls hid his fingers. "I'm sorry." He shivered so violently he staggered a little.

Gytha's heart twisted with a strange sense of protective anger. "Sit down. You must be exhausted."

She reached for his arm, and he flinched.

"I'm sorry," he said, and there was such a weight of weariness and despair in his voice that tears sprang to Gytha's eyes.

"Sit down," she said again. There was a table, but there were no chairs, so she retrieved the blankets and spread one on the ice floor. She sat the lantern down and put the plate of raw meat beside it.

After a moment, Alexander sat across from her, his dark eyes searching her face. "I've forgotten your name," he said. "I'm sorry. Being a bear makes everything...jumbled...and near the end, I nearly forgot I was ever anything but a beast."

Gytha pushed the plate of food toward him. "My name is Gytha Ivarrsdattar. Eat a little, if you can."

He eyed the plate with distaste but picked up a cube of raw fish between two fingers and looked up at her. He put it in his mouth.

"When you were a bear, my father thought you were going to eat my sister and me, and he tried to protect us. He gave you that scar on your nose. Do you remember that?"

He touched the scar gingerly and his gaze went distant for a moment. "You have many sisters and brothers," he said at last. "I called two of them Little Sister, and the smaller one shouted in my ear and woke me out of a sleep like death." He closed his eyes and shook his head as if shaking water out of his ears. "That was in the south, when the queen's magic was burning like ice in my bones and threading my mind with nightmares when I dared try to sleep." He buried his face in his hands and let out a soft groan. "I am sorry you are here. I never wanted the curse on me to cause you such trouble."

When he looked up at her, his face was terribly pale and drawn, and he was still shivering. She pulled her gloves off, and held them out. "Here."

His gaze flicked to her bare hands and then to his own. "Keep them. I haven't lost my fingers yet."

She pushed the gloves at him a little more emphatically, and he flinched. Something twisted inside her. "Please," she said gently.

His eyes were wide and a little wild, and he shook his head. "No. I won't." He folded his arms over his chest.

Gytha bit her lip, torn between fury at the queen and an abyss of grief and sympathy for him. She tugged the gloves back on reluctantly. "Eat a little more, if you can," she said. "Do you remember the place I spent a year? Was it you who came to my bed every night?"

"Yes. I am sorry I frightened you." The grief and sorrow in his eyes tugged at her heart.

"I thought it was you. Your voice is different than when you were a bear, and of course you look different, but..." She looked at his face, really looked. His dark eyes were almost the same, and the way he'd said *Little Sister* with such longing, as if he wanted to claim them as family. "You're not so different after all," she finished.

She stood, and he started to rise too, but she said, "Stay. I'm just getting a blanket." He sank back down, and she wrapped the blanket around his shoulders and over his messy curls, with the ends in his lap. He flinched when the cloth touched his shoulders, and she pretended she did not notice. She sat down again across from him.

He wrapped his hands in the fabric and stared at her. "I don't know how or why you are here," he said at last. "But the queen is angry with you. She thought you would break the terms of the bargain and look at me. She will not be pleased that you are still trying to help me."

"Why is she so angry with you?"

He looked down at his crossed ankles, and there was such weariness and frustration in his posture that Gytha's heart softened toward him even more. His hands clenched in the blankets. "I went out riding many years ago, with my favorite horse and my dog. She approached me and said she would have me for her own, for I was handsome of face and she liked my warmth. She looked human; I learned later it was a glamour. I had thought her words strange, but at the time I thought only that it was unsettling phrasing.

"I told her that my marriage would likely be largely dictated by political concerns, but that I hoped to find love in it too. A life of honor and integrity, with a woman who also held such values dear, would surely lead to affection and love, if we worked toward these things together.

"This did not satisfy her. She took me by force to her father, the ice goblin king, and demanded that he force me to marry her." He looked up to meet her eyes for a moment and then back down at the blanket. "The king was furious with me for refusing her, and with her for choosing a weak and foolish human. He said he would change me into something stronger, something fiercer, and so he changed me into a bear. But only during the day. At night, I shivered as a man. For two and a half centuries, I have refused to marry her. As a human, I despise her and everything she has done, and I will not sully my name by uniting it with hers, nor will I reward such selfishness by conceding a single inch to her."

He shuddered. "But as a bear, I began to forget what it was to be human, and every night, when I lost my thick fur and regained my human form, I found it more disorienting and more terrifying. As a beast, I was able to endure the merciless cold. As a human..." He looked up at her again, his dark eyes anguished. "As a human, I grew more hopeless. The king died, perhaps by Javethai's hand, although I do not know for sure, and his magic is tied up in me, so that whatever selfish version of love she once had for me is now lost in her desire for power.

"I am nothing to her but an obstacle. She still wants to marry me, but only as a show of power, a show of her victory over man, and as a final demonstration that she has taken the full power of the ice goblin monarch for herself."

At this, he subsided into silence, until at last he said, "Frigtirk told me about the blankets keeping me sleeping when you came in before. Thank you for trying again." He met her eyes, and there was such a sweet gratitude that Gytha had the sudden urge to throw her arms around him.

But it was different now that he was shaped like a man, and she felt too shy to actually do it. Instead, she said, "The ice goblin prince is here, and he is going to help free you from the queen."

Alexander stared at her. "The prince? There is no prince."

"Eshkeshken. He was the servant I called Magni when we were in that strange, underground prison."

Alexander frowned thoughtfully. "Eshkeshken," he said to himself. "I've heard the name before. You are sure he's telling the truth?"

Gytha nodded. "I think so. The winds acknowledged him as the prince, as if they knew him, and others here did too."

"The winds?" He looked at her with those soft, dark eyes, so different than the blue eyes of her own people, and she blushed.

"This palace, or city, is at the north end of the world, east of the sun and west of the moon, where only the winds can go," she said. "That's what Eshkeshken said, and the winds each took us some distance closer, and we walked a long way. But they also did something to him, and he's suffering a great deal. More than he will admit."

Alexander studied her face. "You feel for him."

Gytha bit her lip. "Yes. He was kind to me. Not as you were, but maybe with even less reason. He saved my life after the queen took you. He told me to wear my coat and gloves and boots to bed, and when the caves collapsed, he and Dakjudr dug me out and fed me." She looked pointedly at the plate of meat. "You should eat."

He looked down at the plate in surprise. "Oh. Yes. I haven't…" He dragged his fingers through his tangled hair. "I forgot."

"To be hungry?"

"To care that I was hungry." He gave a soft huff of laughter that was almost bitter, but not quite. The huff sounded like a smaller, more human version of the sound he had made as a bear.

"How much do your injuries hurt?" she asked gently.

He put a piece of meat in his mouth and shrugged a little. "I forgot to care about that, too," he muttered.

"Well, I care," Gytha said.

His gaze flicked up to her face again, startled. "Why?"

Her heart twisted with sympathy. "You were kind to my family when we had almost lost hope. Maybe you don't have much hope left, so it is up to me to hold onto hope."

"Hope of what?" His voice broke.

"In the morning, the queen will come. She said that if you remembered me and asked for me, she would let you choose your bride between her and me. She expected you to be enchanted into sleep tonight too, so of course you would not remember me. But I imagine there will be some trick, even if she allows you to choose. Be careful of her."

"You want to marry me?" He stared at her, his eyes wide and shocked. "Why?"

"It was the only thing I could think of!" She felt sick with embarrassment. "Eshkeshken said to offer her a bargain, and I couldn't think of anything else. I was so angry for you! The guards were stabbing you with those spears and lances. It was all I could think of. I argued that you hadn't had a real choice, and you would choose me over her if you had a choice.

"One of the goblins spoke up then. He appealed to her pride and said it would be better for her prestige if you chose her rather than being coerced, and he offered me as a much inferior alternative."

He drew back a little, his dark eyes flicking over her face again and then down the floor, as if he were embarrassed. Why would *he* be embarrassed?

"You don't have to marry me!" she whispered hurriedly. "It just seemed like the only way to get to you at all. Anyway, if you marry me, we can pretend it never happened later. A vow made under duress and threat of death isn't really binding, is it? It's just a ruse to get you free. We just wanted a way to get you away from her. I got her to agree that you should be in your human form, so you could voice your preference clearly."

Alexander pulled the blanket tighter around his shoulders. "Even though no one remembers me, I am still a prince," he said. "My word is my bond. I will not vow falsely." He looked down at the blanket and shuddered. "I'm sorry."

Gytha flinched. "You'd rather let her carve your heart out and eat it in front of everyone than marry me? Knowing that I won't even hold you to it?" Tears welled in her eyes. "What have I done to offend you so? It's not fair!" Her voice cracked, and she tried to bring her unruly emotions under control. "I'm just trying to help you."

He was staring at her with wide eyes. "I think you misunderstood, or perhaps I did."

She bit her lip and watched him compose himself. His eyes were so tired, his cheeks so thin, that she felt her sympathy rise again, stronger than her hurt.

He took a deep breath and raised his chin before he spoke. "You have already sacrificed much for me, coming to this icy end of the world. I will not marry you in a farce to save my skin, no matter how generously you intended the offer. If I marry you, or anyone, it will be with all my heart, for all my life, however long or short that is."

"What if it wasn't a farce?" Gytha felt the desperation in her words. "I can't let you die, Alexander. You said you once thought you could find love with someone who lived with honor and integrity. I will do my best not to disappoint you! I don't want a title or anything, I just want you to live and not let that horrible woman kill you. I—"

"No!" He shook his head, his face even paler than before. "I didn't mean..." He raked trembling fingers through his hair again. "I am sorry. I meant that you have sacrificed so much for me already that it would be cruel to accept this, too."

"Could you love me, if we were married under other circumstances?"

"How can you even doubt it?" He swallowed and met her eyes again. "When I was a bear, I didn't notice that you were beautiful; I only noticed that you smelled of death but still smiled kindly at those you loved. I saw that you were kind to me, even though you were terrified. Your courage and compassion won my heart.

"Now, with human eyes, I..." He gripped the ends of the blankets more tightly. "I am reminded that you must have hopes and dreams beyond this frozen end of the world. Maybe you have a good man waiting for you, ready to give you a happy life. And I have nothing but centuries of painful memories that haunt me and a royal title long since forgotten. No one who still lives, other than you, even knows my name.

"How can I ask you to throw away your good future to save me a quick death? The queen has told me for years she would not let me die before marrying her, and now she is angry enough to kill me. It seems the best way out for both of us. You can go back home, free to marry whom you choose."

A surge of fierce, hot anger made Gytha's voice sharp. "I don't accept that. I didn't come all the way here to watch you die at that evil woman's hand, and you have no right to tell me that marrying you is throwing away my good future! Everything I know of you is good and kind, and that's the kind of man I want to marry. Why should we not find happiness together, if we both choose to love each other well?"

He blinked several times, as if reevaluating everything he knew. "I don't want you to marry me out of pity," he said at last. "Death is a better option than marrying her, and I am willing to accept it."

"Is it really better to die than to marry me?" She swallowed. "And I don't mean out of pride because you don't want to burden me, but do you really think being married to me would be worse than death? You think you'd be so miserable you'd rather die?"

"Of course not!" His voice rose a little in dismay. "I want you to be free to choose whom you marry."

"Then I choose you!" she cried. "Maybe this isn't the best way of starting a marriage, but we can continue better once you're free. Don't you think we could find our way to love, if we both tried?"

"You would really marry me, knowing so little of me, and not feel it a burden or a disgrace?" His eyes were wide and haunted. "How can you be so sure?"

"Please, Alexander," she said softly. "Please. Think of how you would feel if someone had been so kind and generous to you, and then wouldn't even accept your love and gratitude in return. If you marry me, I will have no regrets. If you die, I will grieve for all my days that your pride and hurt kept you from accepting me, and I will feel hurt that you would rather die than attempt to make a happy life with a woman who loves you."

His dark eyes brimmed with emotion. He took her gloved hands in both of his and raised them to his lips and then to his eyes, hiding them. It was several minutes before he spoke, and Gytha could feel his hands trembling as he still held her.

"I am honored," he said in a low voice, "and I will choose you before everyone, now and always. I love you already, and I am sure that, if I survive the queen's wrath, I will love you more day by day. I will endeavor to make you glad of this sacrifice."

"It's not a sacrifice," she whispered. "It is a joy, even if it is surrounded by pain."

He squeezed her hands.

Something in Gytha's heart shifted from fear to determination. She would not leave this place without him. "Eat, please," she said. "I don't know what Eshkeshken is planning, but I think you will need your strength."

He pressed her hands again before he straightened. "Yes. You are right."

For several hours, they talked quietly; it seemed good to both of them to not let the silence draw out too long, because then they felt awkward and unsettled with each other. Gytha asked many questions about Alexander's past, about his time in the north and what he remembered of his childhood.

"I was born in Elestar, the capital city of Eleria, in a beautiful palace built into the side of a cliff overlooking the sea. In the mornings, I watched the sunrise from the windows overlooking the valley to the east, and from my bedroom, I watched the sunset over the water."

"I've never seen the sea, not really. Only that moment at the entrance to the queen's prison."

He blinked and looked at her. "That's right. I suppose you wouldn't have. You saw it covered with ice, and only for a moment. It wasn't free, like I saw it.

"I loved watching the storms roll in over the water, the dark clouds looming like mountains and the waves crashing upon the cliffs. The palace was all stone on the outside, so there was no real danger, but the air crackled with energy, and it made me feel free and alive."

"I would like to see it someday," Gytha mused.

"The smell of the sea is salt and fish and immense open space. It is beautiful and perilous and unpredictable. But the palace was safe.

"When I was young, I heard of other kingdoms in which brother hated brother, and they fought or killed for power. But my brother and I loved each other. We never fought over anything serious; we had only foolish children's squabbles. He was six years younger than I was. Maybe that kept us from feeling like rivals.

"I wish I'd been able to see him rule. He was twelve when I... when the queen took me." He looked down. "The queen's magic kept me alive, but I know centuries have passed. Everyone I knew and loved is long dead. I always wanted..." He stopped again, wrapping the blanket tighter around his shoulders.

When he did not speak again, Gytha asked, "What did you want?"

He swallowed. "To not be forgotten." He met her gaze, his eyes haunted. "Every memory I ever shared with someone, every time I heard my brother laugh, every time my mother sang, every time my father put his arm around my shoulders... they're all gone, and all memory of them is held only in my mind, and my memory was fading. All the warmth of those memories was slowly disappearing, replaced by ice.

"You shouldn't marry me, Gytha. I have nothing left: my name has been forgotten off the face of the earth, my family is dead, my palace is far away and probably occupied by people who never knew I lived at all. I have no home to bring you to, no skill to provide for you other than what little I remember of a prince's education. I have nothing to offer you."

"I didn't ask for anything." Gytha put her hand on his, and when she felt him trembling with cold, her heart twisted inside her, fury and pity and determination mixing in something new. "I'm not going to beg you, Alexander; you already agreed to choose me, and I will hold you to your word." She met his gaze again and said softly, "You were good to me. Let me be good to you."

He nodded jerkily.

The door opened and one of the goblins peeked in. "It is time." His voice was like broken glass and ice. He opened the door wider. "Come now."

CHAPTER 15

Alexander dropped Gytha's hand and stood, his movements a little stiff.

"Can you walk?" the ice goblin said. The question was not sympathetic; there was an edge of irritation in his voice.

"Yes." Alexander straightened painfully and followed the goblin into the hallway. Gytha caught up the lantern and hurried after them.

"I can carry it, if you like," Alexander said belatedly. "They usually don't let me have a lantern."

Gytha handed it to him, and he held it a little to the side so that the light spilled in front of her feet as well as his.

The goblin led them through a series of corridors and then out into a vast courtyard under the open sky, an enormous black expanse full of sparkling pinpoints of light. The air was as cold and still as death.

A thin layer of snow had fallen since they had last been outside, making their steps creak and squeak softly. The goblin said in his rough voice, "You will not see them at first, but your friends are near. Be of good courage."

Alexander looked at him in surprise. "I thought you…"

The goblin's eyes glinted dangerously. "You are not the only one who suffers under Queen Javethai," he hissed softly. "There was little chance for change until now. The lost prince has returned, and the queen has much to answer for."

Gytha's mouth dropped open.

He waved them toward a high wall of ice blocks which glowed softly from the inside. An enormous archway led into another courtyard even larger than the first, nearly full of ice goblins. At the far end of this enormous space stood a dais like the one from a few days before, but even larger. Five lanterns stood on each side of the dais, casting flickering light over the whole front of the courtyard. Queen Javethai stood silently on the top step of the dais, her eyes fixed on them. Even from this distance, Gytha shivered at the hatred in that gaze.

"Follow me." The goblin led them through the crowd, which parted before them with soft, grinding murmurs. Alexander held his head high and proud, as if he were not afraid. Gytha tried to follow this example, but her eyes were continually drawn to the dais, where the queen still stood motionless.

At last the goblin stopped at the bottom of the steps. "Go." He motioned them upward toward the queen.

Alexander raised his eyes to the ice goblin queen and a shudder ran through him. Nevertheless, he raised his chin and strode up the steps toward her.

Gytha began to follow him, but the queen said, "Stay," and ice crept up over Gytha's feet and ankles, binding her to the ground.

"Yes, Your Majesty?" Alexander set the lantern down and bowed courteously to the queen.

The queen gave a faint sneer and tossed her head, throwing her iron gray hair over her shoulder. She spread her arms wide and looked at the crowd. "I have been generous, haven't I? I have been patient." Her voice rang out like the crack of ice breaking upon stone, clear and merciless. "For three nights, a foolish human girl has tried to steal my betrothed! I was patient and generous, allowing this greedy, opportunistic farce to continue.

"Now, bear prince, choose whom you would wed!" Her voice rose, bright and hard. "I don't think you can even pick the human out of a crowd, can you? What good could a human do you here? Choose now: me, Queen Javethai the Glorious, or the common, worthless human?" She gestured broadly at the crowd, inviting Alexander to look out at them too.

Any hint of a murmur in the crowd quieted. The silence was eerie. Chills crawled up Gytha's back, both of cold and of terror. This was not natural, and there was no free choice to be made.

Alexander turned and looked over the crowd. There was an odd stillness in his expression, a blankness that Gytha had not seen before. He swayed as if a wind gusted, but there was no wind.

"Yes?" the queen said.

"I don't…" he whispered.

"He doesn't even remember!" Javethai crowed. Her laughter rang out triumphantly.

"Wait." Alexander gasped and clutched at his head. "What am I supposed to remember?"

"You agreed to marry me, remember?" Javethai laughed again. "Give me the magic, bear. It is *mine*!"

Alexander doubled over, digging his fingers into his hair. "No!"

"Submit to me! Marry me now! Or I will cut your heart out and eat it before these witnesses!"

The queen gripped Alexander by the throat with one hand and lifted him off his feet as she pulled a long, sharp knife out of her skirts with the other hand.

"I will not submit," Alexander gasped.

Several ice goblins shouted, and the knife flashed.

A sudden commotion in the crowd near Gytha resolved into Eshkeshken and several others charging up the steps toward the queen.

A goblin touched Gytha's feet, and the ice around her ankles cracked. She wrenched her feet free with a ferocious jerk, ran up the steps, and lunged at the queen without any plan at all. But the goblin prince was ahead of her.

The queen turned toward Eshkeshken and shrieked in rage. She flung Alexander away and put her hand up toward Eshkeshken, her lips drawn back in a snarl.

Eshkeshken shouted in a voice as sharp as lightning, "Javethai the Usurper, I charge you with treason! I am Eshkeshken, son of Jiehteshken! Stand down and beg for clemency, or die now for your crimes."

The queen cried, "Eshkeshken the Coward? Eshkeshken the Weakling? I thought you long dead. You were hiding in plain sight, I see."

Eshkeshken drew himself up even straighter, but beside the queen's tall, powerful figure, his slim frame was hardly imposing. "Stand down, Javethai," he said more softly. "My patience is at an end."

He took a step forward, extending his hand for the knife.

The queen sidled a little to one side and then sprang.

Though Eshkeshken was smaller and unarmed, he was just as quick as she was, and he sidestepped her stab and gripped the knife with one hand.

She bashed her forehead into his face, and his knees gave way for a moment.

With shocking suddenness, a lance flew through the air and skewered them both.

Locked in their vicious embrace, they staggered and then collapsed half-atop each other, with the lance shaft sticking out of the queen's back. The shaft had penetrated her completely, and stuck deep in Eshkeshken's chest

The queen fought to push him away, but he was as helpless as she was, and instead they fell to one side, so that they faced each other as they lay dying together.

A roar of discordant goblin voices rose like thunder.

Dakjudr ran up the stairs and stood over Eshkeshken and Javethai. "Watch!" she cried. "Watch and see whose claim is just!"

She yanked on the lance, but the weapon would not come free. She put one foot on Javethai's shoulder to brace herself and jerked again, producing agonized groans from the queen and Eshkeshken.

At last, after a few more bone-crunching heaves, she pulled the lance from their bodies and held it aloft. A clear, shimmering orb glittered on the point, dripping with gray blood that sparkled with silvery magic.

The queen gasped, "Give it back! That's mine!" But she could not rise. She reached for Dakjudr's ankle with one hand, grasping and clawing.

"Look! Behold your king!" Dakjudr's voice rang out, sharp and hard. She looked down at Eshkeshken, her eyes gleaming with emotion. "The lance pierced his heart. You saw it. See the ice heart!"

Eshkeshken pressed a hand to his chest and gave a strangled groan. Then he rolled to his stomach and slowly, painfully, pushed himself to hands and knees, and then to his feet.

Dakjudr knelt before him and held out the lance in both hands. "Your Majesty."

Eshkeshken took the lance and straightened, his thin shoulders back and his head high. He cast his gaze over the ice goblins. At last he said, "My name is Eshkeshken."

Perhaps his voice was a little rougher than usual; an ice goblin might have been able to hear the edge of pain or fatigue in it. To Gytha, he sounded as confident as any king. The gray blood that streaked his shirt had already frozen, so that the thin fabric stuck to his skin around the dark, ugly wound.

"Javethai the Usurper is my aunt. *Was* my aunt." He looked down at her.

She lay sprawled upon the ice, her eyes glazed with approaching death.

"I knew she would not give up the throne she stole without bloodshed, and I thought that by letting her have the throne she coveted, I would save you, my people, a bloody war.

"I was wrong. She called me a coward, and perhaps she was right to do so. But I will be a coward no longer.

"I waited and hoped for her to change, but she only grew more wicked. I determined at last that I would be no prince at all if I did not oppose her."

He looked down at her again. Her fingers twitched, and her lips moved, but no one could hear what she said.

Eshkeshken took a deep breath and let it out slowly, looking more regal by the moment. "The winds froze my heart," he said at last. "A unique protection against the lance the winds also provided.

"I did not recognize it at first, but look." He held the lance high above his head, and the broken ice that had encased his heart fell to the ground and shattered. The tip of the lance shifted and glittered, catching the starlight. "The magic kept it whole until you could see it, even as it passed through the usurper's body. Do you see this?"

Eshkeshken moved the lance a little, letting the light catch the tip of the lance again. His thin lips lifted in a faint smile. "It is the lost scepter of my grandfather, the king. Javethai never wielded all the power of the ice goblin monarchy. The winds kept it safe for me, even as I shrank from my duty. But no longer!"

He threw back his head, tossing his gray hair out of his eyes. Then he looked toward Alexander and Gytha, who crouched together some distance away. Alexander's fingers were white and nearly frozen, but he held them against his bruised throat as he watched everything unfolding.

Eshkeshken strode over to Alexander, who looked up at him with wide, dazed eyes. The ice goblin extended a hand to him. "Stand, bear prince."

Alexander reached for him, and when their hands touched, a great crack like thunder rocked the world. Gytha cried out.

The goblin prince gripped Alexander's hand, steadying him as he staggered. "That's better," he said under his breath.

A grinding roar swept over the crowd, and only with effort could Gytha make out that it was goblin voices clamoring for answers. Some sounded angry. The ice goblin king offered Gytha a hand, and he pulled her to her feet, too.

Eshkeshken's silvery eyes focused on Alexander a moment longer. Then he turned to the crowd.

"The North Wind whispered in my ear that if I waited too long, my heart would stop forever. Only the lance could break the ice, and only the ice would save me from the lance.

"Without Dakjudr's courage, all would have been lost.

"The lance pierced my heart, breaking the ice and the queen's hold upon the royal magic at once. The power the queen had stolen poured into me, filling me with life despite the wound, and I now hold what is rightfully mine, the full might and authority of the ice goblin king!" His voice rose, sharp and strong.

"My first act as king is to free the bear prince, unjustly enmagicked and held captive for two and a half centuries. We ice goblins are more than petty tyrants! We will not be defined and known only by Javethai's cruelty." With his head high and proud, he turned to look at Alexander. "On behalf of my people, I beg your forgiveness for the misdeeds of the usurper, and if it is in my power to make some recompense, I will do so."

The ice goblin king, slim and hard and gray, his chest darkened by his own blood, bowed before Alexander.

Trembling and pale, the young man said, "It wasn't your cruelty that kept me here."

"No, but it was my hesitation to act that prolonged your suffering." Eshkeshken straightened. "Be our guest now, and we will aid you to return to your home, when you are ready."

A voice cried out from the crowd, "What of the dead queen?"

Eshkeshken turned to look for the speaker. "Bring your complaints about the usurper's rule to me, and I will seek to do justice."

"What of the body?" Arenenak had made his way to the front of the crowd, and he looked up at Eshkeshken with grave eyes.

"Feed her to the sea. Perhaps the kraken will want her." Eshkeshken's voice was hard.

Other arrangements were made, but Gytha lost track of the voices. She focused on Alexander, who stood motionless as the new king continued to answer questions and direct his allies, of which there were many.

Dakjudr remained kneeling where she had presented the lance to the new king. Her shoulders moved with jerky breaths, but she was otherwise motionless and silent.

When Eshkeshken had answered another question, he turned to look at her. He frowned.

"Get up, Dakjudr." His voice was as soft as Gytha had ever heard it.

Dakjudr glanced up at him and then back down at the ice. "How am I to face you, Your Majesty?"

The goblin king extended a hand to her, but she did not look up again.

"I cannot forget the sound you made when I yanked the lance from your heart." Her voice was low and rough. "I am glad I was able to serve you, but the grief of my crime is too heavy to bear."

Eshkeshken stood over her a moment, as if waiting for her to reconsider. Then he moved to sit beside her. For a full minute he sat in silence, until at last he said, "Well, that is unexpected. How am I to rule without my most trusted confidant beside me?"

Dakjudr chuckled grimly. "There are thousands eager to serve you, Your Majesty." She was still kneeling, her face turned slightly away from him.

"That is true. But none of them were faithful through many long years of exile, not only to my name but to my person, to accompany me into hiding. None of them gave me courage when I had none of my own." He leaned his shoulder against hers for a moment. "I am glad of their support, but I do not need them by my side. I need you, Dakjudr."

Her head dropped even further, and she put her hands over her face. "I am sorry," she whispered.

He tugged her hands away from her face and threaded his fingers through hers. "I grieve because you are grieved. But the pain of the ice in my heart and the pain of the lance are gone."

He stopped and waited for her to say something, but she only shook her head.

"I need you, Dakjudr," he said even more quietly. "By my side. How will I be wise and kind and courageous without you beside me? You have given me hope and courage for many years."

She huffed softly. "You ask a great deal."

He laughed, an oddly bright sound for all its sharp edges. "Yes, I do. You'd have to put up with me. Will you, please? Be my queen? Rule with me?"

She looked at him at last, her gray eyes catching the lamplight. "After what I did?"

"I asked it of you because I trusted you more than anyone else. Can you forgive me for it?"

Dakjudr bowed her head and stared at their clasped hands for several long seconds. "I can," she allowed at last. "But do not ask me to hurt you that way again."

He laughed again. "I hope there will never be a need." Then he sobered. "I would have no one else do the hard, needful thing, because there is no one I trust more. Know that."

"Then I will be your queen."

He drew her to her feet and stood looking out at the crowd. Some of the ice goblins had watched their conversation, but their voices had been so quiet that no one had heard their words.

"May I tell them, or would you like time to reconsider before I make it public?"

She glanced at him. "I know my own mind."

He grinned fiercely, his sharp white teeth flashing.

"Behold now your new queen, Dakjudr my bride!" Eshkeshken's voice rang out like a peal of joyous thunder. "She is worthy of all your respect as a fierce and honorable warrior, a beacon of hope and courage in my darkest moments, and a just and merciful queen."

All this time, Alexander had stood dazed a few feet away. Only the shock of the magic being broken had kept him upright this long. Now, as the crowd quieted and looked toward the new king and his betrothed, Alexander crumpled senseless to the ground.

Gytha bent over him, her eyes filled with tears. "Don't die now," she whispered. "After all this!"

She pulled off one glove to feel for his pulse. The skin of his neck was so cold that she gasped. "He's nearly frozen!"

The ice goblin king knelt beside her.

"What do we do?" Gytha asked.

The hard lines of Eshkeshken's face softened. "I have more magic now. I can warm him a little, and we can build a fire. Come."

He gathered up Alexander's limp body in his arms and carried him into the palace, leaving the crowd behind. Alexander was much taller than Eshkeshken, but the goblin king had no difficulty carrying him. Eshkeshken did not even seem to notice the wound that had seemed so grievous.

The king spoke over his shoulder to Dakjudr and the other goblins, who jogged off in different directions.

A few minutes later, he installed Gytha and Alexander in a room she had not seen before. There was a large flagstone section of the floor in the center of the space with a pile of thick furs near one side. Far above, a small circle in the ceiling showed twinkling stars in the infinite sky.

"Lay out those furs," he directed Gytha.

When the furs were spread upon the stone, he lay Alexander on them. Wirkelshen hurried in carrying several poles and a large piece of thick cloth; he drove the poles into the ice and stretched the cloth upon it to form something like a wall just behind Alexander.

"What is that for?"

"It will reflect the heat back on him." Eshkeshken bent over a box made of stone in the center of the flagstones. A moment later, Gytha felt warmth on her face.

"We have very little wood here," Eshkeshken said. "But I have enmagicked it to burn without being consumed for many hours. The stove is too hot to touch, but you may come close to it. The heat is good for your human bodies."

Alexander still lay pale and unmoving.

"Will he live?" Gytha could not help asking.

Eshkeshken's cold eyes flicked to her and then to Alexander's face. "The magic that kept him prisoner also preserved his life," he said in a low voice. "He has lived far beyond human years, and suffered cold and torments humans were not meant to endure. Perhaps he has suffered too much to continue."

Gytha's heart twisted into a knot, hard and hot inside her chest, and she said fiercely, "No! He can't die now!"

The ice goblin king put a hand on Alexander's forehead. "He can," he said softly. "Perhaps he should."

Gytha pulled off her gloves and took Alexander's icy hands in hers. His fingers were so cold they were stiff, and she thought wildly that he was half-frozen already. Eshkeshken's gray hand rested on Alexander's head a moment longer.

"I have done what I can for him," he said at last. "If he wakes, get him to eat. Whether he lives or dies, we will return you to your people." He turned to meet her gaze. "You have been a friend to me and to my people, and I will repay the debt I owe you."

Silence filled the room, broken only by the muffled hiss and pop of the fire.

"I didn't do much," Gytha said.

Eshkeshken shrugged one shoulder and gave her a sharp-toothed smile. "Perhaps not, but your kindness was given when I most needed it. Out of your own despair and loneliness, you chose generosity and kindness when I had chosen bitterness. You presented a very clear alternative to me when I did not know I had a choice at all."

"Why didn't you say anything to me for so long?" The deadly chill of Alexander's hands sucked the warmth from Gytha's fingers, but she did not pull away from him. She looked at his face and then back at the ice goblin king expectantly.

The king hesitated and then inclined his head in apology. "I was young when the queen took power, and she had not seen me in years. For many years, I watched and waited, avoiding her notice. I knew the bear prince was mistreated, but I did not know how badly. I volunteered to guard your prison for that year, knowing that it would take me out of the city she seemed to own.

"When I presented myself to her, I disguised myself, for I did not trust that she would not think evil of me and try to kill me. Dakjudr, loyal and courageous as she is, followed me in this, though I did not ask or expect it. Javethai did not recognize me, but she required a vow that neither of us speak a word to either you or the bear prince." He showed his teeth in another cold smile. "I was careful with my words; I vowed to not speak to you as long as I served the queen. I said it with such meekness and sincerity that the queen did not realize that when I *decided* not to serve her ends, the vow would lose its power over me."

Arenenak and Wirkelshen erected another fabric wall beside the first at an angle and stretched a cloth over the top.

Within minutes, the air grew warm enough for Gytha to notice the difference. She let down the hood of her coat. The air was chilly, but no longer dangerous to her bare skin. This warmth after so long in the lethal cold felt like a gift.

The ice goblin king sighed. "I should have done more for him, but I did not know how to break the queen's hold on him, and I did not know whether I might not make things worse for us all. And I was afraid." He looked up to meet Gytha's eyes. "I thought my cowardice was prudence and my inaction was patience. But you waited in hope and courage, rather than merely mute endurance.

"The more I think of you claiming me as a friend, the more I am pleased by it." He smiled again, his silver-blue eyes holding hers.

A soft, pained breath caught their attention, and they looked at Alexander. The bear prince drifted toward awareness.

"Alexander," Gytha said.

He blinked, still dazed, and then he saw Eshkeshken, and a shudder went through him. "Don't hurt her," he croaked. He struggled to sit up, and Gytha put her arm around him.

"Why would I hurt her?" Eshkeshken's gray brows lowered in a frown.

Alexander's eyes darted around the room, wide and cautious. "I'm sorry," he said at last. "I thought...I didn't recognize you."

Eshkeshken inclined his head solemnly. "When you are well enough to travel, I will send you home. You are no longer a prisoner here, but a guest. You will have food to strengthen you and clothes to warm you, and if there is any other way I might aid your healing, please be bold in your request."

Alexander nodded. His voice was rough with fatigue when he said, "Your magic is strong, Your Majesty."

The goblin king smiled a little. "Yes. Now it is strong. It was not before."

"Thank you."

"How badly did Javethai hurt you?" Gytha asked Alexander.

"I did not count the beatings. I forgot to care about the hurt. Is it really pain if it doesn't trouble me?" Alexander struggled up to sit with his elbows on his knees. His voice was so soft and weary that Gytha barely heard him. "If I ceased to care about myself entirely, then she had no power over me. No threat of pain, no twist of magic, nothing she could do was worth forfeiting my honor."

Gytha said quietly, "*I* care about your pain."

He hesitated before he looked up. "You don't have to marry me, Gytha," he said softly. "You don't even have to feel guilty about not marrying me. The queen is dead. You have done more for me than anyone in centuries. You owe me nothing except, perhaps, resentment and anger for what I put you through."

Gytha frowned. His eyes were shadowed with exhaustion so deep that she wondered whether he really understood that he was free. He certainly didn't understand the stubborn affection and hope that flared, hot and bright, when she looked at him.

After a moment, Eshkeshken stood. "Take your time figuring out what you will do with your freedom. I must attend my queen." He strode out of the room, his steps quick and sure on the icy floor.

Silence fell over them, and Alexander looked down at his hands loose in his lap.

"I don't resent you, Alexander," Gytha said. "I wish you would stop saying that I should. I would be happy to be married to you, and I would strive to make you happy, too."

He looked up at her again, his face alight with desperate longing. "Even though I ruined your life?"

She took his hands in hers again, feeling simultaneously too bold and not bold enough. His fingers were icy. "You didn't, and even if you did, it was worth it."

He bowed his head and shuddered. "I'm sorry." His words were choked. "I vowed to marry you, and if you accept me, I will gladly do so. But I don't want to trap you the way I was trapped."

Goblin voices in the hallways made a rough, muffled background clamor. Gytha felt the sympathy in her heart shift subtly with this new understanding; she had not wanted to trap him, but she had not fully realized how he might feel that Gytha was also trapped, and how that would horrify him. He would not want to be like Javethai in any way, even by chance.

"If anything, I trapped you," Gytha said. "But you're free now."

His hands tightened on hers, but he did not look up. She could feel his subtle trembling, and she thought it was likely more from exhaustion than cold, for the air in this little alcove the goblins had constructed was warm enough for their bare hands to be relatively comfortable.

Gytha said softly, "If you could have anything, what would it be?"

The silence drew out. At last Alexander said, his voice rough with emotion, "I would... I would want to know that when I die, someone remembers that I lived. That I existed."

This seemed so little, after what he had endured. Perhaps this was what he had wished for when he had been captive, what he had thought of when he was alone and tormented. He had once said he longed for love, for family, but he did not say this. Maybe he could not remember that dream, or did not dare voice it.

Gytha hesitated, but when he said nothing else, she said, "I will never forget you, Alexander."

He sucked in a short, sharp breath. "Thank you. That is enough."

"What if it isn't enough for me?" Gytha said, her heart thumping at her own boldness.

He stared at their hands, still clasped together. She could feel his tension.

She said, "It will take time to know each other better, but I think we could find our way to happiness. I'm willing to try."

His hands tightened on hers. "You don't have to."

"I know."

At last he met her eyes. He took a deep breath and held her gaze before nodding. "I...I had not even thought to hope you would ever love me until now. But I already love you."

The hope in Gytha's heart sparked into joy. "Would it hurt you too much if I gave you a hug?"

He blinked and then, cautiously, he shifted closer to put his arms around her. Tentatively, she returned the embrace. He shuddered and then relaxed a little. Gytha's head was close to his, and she murmured, "It has been a long time since anyone touched you kindly, isn't it?"

"Oh, Gytha," he said in a strangled voice. "When you put your hands in my fur that day, it was the first time in centuries that a hand touched me without intending to cause pain. I think I fell in love with you that very instant."

She felt the pain and exhaustion and despair in his embrace. He shivered and his head sagged.

"Am I hurting you?" she whispered.

"I don't mind at all." He made a strange, choked sound and she realized it was a laugh, rough and unpracticed. "I am utterly yours."

For some minutes they sat in silence with their arms around each other. Their embrace was the furthest thing from passionate, but there was love in it.

CHAPTER 16

Before Gytha was ready to be interrupted, there was a preemptory knock on the door and Iphreshken entered. "His Majesty has used his magic to make you food you might prefer. He commands you eat and be strengthened."

At the sound of the goblin's voice, Gytha felt Alexander tense almost imperceptibly. But he said only, "Thank you," his voice raw and exhausted. The tension remained in his shoulders as Iphreshken put an enormous platter in front of them.

Fresh bread, a pot of creamy herbed butter with a tiny knife, slices of raw fish, a pile of cooked greens, and pieces of steaming, savory sausage filled the air with delicious scents. The ice goblin nodded to them and retreated without another word. This spread seemed to recall both the familiar tastes of Gytha's home and the more exotic tastes of the magically-procured food of the underground prison.

"You should eat," Alexander said, and his voice was strange and rough with emotion.

Gytha withdrew a little and studied his face. "You should, too," she said gently.

Alexander's dark eyes searched her face, and finally he nodded. "If you wish it," he murmured.

For several moments there was only silence. Finally Gytha said, "Eat a bite, Alexander."

Her heart twisted with grief and compassion as she watched him eat. He said little, only looking up at her several times questioningly.

At last, when he had settled with his elbows on his knees and his head hanging down, she said softly, "You must be tired. You can sleep if you need to."

"I am tired," he admitted reluctantly, and he straightened with effort he could not hide. "But I am troubled. I brought you here to the end of the world, and I do not know how to return you to your home."

"I am sure the king will help us. For now, we should rest, so that when the time comes, we are ready to travel."

Soon the goblins brought them more thick furs, both to use as blankets and already sewn into clothes that would keep them warm in the cruelest blizzard.

Once they were wearing this attire, they slipped beneath the furs and slept, together but not touching. To Gytha, this seemed like the only familiar thing in the world. Alexander slept like the dead, and if he trembled at times in his sleep, she knew it was not because he was freezing.

The goblins invited them to explore the city, promising that they would be safe and treated with utmost courtesy. Nevertheless, Alexander and Gytha stayed mostly in the one relatively warm room. Alexander volunteered little of his story to Gytha over the following days, and so eventually she began to probe, little by little.

"Nothing I say can make your life better," he said, his dark eyes holding hers. "Why are you so kind to me, when I have brought you nothing but pain?"

"I wish you would not scorn yourself so easily," Gytha said fiercely. "You brought my family hope in our despair, and you brought me the opportunity to do what was right and good in the face of my own fear."

Alexander swallowed and looked down for a moment before meeting her eyes again. "You have not repented of that kindness and courage yet? Even now?"

"Not at all." Gytha bit her lip as she studied his face. He was still gaunt and hollow-eyed, with a strange, haunted look that made her heart turn over with sympathy.

When he looked away again, she said, "We cannot stay here; this place is too cold for us, and it is neither your home nor mine. So when shall we leave, and shall we go to your home or mine?" She wanted to go to her home, of course, but she could not bear the thought of telling him what to do. He had been a prisoner for so long that she felt it important to give him a choice, even in this.

"I have no home anymore." His voice was bleak. He took a deep breath and smiled, the expression somehow both sad and hopeful. "But I would count it an honor to see your family again, and if you still have not repented of your decision, to marry you in the sight of all whom you love."

The sweetness of his smile caught at her heart, and she said, "I will not repent of it."

210

For quite some time, they stayed with the ice goblins. Though they had more furs, it still seemed reasonable to sleep on the same pallet, though neither of them was bold enough to touch the other once they turned down the lamp. They did, however, talk in the darkness, and their conversations had a careful, hope-filled sweetness that left Gytha smiling as she drifted into dreams. Time was as strange and unmoored from dark and light and sleep and waking as it had been in that unground prison, only there was no need to even attempt to count the days. It might have been a week or a month; neither of them could tell, and they did not try.

Neither did Alexander develop much interest in exploring the icy city. He said he had seen the streets before and had no wish to see either the streets or most ice goblins again. But he did accompany Gytha out several times to a secluded courtyard where they watched the ephemeral ribbons of color dance across the sky, streaks green, gold, pink, and blue.

Eshkeshken came several times to speak with them, to apologize for the slowness of his opposition to Javethai the Usurper and to offer his assistance in their return to the human lands. The goblin king did not change his simple attire much with his new status; his clothes were less threadbare but no more ostentatious than what he had worn as a servant. The only visible sign of his royalty was a thin silver circlet upon his head. The metal was unpolished and set with only a single white gem, and the dull metal was so close in color to that of his hair that the crown did not draw much attention.

One morning, the ice goblin king stepped into their room. His grey eyes flicked over them thoughtfully as they stood to greet him.

"Are you well, Gytha? Alexander?" he asked.

"Yes," they answered.

Eshkeshken bowed gravely to Alexander. "It is my honor to offer you a small token of my regret for what you have suffered here." From behind his back, he produced a bag large enough to hold a brace of hares and proffered it to Alexander.

The bear prince accepted it cautiously, obviously startled by its weight. "What is this?"

Eshkeshken bowed again but said only, "Look, and tell me if you can forgive me."

Alexander put one hand into the bag and drew out a handful of glittering diamonds and rubies. The facets caught the lantern light and threw gleaming points of color around as if by magic. Alexander's dark eyebrows drew downward and he looked at Eshkeshken again. "Gems? Why? This is a king's ransom."

The ice goblin prince bowed even lower. "It is intended to be." His voice had a harsh edge, but it seemed to betray grief and regret rather than anger. "You were a prince in the human lands before you were imprisoned as a bear. You were deprived not only of family, friends, and companionship among your own people, but of your rightful place as king over them.

"No riches can truly repay you for what was taken from you, but perhaps this is enough to show you the depth of my sincerity when I say that no human will be stolen again, not while I am king."

Alexander swallowed. He looked down at the bag again and then back at Eshkeshken.

Eshkeshken added softly, "It is more than I have kept for myself, Alexander. I use your name, because I acknowledge the life you once had and have lost."

Alexander hesitated and finally nodded once. He bowed. "You are generous, Your Majesty. No jewels can pay for what I have lost. Yet you were not my captor, and nothing but your own honor compelled you to give me anything at all. I am without complaint against you."

Eshkeshken hesitated and then said, "I have no standing to offer you advice. You have borne your trial more graciously

212

than I bore mine. But if you will hear me, I would offer one word of counsel."

"What is it?" Alexander's dark eyes were steady on the ice goblin's face. His face was a mask of stillness.

"You are still a prince, even if your people no longer remember you. It is in your blood and your character. You have a duty to your people to ensure that they are not subjugated under an unjust ruler as my people were."

Alexander's face, already pale and drawn, grew even paler. "My brother Tobias would have ruled in my place. He was a good-hearted boy; he would have been a just and gracious king."

"And his son? And his?" Eshkeshken's rough, gravelly voice was soft as Gytha had ever heard it. "I have no right to speak to you of duty; I shirked mine long enough. But I can tell you that this guilt is heavy, and I would spare you that if I could. My advice is to go first to your own country, to take your rightful place if you want it and if you must serve your people by ruling justly. If you see that your country is ruled well, then take your place there as king regent and live in comfort in your own home, or leave and live in anonymity with Gytha's family if you prefer."

Alexander swayed as if he would faint, and Eshkeshken gripped his arm for a moment, steadying him.

For a moment, they locked eyes, and time seemed frozen.

"How will I get there?" Alexander croaked. "It is hundreds of miles away."

"I have the magic of the royal scepter now. I can make you a bear for as long as you want."

Alexander shuddered convulsively. "No."

Eshkeshken tilted his head and opened his mouth, but then apparently reconsidered his words. A tense moment passed, and then he said, "It is an offer. Your clothes will keep you warm enough to walk safely, and I can provide enough food for the journey. I can provide an escort to take you safely to the edge of the human lands with all speed." He bowed again. "Think on it."

Then he withdrew from the room, leaving them alone in the fraught silence.

For a full day Gytha and Alexander rested, but Alexander said not a word for many hours.

At last Gytha said gently, "Have you really recovered enough to walk several hundred miles in the snow?"

Alexander buried his face in his hands. "No," he admitted at last. "Not as a human. I doubt I could even with the king's escort. Nor could I keep you safe."

In her heart, she knew she could have pressed him to a quicker decision. She could have asked him to become a bear, to take her home, to do anything at all.

He would have done it for her.

But he had been hemmed in, his honor used as a weapon against him for so long, that she merely waited patiently. He was a man, and a prince, and though he had been imprisoned and tormented for generations, he was still, somehow, not entirely defeated. With quiet kindness and patience, she would help him remember who he really was.

For some time he remained silent, his face still hidden in his hands. Then he took a deep, shuddering breath, and looked up at her with his haunted eyes. "If the king can make me a bear, it is the safest way to get you south. I will carry you as far as I can."

She reached out to slip her hand into his.

Accordingly, they were provisioned with enough food for a month. The food was arranged in a clever pack of soft gray cloth that would fit over Alexander's bear shoulders like saddle bags. Other preparations were made, too; new, warmer clothes had been made that fit Alexander's gaunt frame better, and both Gytha and Alexander were provided with small items such as fat-soaked tinder, flint and steel, bone fish hooks, and strong fishing line.

When Eshkeshken and Dakjudr had showed them everything, the king and queen began to pack it all away with the quiet competence with which they had so long performed their duties as servants.

Alexander said, "This is generous, Your Majesty."

Eshkeshken paused and looked up at him, his pale eyes catching the lamplight. "You have been generous to me. You have every reason to hold me in bitter contempt; if I had been bolder, you might have been free sooner. Yet you have not even thrown my cowardice in my face, much less shown any justified hatred."

Alexander hesitated and then said, in a thick voice, "Your Majesty, if I ought not dwell in the grief and pain of what I have lost, you ought not dwell in regret." His pale lips worked, and he looked down. "That is easier said than done."

The ice goblin king paused, one gray hand on the gray cloth, as if he wanted to say something else. Then he nodded sharply and focused on the work. Without looking up, he said, "When you are ready, I will enchant you into the form of a bear. You can remove the enchantment when you wish."

Alexander's face had that mask of stillness again, almost entirely expressionless. He swallowed. "Do you know how far it is from Elestar to Gytha's home near Langaholt?"

"Elestar?" The ice goblin prince frowned. "It is on the coast, isn't it?"

"Yes."

Eshkeshken folded the top of the pack over and laced it securely. "I don't know Langaholt. Tell me how you got there."

After Alexander had recounted the days he had run to and from Langaholt and the landmarks he had noted on his way, Eshkeshken nodded and said, "I think perhaps two hundred miles? Two hundred thirty? I think Gytha's home is on the western branch of the Skjaldafoss, though farther south than I have ever been."

The ice goblin king raked his gray eyes over them both and said, "You would travel faster if Gytha were also able to run and sleep without fear of freezing."

Alexander flinched. "No."

The king's gaze flicked to Gytha's face.

"Do you mean you would make me a bear, too?" Gytha asked. Her voice felt small and trembly.

Eshkeshken's voice was gentle, and with a distant part of Gytha's mind, she appreciated the effort that it must have taken to soften that sharp, gravely tone. "Only for a time." His gaze slid to Alexander's face and then back to hers. "Your bear prince possesses a strong mind and stalwart character. It is said that when the magic changes a human to an animal, it is difficult for the human to remember what they once were."

The fear in Gytha's heart fluttered like bird wings, and she took a deep breath that stung her lungs. She held Eshkeshken's gaze for a moment and then looked at Alexander.

"I can be stalwart." She raised her chin.

The ice goblin king smiled, his thin lips drawing away from his teeth. A year ago, Gytha would have been frightened by that smile. Now, she saw that he was pleased with her courage and stubborn hope, and he wished to help her. "I will make you both bears," he said. "When you want the magic to be undone, you must wish yourself to be a human again, with a clear and fierce desire for your own natural form."

He hesitated and then said, "I think the magic will be strong enough to allow you to wish yourself to be a bear again, and take the shape off again."

Alexander's eyes widened. "I don't want to be a bear any longer than necessary to get Gytha south, to lands where humans can live."

"What if the magic wears off while we are bears? What if we can't change back?" Gytha asked.

Eshkeshken closed his eyes and tilted his head, frowning thoughtfully, and then said, "You will change back," he said at last, meeting her eyes again. "When the spell wears off, you will return to your natural human form, even if you are not ready. I think the spell should last many years, probably longer than you will live, and while it is upon you, you can change back and forth as easily as thought, if you wish it clearly. Nevertheless, do not stay in bear form for too long. My magic will not have Javethai's malevolence in it, but it is still goblin magic, strange to your human minds and bodies, and it may be difficult to remember yourselves in the bear form. If I were you, and I wanted to live and die as a human, I would not stay in the bear form for more than a few months at a time."

Alexander shook his head hurriedly. "No. I have no desire for that." He swallowed. "You are sure, Your Majesty, that we will be able to change back into humans?"

"I can put it on you now and let you try it before you depart." There was a faint edge in Eshkeshken's voice, as if he were perhaps a little offended but had decided to ignore whatever insult he had perceived.

The prince shuddered and then said, "Yes. I will try it before Gytha." He met the ice goblin king's gaze. "I am ready."

Eshkeshken bowed. He stepped forward and put one pale gray hand on Alexander's shoulder. He grimaced with effort and his fingers dug into the taller man's jacket.

Alexander shivered violently once.

Then the goblin king stepped back. "It is done." His voice rasped.

Alexander stared at him and nodded. Between one breath and the next, his gaunt frame transformed into that of the great white bear Gytha had known first.

The bear turned to Gytha, walked around the room, and then returned to the same spot. Alexander took his human form again. "It is different," he said breathlessly. He sagged and put a hand on the table to steady himself.

Eshkeshken stepped back, giving the two humans a moment for private conversation.

The room was so quiet that the distant grinding sound of goblin voices was heard for a moment as the speakers passed by the end of the corridor. Then the silence fell upon them again, and Alexander looked down. His long hair fell over his face, hiding his expression.

The weariness in his shoulders tugged at Gytha's heart. "Is it too terrible?"

Alexander hesitated and then took her hand. "The king's magic is kinder than Javethai's was, but it is still cold and alien, like ice in my veins. The wild, fierce strength of the bear makes it easier to endure the brutal cold, but harder to remember my humanity. I forgot my home and my mind before, and I do not want to do so again." His dark eyes searched her face. "But you are strong enough to endure it well," he said at last. "It is not that I think it too difficult for you. It is only that I have asked so much of you already, and it is unjust to ask this too. My debt to you piles up like snowdrifts, thick and cold and heavy. I do not want you to suffer for me."

Gytha felt the weight of his regret, his guilt, his grief, and the tenuous thread of hope that he still did not want to voice. "I have not endured what you have," she said, choosing her words with care, for she did not want to hurt him. "Yet I am not easily broken, either. If Eshkeshken can make us bears together, I think we can return to your home." She hesitated and then said, "I do want to see my family, and I think they would like to see you, too."

The desperate longing in his voice brought tears to her eyes. "Do you think so? They must be as generous as you are, to forgive me for taking you away."

She gripped his hands more firmly. "They will love you. You'll see." She took a deep breath and ignored the fear still quivering in her belly. "I am ready."

For another moment, his haunted eyes searched her face, and then he nodded. He turned to Eshkeshken. "We are ready, Your Majesty."

They had nearly forgotten Dakjudr was in the room too, for she had been silent and had stepped back to stand by the door while Eshkeshken transformed Alexander. They remembered her only now, when they saw her at Eshkeshken's side. He had clasped one of her hands in his and bent to speak into her ear.

The goblin king straightened now and stepped forward, still clasping the queen's hand. "Is it painful?" he asked Alexander. "I can make it wear off faster, I think."

Alexander hesitated and then shook his head. "No, Your Majesty," he said in a low voice. "I feel it, but it is not painful. It is only when I am a bear that I feel the tug of madness. Your magic is not like Javethai's was, though it is powerful."

Eshkeshken nodded gravely. "If it troubles you, come back to my lands, and I will remove it. But I think it would be no bad thing if you could transform when you wish, as long as the magic does not cause you suffering."

He glanced at Dakjudr, who said, "Gytha, I wish to give you a token of friendship. You were kind to me when I was a servant. Now that I am a queen, I will give a gift worthy of the friend of a queen." She smiled, and her pale eyes were lit with affection. In the palm of her hand she showed Gytha a golden necklace with a single enormous diamond pendant. Then she folded it carefully into a piece of leather and slipped it among their supplies.

"That is very generous of you," said Gytha, surprised and touched. "I didn't expect…"

Dakjudr's smiled widened, and her sharp white teeth glinted in the lamplight. "I know. That is why it touched me. You expected nothing in return, and still you were kind. You will always be welcome here, Gytha."

Eshkeshken nodded. "Go in peace, humans."

At Gytha's nod of readiness, Eshkeshken put his cold gray hand on her shoulder. A flood of icy chill went through her like the shock of falling into a frozen pond, and she shivered, with sparkles in her vision like snowflakes swirling under the brightest sun.

Then she stood looking down at Eshkeshken. Her feet were wide, white paws, and her ears flicked. She could hear the goblin king and his queen breathing, and the great breaths of the bear beside her.

"Can I talk?" She was relieved to find that she could. She wished herself to be a human, and she transformed in a moment with a rush of icy magic. "How very strange!" she gasped. She wished herself back into bear form, and the transformation was just as quick, with a shiver that ran down her spine and through her mind.

Alexander transformed again, and the goblins put the pack on him. It would be easy to remove it once he took his human form; the straps would fall off him.

A vague memory of Eshkeshken's words to the winds caught at Gytha's mind and tugged at it like an insistent breeze. "Aren't we beyond the edge of the world, east of the sun and west of the moon, where only the wind can go?" she asked. "How can we walk to the human lands?"

Eshkeshken looked up and smiled, bright and proud. "I have my magic," he said. "I can take you across the icy water where only the wind could go before."

Soon they set off into the cold, dark, endless winter night. Ribbons of light danced above them as if in celebration, and Gytha thought that if they listened hard enough, they might almost hear the stars singing. The ice goblins walked side by side without talking, and the bears followed.

For many hours they walked, until at last Eshkeshken stopped. He swept one arm through the air as if sweeping an invisible tent flap aside, and ushered the others through. A slight pressure weighed upon Gytha's fur as she strode past him, and there was a rush of icy wind upon her face.

In that moment they stepped by magic from one place to another far distant. They now stood upon a low, rocky hillside a little way above the snow-swept plains over which Alexander had carried Gytha. The goblin king pointed to the west, where the mountaintops caught the faint starlight above their shadowy sides. "Elestar is that way." He pointed to the south. "Gytha's home is that way, not quite so far."

"Thank you." Alexander shifted into his human form again, perhaps to test that he could, and also to bow to the goblin king. Gytha did so as well.

After short farewells and well-wishes, Alexander and Gytha set off toward the city he barely remembered. As bears, with the ice goblin magic in their veins, it was not difficult to run for hours, and their steps were sped by magic, so they covered miles faster than even the fastest dog sled, much less horses.

Sometimes they ran in silence. At other times, they slowed and spoke quietly of what they had endured. When Gytha asked, Alexander said that Javethai's magic had been cruel, freezing his blood with every step and driving him onward, though his urgency had needed no outside force. He had grown so accustomed to the pain that it was strange and startling to feel only the wild strength of his bear form.

CHAPTER 17

They reached the mountains north of Elestar after nearly three weeks of travel, for they slowed when they reached the warmer, inhabited lands. The air was almost balmy in their bear forms, and they switched to human forms with a sense of relief. They made a fire and ate, speaking quietly to each other. Their conversations were strangely tentative, for in all their time together, they had seldom talked of what might come, of feelings or hopes or dreams. Yet for all their shyness, each was sure of their own feelings, and so they came to a quiet, warm sense of comfort as they walked together toward Elestar.

It was late spring by now, and the golden sun felt like a blessing from the Creator. The road from the mountains wound down through the foothills toward Elestar, the capital city on the coast that Alexander remembered as his home so long ago. At last, when they reached the top of a hill, he pointed to the distant cliff, and Gytha could see the glint of glass in the castle windows. From this distance, the castle could barely be seen otherwise, for on this eastern side it was more cliff than structure.

The road was wide and well-maintained, and Gytha felt that she was entering yet another alien world, so different was this than anything she had ever seen before. The thick northern forests were long behind them, and they walked between prosperous farms on either side, with wide strips of trees to manage the wind and irrigation channels sometimes visible in on the lower hillsides. Gytha looked upon it all in admiration; fat, contented cows grazed in rich fields of grass and clover, and sheep dotted the hillsides. Everywhere was abundance, and she imagined the harvest of such a country must be rich indeed.

Alexander's eyes shone with emotion when he looked at the castle, and she did not press him too much to talk. Gytha's heart went out to him; how strange and terrible must the icy far north have been to him! Gytha had always known the North Lands, but his prison had been even farther north, in an even more cruel and inhospitable land. If he had known this comfortable abundance as home, it must have seemed like a death to be there, alone and forgotten.

Just before noon, they approached the outskirts of the city and stopped to eat lunch. Alexander lay their thick coats upon the ground and they sat on them to eat, looking at the stone buildings spreading out before them. Their travel had been long and tiring, and although Gytha did not know what would come, she was glad to sit down and eat a good meal before entering the city.

The sun was warm upon their shoulders and the tops of their heads, and Gytha closed her eyes. "The sun is just marvelous."

Alexander lay back upon the grass and closed his eyes. "I had forgotten what it felt like on my skin."

Gytha lay down beside him. "You should eat a little more."

"I'm too nervous to eat," he admitted almost inaudibly. "Whoever is king won't believe me when I say who I am, and if he does believe me, he has every reason to want me dead." He swallowed and continued without looking at her. "I trusted my brother without question, but so much time has passed. I don't know this king."

In silence Gytha pondered this. She knew she was ignorant of politics, of kings and powers and borders. On the journey, she had asked him a little about his country, Eleria, and he had told her that the place she had lived was claimed by Eleria, but since it was on the far side of the mountains, it had been essentially autonomous for many years. Boravia, to the south, had little interest in the cold, sparsely populated stretches of tundra and dense forest. Gytha had understood all this to mean that she was Alexander's countrywoman, if she belonged to any country at all, and that Elestar was her own capital city. How strange to think that she somehow had a connection to this place! It felt nearly as strange as the ice goblin city.

They slipped through the outskirts of the city and Alexander led her to the castle built into the great seaside cliff. Some of the streets were different, but many were the same, for the houses and shops were built of long-lasting stone and the cobbled streets would last for generations.

At the gate of the palace, Alexander raised his chin, threw his shoulders back, and strode up to the guard. "I request an audience with His Majesty."

The guard frowned. "What is your purpose?"

"It is a matter of discretion."

The guard's eyes narrowed, but he said, "His Majesty? Not Her Highness?"

Alexander hesitated. "Yes, with His Majesty, the king. The monarch and ruler."

The guard swept a thoughtful gaze over Alexander and then turned his attention to Gytha. She tried not to look as nervous as she felt.

"Very well," the guard said, somewhat to Gytha's surprise.

The two were escorted through the gate, across an open courtyard, through an enormous set of doors inlaid with gold, and through several hallways to a spacious sitting room with no windows.

The room was dazzling in its opulence, with thick, intricately woven rugs on the floor, couches and chairs upholstered in silk in colors like the brightest flowers, and a fire-place laid with logs. Everywhere Gytha looked, there was some new wonder! There were paintings on the walls, and little wooden obscurities, and a set of vases made of the most delicate porcelain and glazed in the color of a stormy sky. She clasped her hands behind her back and turned on her heel, trying to see every corner of the room without giving any reason for anyone to think she had touched or damaged a single thing. Being surrounded by such wonders felt perilous, as if at any moment she might be held responsible for breaking some priceless artifact.

A quarter of an hour passed before a maid came in. "I am sorry for the wait. It will be a little while longer. I've brought refreshments for you." She put a tray of fruit and little pastries on a table, curtsied, and slipped out the door again, closing it behind herself.

Alexander stood over the tray as if in wonder. He offered Gytha the tray first, and then took a slice of juicy green fruit between finger and thumb. He smelled it first, closing his eyes. He put it in his mouth.

"You must have missed this." Most of the fruits were strange to Gytha, but they must taste like Alexander's childhood. The green fruit was indeed delicious, but the pink one with tiny black seeds was even sweeter.

"I did." He said no more, but she could see his mask of control was thin.

It was another hour before the door opened again.

A pretty young woman swept in with two guards behind her, a man nearing thirty and a younger one, clearly lower in rank. The young lady looked not much older than Gytha, perhaps twenty-one or twenty-two. She wore a simple but lovely dress that set off her warm olive skin and dark hair. Her dark eyes shone in the lamplight.

"His Majesty is engaged in other business at the moment. May I help you?" She smiled kindly.

Alexander hesitated. "I think this is a matter for His Majesty. I can wait." He bowed.

"His Majesty has authorized me to address this matter, and I am glad to serve him." The young lady's face was as friendly and warm as before, and she said this with a tone of reassurance rather than argument.

Alexander clasped his hands behind his back and took a deep breath. "As you wish. My name is Alexander Rafael de Gracey, and I am the crown prince of Eleria. I *was* the crown prince two hundred fifty years ago." He frowned. "I might have lost track of the years. My brother Tobias would have ruled in my place." His voice grew quiet and rough with emotion. "I was taken from the forest not far from here."

The young lady looked over him again, her eyes cautious now. "And how did you live so long? Where were you?"

"The ice goblin queen took me for her own, and I have been captive in the north." Alexander's hands were clasped so tightly his knuckles were white. "She is dead now, not by my hand, and the new goblin king freed me."

For a moment, there was a fraught silence. Then the young lady said, "Well. That is…unprecedented." She raised her chin slightly, not in defiance but as if she were controlling her own complicated emotions. "My father holds true to King Tobias's vow. If your story is true, he is prepared to abdicate, and I will cede all power, authority, wealth, and everything to you. However, we must prove your words true first."

Alexander hesitated. "Your father is the king?"

"Yes. My father has been ill for some time, and I endeavor to take as much weight off his shoulders as I can. But he still rules, not I."

Alexander bowed again, more deeply this time, and motioned that Gytha should curtsey. Gytha did her best, although the motion was unfamiliar and awkward.

"This is Gytha Ivarrsdattar. She endured great hardship and loneliness to free me from my imprisonment. I hope to marry her." Alexander straightened his already erect posture. "Your Highness, if the kingdom is ruled justly and well, I have no wish to take the throne from you. The ice goblin king reminded me of my duty to my kingdom: I am honor-bound to ensure that Eleria is ruled with honor, justice, and mercy before I pursue the peace I desire for myself. If I am assured that my nation is ruled well, then I will gladly leave the throne to your father, without any argument or claim to my ancestral title or lands or wealth."

The princess swept her eyes over them again thoughtfully. "I would have thought you would desire the throne," she said, her voice soft. "After all this time, you don't want it?"

"I have no desire for power." Alexander took a steadying breath, his hands still twisted together behind him. "I wish only to do my duty to my nation. If my people are in good hands, I would not change that."

The princess pressed her lips together and her gaze flicked from Alexander to Gytha and back. "I see."

Alexander said, "Your Highness, I know the story sounds impossible. I would not believe me, if I were in your place. But if you believe nothing else, please believe that I only want to do my duty."

The princess nodded. "Thank you." Her dark eyes gave little away, but Gytha did not think she intended to have them hauled off to be executed. She studied them a moment longer and then said, "You must be tired. I will have guest rooms prepared for you, and tomorrow we will speak again."

They were installed in two guest suites across the hall from each other, and servants delivered a warm, comforting dinner. They ate together in the sitting room adjoining Alexander's suite and went to their beds very early, for the fatigue and emotions of the day, and indeed of the past weeks, threatened to overwhelm them both.

The room in which Gytha slept was entirely made of stone and had no windows, so it easily served as prison cell as well as guest room. Nevertheless, it was comfortable, clean, and warmed by the fire in the grate. Bright rugs, paintings on the walls, and numerous lanterns made the space cheery and welcoming.

Gytha woke to a servant bringing a simple but delicious breakfast of flaky, buttery biscuits, sweet berry jam, savory sausages, and a delicious honey custard with a crunchy, sugary crust. When she had just begun eating, the princess and one of the guards from the previous day entered.

"I don't mean to bother you," said the princess, as if she were not allowed to be anywhere in her own palace. "But I wanted to hear your story. Will you speak with me?"

Gytha stood hurriedly. "Yes, miss. I mean, Your Highness." She curtsied.

At the princess's nod, the guard introduced the princess as Her Highness Marin de Gracey and himself as Captain Derek Brighton. Soon Gytha was telling the princess everything, from the desperate deprivation from which the bear prince had saved her and her family, to the year in a strange prison of snow and ice, Eshkeshken's determination to retake his throne, the confrontation at the ice goblin palace, and their travel to Elestar.

"And what do *you* want?" the princess pressed gently.

"I want to go home." Gytha's voice cracked, and she flushed and looked down at her hands clasped in her lap. "I miss my family. I want to marry Alexander and build a homestead near my mother and father. I want to have children with him and teach them how to read, and even buy some books for them, if the farm does well." She did not mention the jewels from Eshkeshken because she did not think of them. "I want to sit in a rocking chair and knit little sweaters for my children and kiss their pillowy little cheeks. I want to listen to Alexander read to our babies and sing to them."

The princess met her eyes. "If you could choose between that and being queen here, which would you choose?"

Gytha swallowed. She felt this was a test, but there was only one answer. "I want to marry Alexander," she said. "I will go where he goes. But I would prefer a simple life in Aoalvik over a crown or a throne."

The guard's steely blue eyes softened at this, and Gytha was belatedly aware of how perceptive his attention had been. But he said nothing.

"Thank you." The princess rose and smiled at her kindly. "Rest now."

Hours later, Alexander joined her, and they were served a generous and fortifying lunch. He had given his story in much the same manner, and he was equally unsure whether the princess or her guards believed him.

For quite some time, they were left alone. Alexander sat and stared at the fire, his elbows on his knees and his hands hanging down. At last he said, "If I were her, I wouldn't believe me. I requested that she let you go free, even if she executes me as an imposter."

"Do you think she will?" Of course it made sense, but Gytha could not bring herself to truly fear that the princess would do such a thing.

Alexander let out a slow breath and then, carefully, reached out and took one of her hands in his. "Don't be afraid, Gytha." His dark eyes held hers. "I trust that whatever Her Highness thinks of me, and does with me, she will let you go free."

The gratitude and love in his expression nearly took her breath away. "I am not afraid," she said.

He swallowed and nodded. "You are courageous."

They ate a similarly quiet dinner, and Gytha felt the warmth of the food as a kindness, as if the princess had personally selected the dishes to provide comfort after many months of being chilled. When they had finished eating, a servant cleared the dishes and another one entered.

"Her Highness requests your presence at once."

Gytha hurriedly smoothed her hands down the front of her dress and over her hair, noting surreptitiously that Alexander was making a similar effort to look more presentable. They followed the servant through many halls and up so many staircases that Gytha's legs burned with exertion. She wondered whether the elevation and exertion were a way to show the power and authority of the throne, or whether the princess was so accustomed to the stairs that she did not mind climbing up so far. Perhaps she never went all the way down! They were accompanied by several guards, though the guards did not seem to expect any rebellion or violence from them.

At last they stopped before a set of wooden doors inlaid with gold and silver. They were ushered into the room.

The room was dazzling, and its occupants even more so. The lamplight glittered on the polished marble floor, the golden threads of the tapestries, and the silver and gold embroidery on the clothes of the princess and her companions.

The princess, as lovely as she was, suddenly seemed like perhaps the least interesting person in the room, excepting Gytha herself. Beside Her Highness was a man of such impossible beauty that it nearly hurt to look at him; his hair was spun gold, and his face was chiseled of alabaster. His full lips turned up in a smile at the sight of them, not exactly in mockery but as if he knew exactly how unsettling his beauty was. His clear, ocean blue eyes sparkled with intelligence and humor. He was barely of average height, but his shoulders were broad and muscular, set off to perfection by a suit the perfect color to make his remarkable eyes gleam.

Near them stood a man and a woman.

"Alex?" the woman said in disbelief. She was dainty and exquisite, like a sparkling jewel. Her dress nipped in to show her tiny waist and bared her delicate collarbones without being scandalous, and her dark hair was caught up in with jewels that sparkled merrily in the light. Her face was as delicate as a rose petal, pale and lovely, with huge dark eyes. She rivaled the blond for beauty, although her beauty was entirely of a different sort, but something about her seemed less perilous, at least to Gytha. The tall, lean man beside her was dressed in attire that matched hers; he had a dangerous elegance that bordered on forbidding. He had a wolfish face that gave away little, and his long, shaggy, black hair was liberally sprinkled with silver. His shoulders were broad and his waist narrow; he gave Gytha the impression of tightly coiled strength with more than a hint of danger.

Alexander gave a soft gasp of surprise. "Miss Woodward?" He took a few steps forward. "Miss Colette Woodward? How are you…"

The tiny lady gave a soft, musical laugh. "It's an odd story, as I suppose yours must be. Where have you been?"

"More like *what* have I been." He closed his eyes and took a deep breath, controlling his emotions. "You haven't aged a day." His voice was filled with soft wonder. He turned to the tall man and paled slightly, ducking his head in reflexive respect. "Mr. Stepanov."

Alexander smiled again; from behind him, Gytha could see the curve of his cheek and the almost imperceptible trembling of his hands at his sides.

"You've had a hard time, haven't you?" Miss Woodward said gently. "I wish I had known, or I might have been able to help."

Alexander looked down. "No one knew." He straightened and forced a smile. "Miss Woodward, Mr. Stepanov, this is Miss Gytha Ivarrsdattar. She freed me from my captivity, and we are going to be married. It would mean a lot to me if I had your blessing."

The woman turned her attention to Gytha, and Gytha felt the weight of her gaze with a shock. Everything in her wanted to obey this woman; her dark eyes were soft, kind, and utterly compelling.

"How do you know Alexander?," Gytha managed. "He said he had been gone for two hundred fifty years." Gytha dragged her eyes away from Miss Woodward to look at Mr. Stepanov; the man's eyes were intent upon Alexander, and he spared Gytha only a quick glance.

"I was an advisor to his father more than once, and I met him when he was young." Miss Woodward smiled kindly at her and then looked back at the princess. "I see now why you requested Mr. Stepanov and me. It is difficult to believe, and I am sure this causes political difficulties, but Alexander truly is the lost prince."

"I see," said the princess. "This does complicate things." She took a deep breath, and her eyes flicked from face to face as she thought. "It is rather late. Whatever we decide, Prince Alexander, we will not make the decision tonight. Please believe me when I say you are safe here, and I have no desire to cause you additional pain. Why don't you rest tonight and perhaps all day tomorrow, and then we can discuss what we will do, together, for the good of the kingdom."

Alexander bowed. "Thank you, Your Highness. Thank you, Miss Woodward. Mr. Stepanov."

The trembling in his hands had become more obvious. Gytha slipped her hand into his and felt him relax a little. Only now did Gytha notice that two other people, in addition to the guards, were present: a youth of about her own age, and a girl of perhaps eleven. Both of these were observing with naked curiosity and fascination, but neither seemed to have any role in the conversation.

When they turned to leave, Mr. Stepanov stepped forward and put a hand on Alexander's shoulder. His dark eyes swept over Alexander's face, and he frowned. "You smell like a bear," he said softly.

Alexander nodded. "Yes, sir."

The man's gaze flickered, and he nodded. He squeezed Alexander's shoulder and stepped back, bowing slightly.

CHAPTER 18

T wo days later, after Gytha and Alexander had slept, eaten, rested, been provided with new clothes, and been treated with every possible courtesy, they were escorted to a room even higher in the stone castle. Great windows all along one wall offered an expansive view of the land to the east, now shadowed, with gold fading on the distant hills as the sun slipped beneath the waves on the opposite side of the palace. They were provided a meal, and soon they were joined by the king, who appeared frail and blind but mostly clear-minded, the princess and her blond betrothed, Miss Woodward, Mr. Stepanov, and several of the princess's royal advisors, including the steely-eyed guard.

What followed was not exactly a negotiation, but rather a conversation with a remarkable degree of generosity on both sides. The advisors presented Alexander with an account of the diplomacy, political struggles, and economic progress of the years since he had been kidnapped, with an emphasis on the most recent conflicts with its neighbors, the assistance of the blond prince, Kaerius, and the agreement he had arranged between Eleria and his own people, the Mer Folk. At this, Gytha looked at him curiously, and he smiled and winked at her with such impudence that she blushed furiously and looked down. He was *too* gorgeous; it was not comfortable to look at him. She fixed her attention back on Alexander, and from the corner of her eye, she saw that the Mer prince's smiled softened and warmed, as if he had been teasing her and was pleased by her fidelity to Alexander.

Various officials briefed Alexander on the defenses of the nation, of the pay of the soldiers, of Eleria's trade agreements, and on various other elements of statecraft that Gytha had little interest in. She enjoyed watching the people more. Each of the participants was fascinating in their own way.

The princess was unfailingly sweet and courteous. The Mer prince would have been dangerous to anyone, and when he opened his mouth, his voice was like the purest gold, and it would have been easy for him to command or beguile the group to his own ends. Despite his easy power, he was too occupied by admiring the princess to be troublesome; indeed, he seemed to enjoy watching her graciously lead the proceedings. The various military leaders and administrators seemed to like and respect the princess, and Gytha thought there was something beautiful in that. They could have discounted her for her youth or her sex, but they both treated her as a lady and respected her as a leader. Miss Woodward and Mr. Stepanov spoke rarely, but when they did, everyone listened.

At last, when Alexander had heard everything, he looked up to meet the princess's gaze. "It seems the country I longed for so desperately does not need me." There was a strange, empty grief in his voice. He swallowed and raised his chin. "I am glad of it. Thank you for your generosity and trust in revealing such detail to me. I am glad to have you at the helm."

The princess said, "Will you take your throne? It is yours by right. I ask only that you treat my father with the honor and gratitude he deserves for how he has served Eleria so selflessly, and that you respect and honor the work of the palace staff, advisors, guards, and military personnel."

For a moment, there was only silence, and everyone watched Alexander. He swallowed and said thickly, "I am content."

The king rose to his feet, clutching the edge of the table for support. "You want nothing?" he breathed.

Alexander bowed deeply to the older man. "I wanted...I wanted to know that I had fulfilled my duty." He cleared his throat, for his voice was still choked with emotion. "I had not anticipated that I would be so deeply grateful that you believe my story. That you know me, or know of me, at least, and that I am not entirely forgotten. I have received more than I dreamed possible."

He did not sound as happy as his words seemed to say, and Gytha studied his face. When he said nothing else, she slipped her hand into his. He flashed a quick, nervous smile and said, "There is one thing I had hoped, when I was alone and despairing. If I ever returned, if I ever saw Eleria again, I wanted someone to know that I was broken and still I did not bow to injustice. I upheld the honor of my father and of Eleria."

The king, standing across from him, said, "You did. You honor Eleria with your courage."

The princess said, "We will remember your courage, Your Highness. I am glad you returned from the North so that we know of it. King Tobias wrote of you. He said that everything he did, every decision he made, was done in the hope that if you returned, you would be proud of him. His reign was a testament to the love and esteem he had for you."

Alexander swallowed hard. "I loved him very much."

"He loved you, too, and he always hoped for your return."

The king's voice was weak, but there was steel in his face. "The coronation vows are a testament to that."

Alexander let out a trembling breath. "Thank you, Your Majesty. Your Highness."

Marin glanced at servant and nodded before looking back at Alexander. "When we finish here, you should see the portrait gallery. What else can be done to satisfy your honor and duty or make you comfortable?"

"The only thing I lack now is Gytha's hand in marriage, and to fulfill my word to see her home safely." Alexander smiled sweetly and looked down at Gytha.

The very air in the room changed, as if everyone but Gytha had been holding their breaths as they waited for his decision.

"That is generous of you," murmured the king, his trembling voice almost inaudible. "But what of your children?"

Alexander looked at Gytha again, his eyes searching hers. "I love Eleria. But, if I am blessed with children, I would have them grow up surrounded by family. Near Gytha's family. I suppose you, Your Majesty and Your Highness, are family, but..." He looked up. "There is nothing for me here. Staying would cause political trouble for you and cause Gytha grief to be away from her family. I owe her everything, and I promised to see her safely home.

"I will sign whatever papers you wish to renounce all claim, now and forever, to the throne of Eleria. Thank you, Your Majesty. Your Highness." Alexander bowed again to the king, then to the princess, and then to the others in turn.

Papers were signed, and Alexander and Gytha were thanked and congratulated by everyone. They were offered a great deal of gold to provide for their future, not to purchase their cooperation but because the princess said it was unreasonable to send them away with nothing after Alexander had shown such open-handed generosity with what was rightfully his. At one point, Mr. Stepanov, tall and grave, put one hand on Alexander's shoulder and bent to speak in his ear for a moment. Alexander looked up at him in surprise and then nodded.

On their way back to their suites, Marin led them through a wide corridor with portraits on either side. "This is the portrait gallery," she said. She gestured graciously for Alexander and Gytha to continue at their own pace; one servant strode to the end of the hall and waited for them, while the king, princess, and the others bade them courteous farewells.

When they were alone, save the servant some distance away, Alexander looked around with something approaching trepidation. Soon he found one portrait and stood in front of it, studying the king's face. *King Tobias Ulrich de Gracey* read a brass placard beneath the painting, along with a brief summary of King Tobias's life and reign.

The king in the portrait bore a marked resemblance to Alexander, but he was older, with a few wrinkles by his eyes and a dusting of gray at his temples. His lips curved in a quiet, restrained smile. Alexander reached out to touch the painting, his fingers brushing over the king's elegant boot. A brass placard beneath the first caught Gytha's eye.

"Alexander, read this." She pointed.

Alexander tore his eyes away from his brother's face to the placard. *Whatever fate took my brother, I know that his honor and courage could not be broken. Every good deed I have done, I have done in his honor. Every poor decision is my own. May the Creator bring Alexander home someday. When he returns, I will fall on his neck and give him his crown. If he is kept away for many years, I will require such a vow of my son and all my descendants. Alexander was my hero and my best friend, and I await the day we meet again.*

Tears rolled down Alexander's face, and he fell to his knees. He wept, head bowed and shoulders shaking. Tentatively, Gytha put a hand on his shoulder, but she said nothing. In his tears, there was a release of grief held long and close.

After a very long time, Alexander's quiet sobs subsided into jerky breaths that tugged at Gytha's heart. "I'm sorry," he said at last, covering his face with his hands. "I missed him so much."

"What did you love most about him?" Gytha asked gently.

"He was just...fun. I prayed for a little brother for years, and he was everything I'd hoped for and more. He was intelligent and witty; he loved to make us laugh. He hugged me when I left for the forest the day I was taken, and it was the last time someone touched me kindly before you. He had so much love in his heart, for me, for my parents, for Eleria." Alexander swiped his hands over his face and glanced at her, then back up at the portrait of King Tobias. "You see it in his face: the sweetness, the love, his character. He would have been a gracious, merciful king."

Alexander stood and leaned both hands on the wall for a moment, his head down. Then with conscious effort, he straightened and looked at the other portraits. There was a portrait of his brother's wife, the queen. "Kiersten!" Alexander gave a damp, surprised chuckle. "She was a little doll when I saw her, with little ringlets and big green eyes." He gazed up at the portrait, studying the dignified smile on the queen's face. "She would have been happy with him." King Richard was much older than his father upon his coronation, for King Tobias had reigned for many years. His expression was grave, but his eyes held kindness and nobility. The placard indicated that he had been crowned just after his father's unexpected death rather than a planned succession. "That's my nephew," Alexander said, as if he could not quite comprehend it.

For well over an hour, Alexander examined the portraits in the gallery. He showed Gytha the portraits of his parents and found the smaller gallery off to one side, which held more portraits, mostly of the families together. Alexander spent quite some time in front of the portrait of his brother, his brother's queen, and their young son. He smiled through his tears, and he sighed, full of grief and love and resignation. "They were happy together. Good."

Another portrait showed King Tobias with his queen some forty-five years after his coronation, Prince Richard and his bride Princess Lirael, their son Prince Corentin, a slim, handsome youth with an infectious smile, and two of his three young sisters. According to the placard, the portrait was done before his fourth sister and second brother were born. Alexander studied this portrait for long minutes, taking in every detail of their faces. "What a beautiful family," he murmured to himself. "I am glad."

There was a portrait of Alexander himself as a youth, with Tobias by his side. Alexander stood in a regal pose, his dark, curly hair pulled back with a velvet ribbon. His right hand thumb was hooked in his belt, and his left hand rested on his young brother's shoulder. "I remember posing for that," Alexander said quietly. "I was sixteen, I think, and Tobias was eight. He was getting restless, and I kept tickling his ear to make him wiggle, and Father tried to fuss at us but he kept laughing."

Without a word, Gytha slipped her hand into his. She studied the portrait, glancing at Alexander's profile at intervals. In the portrait, his dark eyes were bright with mirth, and his lips turned up in a sunny smile. But Alexander's attention was entirely on the faces of his brother and his parents.

At last Gytha said, "He loved you."

Alexander nodded jerkily. "I...I did not know how much seeing this, reading that he remembered me, would soften my grief. I will miss my family all my life, but I...can...grieve with joy, knowing they were happy." He looked down at Gytha, his eyes red and damp. "The Creator was good to me, even in this."

She smiled up at him and then, gently, slipped her arms around his waist. When she put her head against his chest, she could feel his heartbeat, strong and steady. He put his cheek against her hair and breathed deeply. "Thank you, Gytha."

CHAPTER 19

Though the political discussions had concluded, they did not depart the city immediately. For another week, they remained as guests of the crown. The palace physician had examined them both and prescribed a great deal of rest, sunlight, and good food, and they were provided with all of these. They were shown several balconies protected from the wind on which they rested in warm early summer light. Nourishing, delicious food and drink were brought to them at short intervals. One morning after breakfast, with the early light warm upon their faces and gilding the city below, Alexander told Gytha that he intended to spend much of the day conversing with Mr. Stepanov. At her surprised look, he said, "He has maintained his humanity through more years of affliction than I endured, though his hardship is different, and he offered a listening ear if I wanted it.

"I do. I remember him as a man of great integrity, though I did not recognize his other qualities when I was a child. If he has no advice for me, then I will still benefit from letting him decide that rather than forgoing any chance of benefiting from his wisdom."

"I thought him rather frightening" Gytha admitted. "Though I suppose Miss Woodward is not one to suffer a cruel man to accompany her as he does."

Alexander laughed softly. "She is not, but I thought ill of him, too. He spoke kindly to me. I think I would like to hear of another man's courage. To know a brave, compassionate man, and to spend time with him, is to be reminded that it is possible to be brave and compassionate. I feel in need of courage. Mine is worn quite thin."

Gytha, feeling rather courageous and bold herself, took both his hands in hers. "I don't doubt your courage." She looked up at his dear, sweet face, illuminated by the morning and smiled. "But I am glad if he can encourage you, and I will be even more glad when we see my family and they have the chance to love you, too."

Alexander smiled down at her. "Thank you, Gytha. I would like to see your family again."

When he returned that evening from his visit with Mr. Stepanov, he looked more relaxed and hopeful. He was still gaunt and pale, with tired eyes, but the fatigue and grief seemed to weigh on him less.

"Was it a good conversation?" Gytha asked.

"It was." He smiled ruefully and settled in the chair across from her. "Someday I may be brave enough to tell you some of what I told him, of my fear and despair and the utter desolation of believing my torment would never end. Of the temptation to end it myself." He swallowed and looked away. "Telling him helped me put it a little behind me, so that I could think of who I want to be for you."

"You can tell me when you want to." Gytha leaned forward. "But you don't have to. I am glad it helped you, though."

He met her eyes and smiled again, sweet and sincere. Then he leaned forward to take her hands. He pressed one to his cheek and sighed, as if a great burden had been lifted from his shoulders. "I know. I did not want to put the weight of it on you, but I did not think I could bear it myself. Mr. Stepanov is strong enough for a hundred men, and he gave me what I needed: a good deal of courage to find my way back to living again, a compassionate ear, and wise words about love and sacrifice." He shifted, close enough that she almost thought he intended to kiss her. But he hesitated. "I don't know who I am anymore, other than that I am free. But I don't really know what that means." His dark eyes held hers, and if he still looked worn and tentative, he no longer had that shattered look that had so grieved her.

"I have loved you since I met you, but I intend to love you more fully and more deeply with every day that passes. I will fail, I am sure of it, but my mind is set upon this end, Gytha. I cannot promise I will make you happy, but I will promise to love you before myself, forever and always. Will you still you have me?"

"I already said I would!" Gytha laughed, and Alexander's smile widened.

For another two weeks, they stayed in Eleria to rest and regain their strength. Alexander showed Gytha some of his favorite places and told her of his memories of his family. Even in the melancholy moments, when Alexander's voice choked with grief over those he had lost, there was a sweetness between them that grew by the day.

At last they determined to leave. They bid the princess and all their friends in the palace farewell and set off in human form until they reached the cover of the woods. Then they transformed into bears and ran toward the mountains, their steps quickened by magic.

CHAPTER 20

For three weeks they traveled, transforming every now and then just to prove to themselves that they could. They made camp and had long, quiet talks by a campfire, enjoying the crackling of the wood and the sound of the breeze whispering through the tree branches above them. Their pace was easier than when Alexander had sped north with Gytha, but still they covered ground far more quickly than Gytha could have imagined.

At last they reached the top of a hill, and Alexander stopped, his great white head turned toward Gytha. "This is where I stood when I saw you for the first time."

Gytha strode up to stand beside him. Her bear form felt more familiar now, and with her animal senses, she could perceive more of the town than she could see. The voices of the men by the river were almost clear, though they were far down the hill and out of sight among the trees. The lake Alexander had painted was visible in the distance, though it would be out of sight once they descended into the valley. The scents of pine and spruce and loam mingled with the faint hint of woodsmoke.

With a huff, Alexander transformed from a bear into a person, and Gytha followed. He slung the pack over his shoulder and looked at her.

"I'm terrified," he said abruptly.

Gytha blinked. "All this time, and all the courage you've shown, and you're terrified now? Why?" She stepped closer, looking up at him.

"Your family has every reason to hate me," he said, gripping the straps of the pack as if to steady himself. "I took you away from them. Dare I ask your father for your hand in marriage?" He looked across the valley at their little homestead nearly hidden in the trees, and his jaw tightened. Then he looked back at her. "For you, Gytha, I can face anything." And he smiled, sweetly and shyly, and put out one hand.

She slipped her hand into his and they set off toward home.

Together.

CHAPTER 21

The woods were so thick, and everyone so busy with chores, that no one saw them coming until they were nearly at the edge of the clearing. Then Dagney looked up and cried, "Gytha! Gytha's coming!" and everyone dropped what they were doing and ran toward them.

For a moment, Gytha was so engulfed in hugs and arms and voices that she could barely speak. But she managed, "Just a moment! Let me introduce you!"

They had not entirely ignored Alexander, but now everyone turned their attention to him. A flush came to his thin cheeks, and Gytha took his hand. "This is Alexander, who was a bear and a prince." There were exclamations, and when Gytha could get a word in, she said, "Alexander, this is my family: my father Ivarr Bjornsson and my mother Hlif, Sigrid, Solveig, Ashild and Dagney, Randulf, Halvard, and Brinja."

Ivarr's gaze had caught on the scar that marred Alexander's nose, dragging from the corner of his eye downward.

Gytha could feel Alexander's tension in his hand. He spoke in a quiet, courteous voice. "I am honored to meet you again." He met their eyes in turn, and when he caught Solveig's gaze, she smiled at him.

He smiled shyly, and at that, Ivarr shook his head as if he had just come to his senses. "I owe you an apology."

Alexander blinked and ducked his head a little. "It isn't necessary. I—"

"It is," Ivarr said firmly. He stepped forward and put both hands on Alexander's shoulders to look him in the face. "I am sorry for hurting you, and I ask your forgiveness. More than that, I owe you my deepest gratitude for what you did for Hlif and Gytha, for healing their fevers. Without you, we would have lost them both, and maybe others, to fever and hunger that winter. Thank you."

Alexander's lips trembled, as if he were trying to think of what to say. Then he nodded. His voice was choked when he said, "I didn't expect gratitude. It was an honor. Thank you for not hating me for taking Gytha away."

Ivarr let his hands drop but remained close, his blue eyes taking in Alexander's ragged scar, his dark eyes, tired and apprehensive, and the dark curls pulled back in a bit of ribbon. "I see now that you are a man of honor," he said. "I would like to hear your story."

"It is a not pleasant tale." Alexander's gaze flicked toward the younger children and then back to Ivarr. "But I would have no secrets with you, if you will hear it."

Ivarr blinked in surprise, and Alexander took a deep breath.

"I want to marry Gytha. I loved her from the moment she put her hands in my fur, and I grew to love her more over many months of observing her character. She is beautiful beyond words, but that is not what I love most about her. She is lovely in her heart, and I want to spend the rest of my life, however long it is, in knowing and loving her. With your blessing, I will wed her when she is ready." Alexander's fingers squeezed Gytha's nervously, but he held Ivarr's gaze.

Ivarr studied him and then looked at Gytha, taking in her hopeful look. "Is this what you want?"

"Yes!" Gytha's lips curved in a smile, and she leaned closer to Alexander's side. "I love him, Pabbi, Mamma." She glanced at her mother. "You will too, when you get to know him." She smiled up at Alexander reassuringly, hoping he could see the affection in her eyes. "We still have much to learn about each other, but I know enough to be sure about my choice." She looked back at her father. "Please, Pabbi. Love him, and get to know him, and welcome him as a son."

Ivarr glanced at Hlif, who smiled warmly. He said, "If Gytha loves you so well, I am sure we will, also. It will be good to spend time growing close." He kissed Gytha's forehead and then put a strong arm around Alexander's shoulders. "Come, Son, and have some lunch. We have much to talk about, and plenty of time."

Alexander stumbled forward at the strength of Ivarr's arm, and the man gripped his jacket to steady him. "You want to know me?"

Solveig said, "Of course we do! If you're going to marry Gytha, we need to know everything. You're going to be family."

Alexander's tentative smile widened, and a pink flush rose in his cheeks. He looked back at Gytha. "I didn't know what I wanted, but now I do. I wanted this. Only this, and everything that comes after. You. Your family. Little sisters and brothers. Home."

Ivarr let him pause, no longer urging him toward the house. "If Gytha accepts you, then this is your home, and we are your family," he said, his voice warm and deep. "Have no fear of being separate or apart."

"I was afraid," Alexander admitted. He looked down at his boots.

"Well, don't be," said Solveig. She smiled at him. "I liked you as a bear, and I think I shall like you even more as a big brother."

Alexander's flush deepened. "Thank you, Little Sister."

"Come, come!" Hlif urged. She took Gytha's free hand and said, "You must help us draw him out, so that we know how to make him feel at home."

Alexander chuckled a little, as if he were rusty at it, and said, "Thank you, madame."

Hlif stopped in shock. "Never in my life!" she said, surprised but not displeased. "'*Madame*,' indeed! Call me Mamma! You're to be a son by marriage if not blood, and we will have no artificial distance of titles and formality between us."

They started toward the house, with Alexander engulfed in the happy group. The children began asking questions so quickly that Gytha could not answer them, and Alexander was so choked with emotion that he could not answer either.

Gytha kept her hand in his, and Ivarr kept his arm around Alexander's shoulders, and soon they were settled at the table with tea and honeycakes.

"Now, then," Hlif said. "There's no hurry to tell everything. It's not a race. This is the beginning of your life together. How shall we begin?"

Alexander could not speak; tears filled his eyes, and he looked down at the table before Gytha caught his hand again.

She smiled at him. "Welcome home, Alexander."

Wait! Before you go! The authors from All That Glitters have banded together to create the ultimate bookish Treasure Hunt. Go here: **https://cjbrightley.com/all-that-glitters-treasure-hunt** to unearth a treasure email full of digital gems, games, and fantastical surprises. Play now and unlock the ultimate prize!

ABOUT THE AUTHOR

Thank you for purchasing this book. If you enjoyed it, please leave a review at your favorite online retailer!

C. J. Brightley lives in Northern Virginia with her husband and young children. She holds degrees from Clemson University and Texas A&M. You can find more of C. J. Brightley's books at www.CJBrightley.com, including the epic fantasy series Erdemen Honor, which begins with *The King's Sword*, the Christian fantasy series A Long-Forgotten Song, which begins with *Things Unseen*, and the Regency-esque fantasy romance series The Wraith, which begins with *The Wraith and the Rose*.

THE
SILENT
PRINCE

Chapter 1

L ight danced through the water in a thousand shades of blue and gold.

Kaerius burst from the waves in an exultant rush, and his song might have split the sky with its beauty. His tail flashed in the brilliant dawn before he dove deep only to twist toward the surface for another joyful leap.

He sang for the joy of the morning, for the thrill of the icy water upon his skin and scales, for the ecstatic bliss of a new day full of possibilities. He sang for the deep tones of a whale song and the joy of fish flesh between his teeth, for the joy of leaping between sea and sky, and for the beauty of the droplets that caught the sunlight and cast it around in a thousand little rainbows.

He sang for the splendor of the Mer voices that echoed through the water around him, high and pure and enchanting, and for his exhilaration and pride in knowing that his voice was the loveliest and most irresistible of all.

The prince of the Mer was not humble, and he had no reason to be, for he was the fiercest, strongest, cleverest warrior his people had ever known, and he sang with power and beauty that surpassed any other. He sang with lust for all that the world offered and all that he would take from it, and for the pride of the life within him. For what reason would such a prince be humble?

Kaerius sang until the sun was well above the water, and the other Mer had retreated deeper beneath the surface to the quiet, dark depths to hunt. He admired the coruscating flash of the scales upon his tail in the sunlight. He danced in the shallows, turning circles and twisting around and around to let the light play on his scales to dazzling effect.

"Kaerius!" His father's deep voice rang through the water, and the young prince scowled.

His tail flip was sharp with insolence, but when he reached the Mer king some three miles away and a mile beneath the surface, he said only, "What is it, Father?"

"The sun is up. It's time to stop singing and focus on the hunt."

Kaerius snarled, "Why can't I appreciate the beauty of the sunrise, Father? Why do you hate it so much?"

The Mer king took a deep, slow breath of water; every muscle of his chiseled body was tight with anger. "I do not hate the dawn, insolent child," he said quietly. "I am glad that my sacrifices in war, and your mother's sacrifice of her life for yours, have afforded you the luxury of spending your time singing to the uncaring sun. However, I had hoped that when you reached the age of majority, you would understand that ruling requires more than a beguiling voice and a pretty face. It requires sacrifice, Kaerius, and you've been sheltered from so much that I wonder if I've ruined you entirely."

The young Mer prince's mouth dropped open. "This is how you insult your best warrior? How many times did I go to battle for you?" His voice cracked with offended fury. "I haven't been a child for years. But you wouldn't know, would you? You stay in the depths, hiding from the light, and from me, just because I look like Mother."

"Enough!" roared the king. "You speak of what you do not know."

"Then tell me!" cried Kaerius. "How many times did I ask for you to give us better guidance? We won the war, and still you stayed down there, as if nothing in the light had any appeal for you."

The Mer king's chest heaved with the effort of keeping his temper, and his silvery hair made a pale cloud around his grim face. "Did you ever think that others made greater sacrifices than you did, and our healing comes more slowly? The war did not end as quickly and easily for me, or others, as it did for you.

"Nevertheless, I did not call you here to reprimand you for your appreciation of beauty. I called you here to focus your attention on your responsibilities. The hunt. Your life is not your own, Kaerius. You are a prince. Act like it."

Kaerius trembled with rage. "I am acting like a prince! Is it not our life's work to sing and bring joy and beauty to the world? You've forgotten the very purpose of our existence!"

The king snapped, "It isn't all about you and what you enjoy! It is and has always been about sacrificing oneself for one's people. That is why I stay in the depths. I guard our people against the Lord of the Deep! Do you think I do not miss the light upon my face, or the taste of shallow waters? I give myself for my people day by day, and you are too self-centered to even see it."

Kaerius's nostrils flared. "Then you should be glad I sing to the dawn, since you have apparently delegated that task to me, the inadequate prince. At least I sing well." The prince knew this was a horrible thing to say; his father's throat had been nearly ripped out by a warrior of the southern Mer during the war. The king had escaped with his life only because of his exceptional strength and ferocity, but his exquisitely beautiful voice had never recovered its purest tones. The king could still sing, and his voice rippled with beauty and magic, but it was a far cry from its former glory.

Guilt twisted within Kaerius's offended anger at the sight of his father's wounded fury. He wanted his father to say something horrible in return, something that would wound him in similar manner, so that he could focus on his anger rather than his guilt and regret.

Instead, his father said stiffly, "I am glad you have not suffered as I have, Kaerius, and I am glad you recovered so easily from the pain that still troubles me. I wish you had learned a little empathy and compassion along with your skill as a warrior. Now go and hunt. The little ones are hungry."

The king disappeared into the depths before Kaerius could say anything else.

At this depth, even sharp Mer eyes could see only a short distance, and he imagined that his father was not yet far away. But he could not think of what to say.

He darted off to begin the hunt, his heart full of wounded pride.

By late afternoon, Kaerius had brought the little ones more than enough fish for their evening meal. Their mothers were capable of hunting, and their fathers… well, there were fewer Mer men of age after the war, but those who remained were easily capable of feeding their own families and the orphans and widows. The king had given Kaerius this task on principle, not out of any real need for another Mer in the hunt.

When Kaerius turned away from the nursery, he rolled his eyes and sighed in annoyance. He liked hunting, but being told to do anything rankled.

"Thank you, Your Highness," one of the Mer maids sang, her voice laced with magic to draw his attention.

"You're welcome," Kaerius said, his sharp teeth bared in a forced smile.

The maid drew closer and darted in front of him, waving her tail gracefully as if she wanted to draw his attention. "You are so gracious to the widows." The maid reached for his hand, and he turned away, ignoring her admiration.

A sharp pain in his tail made him flinch in surprise, and he whirled to see a young Mer grinning at him.

"What?" Kaerius snarled.

"Oh, did I tweak your pride?"

Kaerius bared his sharp teeth and darted after Tehrgil. "You insufferable upstart!"

The Mer child, barely into adolescence, screamed with mirth as he swam away. He had dared nip Kaerius's tail with his needle-sharp teeth, drawing a few drops of blood. "Prince of pomposity! Thought it would do you a little good!" His laughter tinkled through the water like the song of a newborn whale.

The prince surged forward and caught the little prankster by the tail. He turned toward the surface, hauling the now-frightened child behind him with a roar of anger.

"I AM a prince, you insulant brat! Never forget your place!" As his head broke the surface, he gave a furious flick of his tail, sending them both high into the air. At the apex of his leap, he flung the child away from him to tumble through the air and flop back into the water with an undignified slap of his tail.

Tehrgil was not hurt, of course. Mer skin was far too tough to be stung by the slap of water, even from such a height. But the young royal, a cousin much lower ranked than Kaerius himself, was suitably chastened and fled without a backward glance. Tehrgil often sought attention, usually by causing trouble, but to actually bite the prince was bold, even for him.

Kaerius roared after him, "And never draw blood near the nursery!"

If Tehrgil had looked back, he would have seen the prince twist beneath the waves with a graceful arc of his tail and then slip his head above the surface again.

A small sailing ship had been close by.

Ships were rarely of interest to Mer. If there were a storm, the ship might be dashed into pieces among the rocks and the sailors would drown. But on this coast storms were rare. Moreover, three hundred years ago the humans had built a lighthouse on the nearby promontory. Since the lighthouse, there had been only two wrecks, both before Kaerius's birth.

He had seen ships, of course, but only from a distance. Little fishing boats hugged the coast, dragging their nets behind them. Nets were dangerous; rumor said that once a mermaid had been caught in a net and killed by humans, an ocean away and several generations before. Kaerius couldn't remember the details, and imagined it was a myth anyway. If he were caught in a net, he would cut himself free with his knife or his teeth! A warrior such as himself would never fear a human. Still, the Mer folk had always been cautious of contact with humans.

The sun setting behind Kaerius seemed to gild the entire ship, and he drew closer without realizing it.

A sound carried across the water.

A strange instrument made a sweet, pure sound unlike anything Kaerius had heard before. It was like sunlight in his ears, warm and bright, sliding liquid through his veins. Another swish of his tail brought him closer, and he shook his head to fling his wet hair from his eyes.

Then another sound joined the first, a voice of dawn as the sun settled below the waves. The words were a little breathy, as if the singer were young and nervous in the most charming way, and then the singer found her confidence and her voice soared.

Waves slapped the side of the little ship, and Kaerius followed it as it drew close to the rocks, caught as surely as if he were entangled in a net.